THE GRACIE CHRONICLES

A Novel

Irene Williams

ISBN
978-1-7360803-0-6
978-1-7360803-1-3

Website:
Irenewilliamsbooks.com

Cover design by Lindsay Heider Diamond
Formatting by Polgarus Studio

To all in the body of Christ who stay on the straight and
narrow road in spite of adversity.

ACKNOWLEDGEMENT

I have to start by thanking Jesus, for giving me the inspiration to write. Only he knew how much I would enjoy it. I owe a great deal of thanks to my husband Clive and daughter Jasmine for their continuous support and patience. I'd also like to thank Dana, Chelsea and Celeste for their unceasing encouragement and honest feedback.

THE GRACIE CHRONICLES

Chronicles I

CHAPTER ONE

"You're kidding me, right?" Gregory shook his head in disbelief as he listened to Jennifer's landlord. "Yes, yes, I understand. I'm leaving now. I'll be there as soon as I can."

The other members of Gregory's band, GMAC, looked up from their cards and waited for an explanation. They'd just finished a set at Dizzy's, the upper west side club they played at regularly. The band would always wind down from their sessions by drinking scotch and smoking cigars until the place closed. Still shaking his head, Gregory pursed his lips as his six-foot two-inch frame stood up from the table.

"This woman is gonna drive me crazy," Gregory said between clenched teeth.

"Now, calm down Greg. You'll never win Jennifer back with that face," said Gregory's 65-year-old percussionist, Eddie.

Eddie's comment reminded Gregory of how much he'd stretched the truth to his band mates. He told them Jennifer would be back within the year. After all, he knew she still loved him. She just needs to get over her issues and come back home where she belongs. Gracie will be three years old soon. Gregory envisioned himself back together with Jennifer as a family, celebrating Gracie's third birthday.

Gregory remembered when Jennifer was the new waitress at Dizzy's. She didn't care that a Grammy award-winning artist was asking her out. With attitude, Jennifer told him that she was not on the menu. Normally, Gregory moved on when a woman turned him down; he never had a problem attracting women. They checked him out all the time. Even at 42 years old, strange women would slip phone numbers into his palm.

But there was something different about Jennifer. She wasn't just a beautiful, curvy woman with a tough attitude. She was a sweetheart. Gregory had watched Jennifer interact with the other patrons, most of whom were seniors who'd patronized Dizzy's since they opened five decades ago. Jennifer was very caring to them. The more Gregory observed her, the more he fell in love. Jennifer must have seen the love in his eyes because after a month of asking her out, she finally relented.

Jennifer was his queen. She was the only woman who inspired him to write love poems. After six months of dating, Gregory asked the question. "Will you marry me?"—for the first time in his life; and Jennifer said yes. The couple purchased a two-family home in Brooklyn and converted it into a large one-family home with plans to fill it with children. Gregory and Jennifer tried their best to conceive, but after three years went by with no pregnancies, Gregory gave up. He had enough of doctor visits and fertility treatments. Who knows why it wasn't happening. Maybe he was too old, or maybe Jennifer's past history as a heroin addict had damaged something. In any case, Gregory spent more time with his young protégé, Jamal, than with Jennifer, believing that mentoring the young man was as close to parenthood as he was going to get. Jamal's father had abandoned the boy when he was only four years old; so, he wasn't stepping on another man's toes.

When Gregory made plans to convert the house back into a two-family home, Jennifer was livid. They argued for days before Gregory said the words he'll forever regret. "This is not your house. I bought it with my money!" The change in their marriage was immediate.

Jennifer had been cold with him since that day. Then, ten months after the argument, Gracie was born. Just when Gregory believed things would get better, Jennifer served him with divorce papers. He lied to the band and told them that it was a temporary separation. At least, that's what he believed at the time.

Gregory tried to get back with his ex-wife, but the real truth was, Jennifer had moved on. He'd known for weeks that she had started seeing some shady looking guy. He didn't want any strange men around his child, but what could he do now? Their relationship and marriage were over.

"Sorry guys, I have to find out what's going on with Jennifer," Gregory announced. "That was her landlord. The neighbors heard Gracie crying all day. They think Jennifer may have left her alone."

"That's crazy man. Jennifer loves Gracie too much to

neglect her. I can't see her leaving Gracie alone for one minute," said Eddie.

"Honestly, I can't see it either," Gregory said, "but thanks to her 'need for space,' I'm not around to see what's going on." Gregory pushed back his chair. "We're gonna have a serious talk when I see her. No child of mine is going into Child Services. Keep my seat warm, fellas, I'll be back to take your money." Gregory put on his leather coat before heading for the door.

The band mates laughed as Gregory stepped out of their private room. He stopped by the bar and ordered another bottle of scotch to be sent to their table before heading for the exit door. Some of the patrons waved as he walked by. Gregory nodded in their direction and slapped hands with the front door bouncer before stepping out into the chilled December air.

Eighth Avenue was filled with yellow taxis. Gregory hailed one and was immediately on his way to Brooklyn, but his easy-going smile left his face as the taxi slowed in traffic. He remembered calling Jennifer's cellphone two days ago. She didn't answer, but that wasn't unusual. Not answering her phone had been her M.O. since she'd gotten with the new guy. The rage Gregory felt when he saw them talking in front of her home two months ago was so strong that he had to keep his distance. The last time he picked up Gracie, he made Jennifer meet him outside because he wasn't ready to see some man cozying up to his former wife.

This was the worst possible time for Jennifer to get slack with Gracie, Gregory thought. The band had to fly out for their tour in two weeks; he didn't have time for drama right now. Gregory busied himself by watching a game on his phone, but the closer the taxi got to Jennifer's home, the more anxiety he felt. The knot in his stomach told him something wasn't right.

Gregory entered the building and quickly climbed the stairs to the second floor. Standing next to Jennifer's door were two police officers, a male and female. The landlord stood next to them with the keys. That angered Gregory. He told the landlord he was coming right away. He also told the landlord that he would take care of Jennifer's lapsed rent. Gregory saw no reason for the cops to be there. Some of Jennifer's nosy neighbors stuck their heads out into the narrow hallway with questioning looks.

"Sir, are you the husband?" asked the female officer.

One of the neighbors stepped forward. "No, they're not married; that's the baby's father. He picks her up every week," she said before Gregory could reply. Gregory's look of disdain made the bold neighbor back up into her apartment entrance.

"Jennifer and I are separated," said Gregory. The male officer turned and knocked loudly on the door. Then he called Jennifer's name several times. When there was no reply, the officer motioned for the landlord to unlock the door.

Gregory was the first to walk into the cramped apartment; the officers followed closely behind him. There were no lights but he heard faint sounds of a television playing in the back of the apartment.

"They must be in the bedroom," Gregory said as he headed in that direction.

The female officer flicked on the light before they followed. "Jesus," muttered the male officer under his breath. Gregory was halfway down the apartment hallway when he looked over his shoulder to see what had caused the officer's reaction. He turned around and headed for the living room. Jennifer's body laid still on the sectional sofa. Only the cloudiness of her eyes gave it away that she was deceased. Little Gracie laid on top of Jennifer's stomach with her head down.

"No!" Gregory shouted as he ran to Gracie. He picked her up quickly and repeatedly called her name until she wearily opened her eyes. Gregory exhaled a sigh of relief. "D-d-daddy's here, baby." He held onto his baby girl tightly as he wept for Jennifer.

The female officer retrieved a sheet and extended it over Jennifer's body and face. After viewing the lighter and cotton balls on the sofa table, the second officer searched for and located a spent hypodermic needle under Jennifer's couch. He held it up for the other officer to see.

When the ambulance arrived, the medic had to pry Gracie from Gregory's arms. "W-where are you taking her?" he demanded.

"Sir, we have to take your daughter to the hospital to make sure she's okay."

"Oh, alright," said Gregory as he released his hold.

"Sir, I'm sorry for your loss. I'm going to pack a few of the baby's things for you to take," said the female officer. Gregory just nodded his head absently.

At the hospital emergency center, the nurse wanted him to wait outside the hospital room as they examined Gracie.

Gregory refused to leave, he needed to know why Gracie was so lethargic. Finally, the doctor told him Gracie was just dehydrated from not consuming fluids or foods, but was otherwise unharmed physically.

That night, Gregory sat in the chair next to Gracie's hospital bed with his head in his hands. He couldn't get the image of Jennifer's deceased body out of his head. The same taunting questions kept coming to his mind, *why did she do it? Why did she return to heroin? Was it my fault?*

Gregory's vibrating phone woke him up. Early morning sunlight peeked through the window when he accepted the call. It was Eddie. Gregory had forgotten all about the band. He told Eddie everything that happened. His friend gave him comforting words and told him not to worry, but Gregory didn't see that as an option. Now he had new thoughts running through his mind. *How do I bury my ex-wife? Jennifer grew up in foster care and had no family. How can I tour when Gracie doesn't have a mother?*

Gregory sighed as he realized his little sister was his only choice. Loretta was the only person he could think of to watch Gracie for him. *Yeah, she's unpredictable and supports a deadbeat boyfriend, but what else can I do*, he thought.

When Gregory's mother passed away, Loretta was just 18. Gregory supported her financially, expecting her to attend college. Unfortunately, Loretta hooked up with Terrance and pushed her college plans aside without even consulting him. They argued about Loretta allowing Terrance to live with her rent free while Gregory helped her financially. Gregory told Loretta to get rid of him, but she refused to listen. After Gregory and Jennifer married, he cut Loretta off financially. Loretta had disliked Jennifer since the wedding and she accused her of making Gregory end her checks.

Gregory loved to tour. He enjoyed meeting different people and travelling to cities all over the world. The GMAC band was his creation. The band and the Grammy award were his prized possessions. On stage, the feedback from the audience gave him the euphoric energy he needed to outshine every night. But this tour was filled with anxiety and worry. Gregory felt tremendous guilt for leaving Gracie behind so soon after her mother's death. The sound of Gracie screaming daddy over and over behind Loretta's closed door made him regret every day of the tour. It became the longest six weeks of his life.

In the middle of his tour, Gregory made the decision to quit travelling on the road and retire from the band. He was going to stay home to raise his only child; this was the desire of his heart. When Eddie said he understood, Gregory knew he had made the right decision. When the band flew back to NYC, Gregory rushed to Loretta's house to pick up his daughter. Gracie was so happy to see him that she wouldn't let him put her down after he picked her up for a hug.

Back at home he noticed Gracie's behavior had changed. She wasn't speaking and she was wetting herself at night. He blamed himself for the regression in Gracie. Besides the lack of speech and bed-wetting, Gracie would cry whenever he went over to his sister's house for a visit. He didn't understand it. Maybe she thought he was leaving her again, he surmised, but she never cried when he would visit Jamal and his mother, Felicia. He was relieved when Jamal's grandmother offered to be a daily babysitter when he took on a teaching job. She stayed home and looked after Jamal while Felicia was upstate at work. Gregory took her up on the offer and he's happy that he did. Gracie loved staying with Jamal and his family. It was a huge weight off of his shoulders. Now he focused on raising his child for him and Jennifer.

CHAPTER TWO

"Daddy, look at me! Daddy … daddy, look at me!" Gracie tried desperately to steal her father's attention away from Jamal. She practiced diligently on the small keyboard her father bought for her.

"I'll be right there, sweetheart. Jamal, what are you doing? You just skipped a semi tone."

"Mr. Mitchell, I'm trying to concentrate, but Gracie keeps shouting," said Jamal.

"Gracie, it's time for you to get ready for bed."

"But daddy, you …"

"No buts, Gracie, get ready for bed," said Gregory.

Gracie pursed her lips and stomped her feet as she walked by Jamal. When Jamal looked at her with a triumphant grin, she stuck her tongue out at him.

"Mr. Mitchell, she did it again," said Jamal.

"Gracie, I told you it's not nice to stick your tongue out at people. Now apologize to Jamal."

Six-year-old Gracie approached the piano with downcast eyes and mumbled, "I'm sorry JJ," in the lowest tone possible.

"Okay, Gracie, now go brush your teeth. I'll run your bath in a minute."

"Okay, daddy," she said with eagerness in her voice.

"Jamal, I told you before that you have to get used to distractions. One day you'll be on stage while your fans are shouting your name. You have to block all of that noise out when you play; mistakes won't be forgiven." Gregory continued to talk while 16-year-old Jamal daydreamed. He imagined being on stage while a stadium filled with fans shouted his name.

"Jamal? Are you paying attention?"

"Ahh, yes, Mr. Mitchell."

"Now, play the song through one more time; then we'll wrap it up."

"Um, okay, Mr. Mitchell."

As Jamal played, Gregory left the living room to check on Gracie. With the bathroom door open, his trained ear focused on every note Jamal played. Gracie stood on a small wooden stool. She looked in the mirror to check her mouth for left over toothpaste, just like daddy showed her.

"Gracie, the water is ready sweetheart," said Gregory.

"Okay, Daddy."

He closed the door as he walked out of the retro styled bathroom. The black and white penny floor tiles always made him think of Jennifer. She had searched all over New York City to find that specific design.

"Jamal, when you call your mother, can you ask her if she can watch Gracie for me tomorrow evening? I've been invited to play a gig at the club."

"Sure, I'll ask her Mr. Mitchell." At 5 foot 10, Jamal Bliss was tall enough to look Gregory in the eye, but his slim lanky build was definitely that of a teen. Jamal was proud of the full peach fuzz mustache above his lip. After Tasha noticed it, he oiled it every day, hoping that doing so would encourage more growth. Jamal's mother, Felicia, worked as a corrections officer 250 miles away at the Marcy Correctional Facility. She'd already instructed him not to bring anyone, especially girls, to their home. When Jamal's grandmother passed, Felicia was ready to pack up and move her son closer to her job, though neither Jamal nor Gregory agreed with that plan. When Gregory requested Jamal stay with him and Gracie so that he could continue his apprenticeship, Felicia relented. Not because of the music, but because she didn't want to take Gregory away from Jamal.

Jamal's apprenticeship began early in his life. Whenever little Jamal came visiting with his parents, they would have to chase him away from the piano. One day Gregory said, leave him alone. While the adults conversed in the kitchen, Gregory heard burgeoning talent in his living room. That was the first day of Jamal's lessons. Later that year, Jamal's father left for a tour and never came back. His parents' marriage ended when his dad admitted he fathered a child in Germany. That year, Gregory became the sole male role model in Jamal's life. Music was Jamal's sole activity. Felicia enrolled him in various sports programs throughout the years, hoping he'd find something else he'd like, but Jamal had no interest in them. Music consumed all of his free time with the exception of the time spent with Tasha.

Confident in his skills, Jamal created a music video with his best friend Brandon. The video was of Jamal playing the keyboard while singing a song that both he and Brandon composed. They uploaded the video on YouTube in the beginning of the year and had received over 4,000 likes so far. Jamal showed the responses to Felicia, hoping it would make her understand that his music meant something to people, but she brushed it off and reminded him to keep up his schoolwork.

"Daddy, I'm ready for bed now," said Gracie with her arms outstretched. Every night, Gracie expected her daddy to carry her to bed. It was the bedtime routine Gregory had started since Jennifer's death three years ago. Gregory lifted her up so she could put her arms around his neck and lay her head on his shoulder as usual.

"Goodnight JJ," she said as they walked through the living room.

"Night Gracie, see you tomorrow," said Jamal.

After she said her prayers, Gregory helped her into bed. Gracie snuggled with her favorite teddy bear, Mr. Pockets.

"Sweetheart, tomorrow night you're staying with Jamal and Aunt Felicia because Daddy has to play a gig. I want you on your best behavior, okay?"

"Do you have to go, daddy? When will you be back?"

"I'll pick you up Saturday morning. When we get home, I'll make you my famous chocolate chip Mickey Mouse pancakes."

"Yayyyy! I like pancakes, daddy."

"I know you do, now get some sleep." Gregory kissed

Gracie's cheek before she turned over. The bedside lamp stayed on. It was another bedtime request from Gracie.

Gregory closed her door and walked to his bedroom. The March wind chilled him as he opened the window, but he was used to it. He needed to smoke. It was the one vice he allowed himself to keep after Jennifer's death. Though deep in thought as he exhaled, Gregory's trained ear assessed every note Jamal played. They were all perfect as usual. If he had his way, Jamal would be enrolled in college level music courses, but that decision was up to Felicia.

****

"Gracie, your brother's here. Don't forget your book bag sweetie," said the teacher's assistant. At the end of the school day, the first graders waited in the cafeteria until their guardians picked them up. Gregory thought it best to list Jamal as Gracie's brother so they wouldn't give him any problems with taking her home. Gracie waved goodbye to her friends before she ran to catch up with Jamal.

"Hi JJ, I want to go to the store," she said as she grasped his hand.

"Do you have money?"

"Yeah, daddy gave me three whole dollars."

"Alright, we'll go to the store after I pick up some burgers and fries for dinner."

"I don't want hamburger and fries, I want pizza."

Jamal exhaled. "Okay, we'll pick up a slice of pizza for you if that's what you want. Don't ask me for my fries though. Now we have to make an extra stop."

They walked to the corner grocer after picking up their meals. Gracie turned around and put out her hand to stopped Jamal from following her into the store.

"JJ, I'm a big girl now. You don't have to help me in the store. I can do this all by myself. You stay here."

"Okay, if that's what you want."

After Gracie entered the store, she turned to make sure Jamal was not watching her. Then she ran to the beverage refrigerator and took out a can of cola, but when she turned around, Jamal was blocking her path.

"You know you're not supposed to drink cola, so put it back, now," he said authoritatively.

"But I want it," she whined.

Jamal didn't flinch, he stood staring down at her with his arms folded.

"Fine, I'll put it back. You're mean JJ!"

When she returned, Gracie brought a bag of Cheetos and a candy bar to the front cashier.

"You know you can't eat those until you eat your dinner, right?" Gracie rolled her eyes after Jamal turned around.

When they arrived at Jamal's home, he left his burger and fries on the table while he went to the refrigerator for a can of Coke. Gracie seized the opportunity to steal some fries; she wolfed them down before Jamal returned. Gracie turned the TV on to her favorite cartoon before sitting down to eat her Cheetos.

"Gracie, stop eating those Cheetos and eat your dinner." Her face and hands were already covered with orange cheese dust. Jamal sighed, "Gracie, go in the bathroom and wash your mouth and hands. When you come back, you better eat this pizza or I'll tell your dad."

She got up and quickly ran to the bathroom. When Gracie returned, she saw that Jamal had retreated to his room. She could hear him practicing on one of his keyboards. Spotting Jamal's opened can of cola on the kitchen counter, Gracie ran to the can and gulped down the contents. Though her dad told her that cola was off limits because it made her too active, Gracie couldn't resist. She loved the flavor. Gracie belched repeatedly; then she felt bad about drinking all of Jamal's soda. She threw the empty can of cola in the garbage before retrieving a new can to leave on the table. Gracie opened the tab and placed the can where she thought the old one was placed.

Gracie was dancing to the theme music of her cartoon show when Jamal came out of his bedroom. His cellphone was glued to his ear and she could tell from the silly grin on his face that he was talking to Tasha. Jamal picked up the can of cola and headed back to his bedroom. Amused with his good mood, Gracie decided to ask for something she wanted.

"JJ, when I finish my food can I play Nintendo in your room?" she asked.

"No, absolutely not. I don't want you in my room anymore, you trashed it the last time."

Gracie opened her mouth to protest, but instead of words a huge burp came out. Jamal grimaced and fanned his hand in front of his nose.

"Gracie, did that come out of you? You know what, you don't have to eat any more of your dinner. Just stay out here and watch TV until my mom comes home. DO NOT come in my room!"

"You're mean JJ," she yelled as he shut his bedroom door.

It was 9 p.m. when Felicia called to let Jamal know a heavy rainstorm was making her late. Jamal walked to the living room to check on Gracie. She was passed out on the couch. *Good, now I can have some peace,* he thought. Jamal turned off the television and placed a blanket over Gracie. He cleaned up before returning to his room to go to sleep.

Hours had passed. Intense rain poured onto the Brooklyn streets, pelting the windows and flooding the gutters. The storm brought high wind gusts and ear-splitting thunder that made the windowpanes tremble.

Jamal slept peacefully until a close lightning strike jolted him out of his sleep. Turning over, he saw his door was left partially open. Now fully awake, he swung his legs out of the bed to investigate, but his feet landed on something soft. Then he heard a burp. Gracie was sleeping on the floor with the blanket he laid over her. Her gas indicated that she somehow drank soda that night. Then Jamal remembered thinking his can of Cola seemed too full when he picked it up. *She did it again,* he thought. "Outwitted by a six-year-old," he mumbled as he shook his head. Jamal picked up the 32-pound Gracie as gently as he could to keep from waking her. Back in the living room, he lowered Gracie on the couch and spread the blanket over her again.

There was light filtering under the closed door of his mother's room. "Mom, are you in there?" he whispered as he knocked on her door.

"Jamal, what are you doing up? I thought you two were sleeping," said Felicia.

"I was sleeping until the lightning and Gracie's gas woke me up."

"Jamal, don't talk about Gracie like that, her gas did not wake you up. Why are you being so mean? Don't you know Gracie looks up to you?"

"Mom, I'm not mean to her, it's just that she's always touching my stuff."

"Well, like most kids she wants attention. Maybe not having a mother makes her want even more attention."

"Mom, lots of kids are growing up with only one parent, take me for instance."

"Jamal, it's not the same. Her mother OD'd in front of her when she was two years old. That's a very traumatic experience for any child to go through."

"I don't understand how someone could do drugs in front of a two-year-old," said Jamal.

"Addiction is a tough thing to give up; it makes you do things you'll always regret. Her mother was clean for years before she had Gracie, but after she divorced Gregory, she started again."

"You knew her mother? What was she like?"

"Jennifer was nice, very quiet and very pretty with lots of curly hair. She grew up in foster care and lost touch with her family, so she had no relatives at her wedding. They made a great couple but had such a sad outcome. So, you be nice to that little girl, she's had a rough start."

"I am nice to her, except when she sticks her tongue out

at me or interrupts me when I'm with Mr. Mitchell," said Jamal.

"Gracie doesn't like sharing her father with anyone. That's probably why she only does those things to you when you're with Mr. Mitchell. Anyway, why don't you pick her up off the floor and put her in my bed?"

"I've already put Gracie on the couch," said Jamal.

"I don't want her to roll off of the couch and hurt herself, just put her in my bed. I would pick her up but I'm so tired from driving through the storm."

Jamal went back into the living room. When he picked up Gracie and placed her head on his shoulder, she jolted out of her sleep and frantically looked around until her eyes fixed on Jamal's face.

"JJ?" she asked.

Before he could reply, she dropped back into a deep sleep with her thumb lodged in her mouth. He tried to pull it out gently, but the low whining noise she made forced him to stop for fear of waking her. Jamal walked slowly into his mother's room.

Felicia pulled back the covers before Jamal lowered Gracie into the king-sized bed. He sat on the edge of the bed and made another attempt to remove her thumb. This time he was successful. Happy with his accomplishment, he kissed her forehead before getting up.

Felicia watched the exchange with a smile. "You know, you two are becoming more like brother and sister every day."

"Mom please, I'm just taking care of her for Mr. Mitchell.

He's always trying to get that thumb out."

"Jamal, it's okay to have feelings for Gracie. It's good that you two are close. Maybe you can look out for each other in the future since neither of you have siblings." Felicia said this ignoring the fact that Jamal's father had a second child before deserting them.

"I don't know mom. Maybe if you did something with that hair, I'll think about it."

"Jamal, why do you say things like that? I think her curly hair is cute."

"Cute? You try walking down the street with the human troll doll, there's nothing cute about it. That hair flies everywhere," Jamal joked.

"Stop it, Jamal, Gregory brushes her hair every morning before she goes to school."

"Yeah I know. It looks okay in the morning, but when I pick her up in the afternoon, it's out of control."

****

Gregory was in good spirits that morning. He treasured any chance he got to play with his old band mates. Last night's gig was great; they brought the house down just like old times. No one could say his skills were rusty. Gregory rang the buzzer at Felicia's house. He heard someone running down the stairs before the door opened.

"Mornin' Mr. Mitchell."

"Hey Jamal. Hmm, I smell something good." They both went up the stairs to Jamal's home.

At the sight of her father, Gracie jumped down from the

island stool and ran over to give her tall bearded father a hug. Felicia had brushed her curly brown hair into two neatly braided ponytails.

"Felicia, thanks for watching Gracie and doing her hair. You didn't have to go through the trouble to make her breakfast."

"Nonsense, I was making breakfast anyway and Gracie likes waffles. I have more if you're hungry."

"Ahh thanks, I would love some. They really smell wonderful." Gregory sat at the island next to Jamal and Gracie. "Is that real maple syrup over there?"

"Yes, it is. One of the perks of working upstate; I buy my syrup straight from the farm," said Felicia.

"How did you make it through that storm last night?" asked Gregory.

"I barely made it. The rain was coming down so hard I had to pull over and nap in my car for about an hour. After the rain let up, the highways were flooded. I had to drive through a few back roads; that really added to my driving time. I didn't get here until one in the morning."

"That was an extra-long commute. Felicia, are you certain you can't transfer to a closer facility?"

"I checked again last year. I could switch, but I would lose my seniority, which means I would have to start at a lower level and take a sizable cut in pay. It would make better sense for me to move closer to work."

"Absolutely not. Mom, there's nothing and no one near your job. Besides, all of my friends are here in Brooklyn. I won't have anyone to talk to while you're at work," Jamal protested.

"Jamal, I've been thinking a lot about moving. I don't like leaving you alone all week and the driving wears me out," said Felicia.

"What about our house mom, we can't just give it up. And I'm not alone, I'm at Mr. Mitchell's all the time."

"But I don't want you bothering Gregory all the time."

"It's no bother, Felicia. Jamal helps me out a lot by picking up Gracie. Also, you and Jamal are the only people Gracie likes to stay with. She won't even stay at my sister's place," said Gregory.

"I don't know, Gregory. Sometimes I feel like I'm neglecting my son."

"Mom, I'm sixteen, practically a man. I already have a mustache."

Felicia laughed. "Boy please, that little fuzz under your nose does not make you a man. Anyway, Gregory how was your session last night?"

"It was great, I miss playing with the guys. It's nice of them to invite me when they're in town."

"Do you ever think about going back on the road?"

"No, that chapter in my life is over," said Gregory as he looked over at Gracie. He thought back to his marriage and how touring took time away from his wife. If he could go back, he wouldn't have left Jennifer to tour when their marriage was shaky. He would have taken her with him. *Maybe they'd still be together today*, he thought.

After finishing breakfast, Gregory and Gracie said their goodbyes. Gracie gave Felicia a huge hug and kiss on the cheek.

"Thank you for the waffles, Aunt Felicia."

"You are so welcomed, Ms. Gracie," Felicia replied as she kissed Gracie on the forehead. Jamal walked them down the stairs to the front door before saying goodbye.

Jamal dashed back upstairs to his mother after locking the door. Felicia was in the kitchen singing while she cleaned up. Jamal decided this was a good time to ask her a question. "Mom, is it okay if I go to the John Legend concert on Sunday evening? Brandon is going too."

"Jamal, that's tomorrow. Why didn't you tell me about this sooner? Where is he playing and what time does it start?"

"Darrel just told us he had extra tickets. The concert is at the Beacon theatre at 9:00 p.m."

"I don't know Jamal; I don't want you coming home late and you have school on Monday."

"Mom please, I don't get to go anywhere! Everyone else goes out all time. I'll be fine; I'll call you when I get home, okay?"

"Well alright, but I want you and Brandon to come straight home, you hear me?"

"I will, thanks mom," he said before kissing Felicia's cheek. Jamal hurried to his room to call Brandon.

"Hey, guess what? My mom said I can go to the concert; I'll pick up the tickets in the morning."

"Man, I'm happy for you, but my dad told me no," said Brandon dejectedly.

"Come on Brandon, he's always telling you no to everything. Can't you just convince him that this is something he should allow you to do? You do everything else he says. I know my mother's not going to let me go alone."

"What if you ask Tasha to go, she's your girlfriend. I'm sure she'll go with you," said Brandon.

"Are you serious? Her mother won't even let her walk down the street with me. What makes you think she'll let her go with me alone at night. She swears I'm up to no good because my mom's not here during the week."

"I'm sorry man, there's nothing I can do. You know how my dad is, he won't budge."

"Well, that's you. I'm going no matter what; see you on Monday," said Jamal before he disconnected the call.

Jamal was extra helpful to his mother all Sunday. He volunteered to do the laundry as Felicia prepared meals to leave for him.

"Jamal, I really need you and Brandon to come straight home after the concert, okay? No matter what time it is, I expect you to call me," said Felicia.

"Okay, Mom."

Felicia was so grateful that Jamal was a good kid. There were never any bad calls from Jamal's teachers and he's never given her any trouble. Long ago, she realized Gregory had a profound impact on Jamal's life. The many years of piano lessons, combined with Jamal's father not being in his life resulted in Jamal imprinting his character from his mentor. And though music was not a field she wanted Jamal to make a career of, his music kept him happy and out of trouble.

Time has certainly moved on since the death of her mother two years ago. Jamal grew up in many ways since then. Now at sixteen, he's matured into a handsome young man. Thankfully, his girlfriend's mother doesn't let Tasha out of her sight. The last thing she wanted was for her son and his girlfriend to spend time alone in her home when she's away.

****

It was 7:30 p.m. Felicia left earlier that afternoon to make her long journey back upstate. With knots in his stomach, Jamal prepared himself to go out alone. He showered, then debated with himself on what to wear. Nervous about the lie he told his mother, Jamal texted Brandon that on the off chance that his mother called, he was not to let on that he wasn't with Jamal at the concert. This was supposed to be an exciting occasion, but he was filed with anxiety. Like Jamal, Brandon didn't feel comfortable with lying. Both were raised in the church from when they came home in diapers. The years of Sunday school and bible study instilled morals in them they didn't realize they had. The two friends played music for the Youth Ministry services every Sunday. Jamal's goal was a career in music. Brandon was great on the drums, but his future goals were unfocused because he had other things on his mind.

At 8:30 p.m. Jamal was decked out in what he considered concert wear. The show was great. It was an awesome but lonely experience. Jamal decided that concerts were not meant to be attended alone; you need to be with someone to share the experience. He thought John Legend's performance was magnificent. Even the backup singers had great vocals. Legend sang half of his songs standing up and away from the piano; he encouraged and motivated the crowd to sing along. *That man is a true professional with class and presence. I want to be like that,* Jamal thought. He imagined feeling the hot stage lights beating down on him like the sun until he dripped with sweat from exhaustion; feeling the emotional high one can only receive from throngs of adoring fans yelling your name.

As the concert ended, hordes of fans left their seats at the same time. Long queues filled every exit. Jamal took his time exiting the venue. He walked alone down the subway stairs, yet he was still hyped and energized from the concert experience. He couldn't wait to tell Brandon about it. Being a drummer, of course Brandon will ask about the percussion quality. Jamal planned to irritate him by saying he didn't have a chance to analyze the percussion because he was so focused on the vocals and pianist. *Maybe next time Brandon will find a way to come,* he thought.

It was after midnight in Manhattan. The number two train was filled with passengers, many were from the concert. Large groups of passengers exited at each stop. By the time the train reached the first stop in Brooklyn, Jamal remained as the sole passenger in the train car.

Three stops away from his destination, two young men came into his train car. Jamal never looked up as he played candy crush on his phone. One of the men nonchalantly peered into the other train cars before both looked in Jamal's direction. The other man walked down the car and quickly snatched the iPhone out of Jamal's hand. He then ran in the opposite direction. Without thinking, Jamal jumped up in pursuit, but the second man blocked his path and punched Jamal in the face. Enraged, Jamal lunged at the man, but he was halted by a piercing pain in his abdomen. In shock and disbelief, he fell to floor of the train as it continued through the tunnels of Brooklyn. His attacker went through his pockets and removed his wallet before running off to the next train car. Jamal's hand splayed over the source of pain in his abdomen. Blood trickled through his fingers as the pain intensified. Lying on the floor of the train, Jamal's thoughts were of his mother. He knew she would blame herself for letting him go to the concert if he were to die here on the floor. Jamal desperately tried to crawl, but the pain was excruciating. Somehow, he found the strength to grip the train pole with his free hand and pull himself into a standing position. When the train pulled into the next station, Jamal shoved himself through the opening doorway, knowing that the conductor would check the doors for people before closing it. As he turned his head to the right, he saw the conductor looking at him from two cars down. Jamal tried to yell "help," but a sudden intense wave of pain gripped him and he fell down again. This time, he fell outside the train on the hard concrete station platform. His legs were still inside the train car, preventing the doors from closing. Jamal's last memory was of the conductor looking down at him before he passed out.

The ringing phone jolted Gregory out of his sleep. With one eye open, he glanced at the clock. It was 3:18 in the morning. He hated receiving calls that woke him up in the middle of the night. They usually meant someone had bad news. Gregory wished he could let it ring, but he didn't want the noise to wake up Gracie. Looking at the caller ID, he saw that it was Felicia and quickly picked up.

"Hey Felicia, is everything okay?"

"I don't know, Gregory. Jamal hasn't called me and no one is picking up the phone at Brandon's house. I hate to ask you this, but could you check my house to see if he got home and went to sleep without calling me? And if he is there, could you knock him upside his head for not calling to let me know he's okay?"

"Don't worry, Felicia. I'm sure he's there and I'd be happy to throw in a lecture for not being responsible, after I knock him upside his head."

"Thanks so much, Gregory. I don't know what I'd do without you."

"You don't have to thank me. I want to make sure he's okay, too. Call you back in a bit."

Gregory hung up the phone and dressed quickly before picking up the still sleeping Gracie with her blanket. As he placed her on his shoulder, she briefly opened her eyes before drifting off again. Gregory dragged out an old umbrella stroller from the closet, grateful that he never had the time to clean out the closet and throw it away. He placed the blanket wrapped Gracie in the stroller and walked the two blocks to Jamal's home. It was a chilly April night; the streets in Crown Heights were quiet and deserted.

Gregory used the key Felicia gave him for emergencies to let himself in her house. The apartment was dark. Leaving Gracie in the stroller, he walked into each room, looking for

Jamal. There was no sign of him to be found. *This is not right*, he thought. Now Gregory was worried. He wanted to search the streets, but this was Brooklyn. Where would he start? He also had Gracie with him. Gregory decided to go to Brandon's house.

It was 4:25 when he reached Brandon's home. Gregory rang the bell and knocked for several minutes before Reverend Maddox appeared in the doorway with a confused expression.

"Sorry for waking you up Reverend, but Felicia and I can't find Jamal. I'm hoping that he just forgot to call his mother when he and Brandon came here from the concert."

"Greg, Brandon's upstairs in bed. He wasn't with Jamal today."

"Wait, Jamal told Felicia he was going with Brandon to the concert," said Gregory.

"We told Brandon that he couldn't go to a secular concert. You know what, come in and let me find out what's going on. I'll wake up Brandon and get to the bottom of this."

A few minutes later, Brandon came down the stairs with a guilty expression on his face.

"Hi Mr. Mitchell," he said while looking at his feet.

"Brandon just told me that Jamal went to the concert by himself. He also told me that Jamal said not to let on to anyone that he would be alone," said the Reverend as he looked at his son angrily.

Gregory sat down and put his head in his hands. He knew in his heart that something bad had happened.

"I'd better call Felicia and then start calling the authorities to locate him," said Gregory dejectedly.

"I'm sorry Greg, I wish he were here. Let me know if there's anything I can do. I'll have Brandon call Jamal periodically. Brandon did text Jamal before he went to bed, but he never received a response."

"Thanks Kevin, please let me know if Brandon hears anything."

"Hey Greg?"

"Yeah?"

"I know you don't come to church anymore, but if you ever need help or just someone to talk to, I'm here for you."

"Thanks Kevin, I appreciate the offer."

Gregory returned home and placed Gracie back in bed before sitting down to make the call he wished he didn't have to make. *How do you tell someone their child is missing?* he thought.

Felicia was panic stricken when Gregory told her the little information he did have. She was on her way, making the long drive back to Brooklyn. Gregory didn't want her to make the drive in her current state, but he couldn't tell her not to come. He only told her to be careful.

His next call was to the local police station. They asked if there was any possibility that Jamal ran away. "No way, Jamal's a good kid and he had no reason to run away. He was given permission to go to the concert," said Gregory. He was then transferred to a Lieutenant Hamilton. He gave the Lieutenant a description of Jamal and the details of where he was expected to travel.

"Wait a minute, I see that there was a stabbing on that train line last night. Let me check it out, hold on a minute," said the Lieutenant.

Gregory closed his eyes and thought, *no, please don't let it be Jamal.*

"Mr. Mitchell, do you know what kind of coat Jamal was wearing?"

"Umm, probably his grey pea coat," said Gregory.

"That's him," said the Lieutenant triumphantly.

"What! Are you certain?" asked Gregory.

"Yeah, Transit Police received a call from a conductor on the number two train to Brooklyn. A teenage boy with a grey peacoat was mugged and stabbed in the abdomen. They took him to Brooklyn Hospital on DeKalb Avenue. You know what, let me pick you up. I'll take you down there to identify him."

"I-I-I Identify him?"

At the sound of Gregory's voice, the Lieutenant quickly clarified. "Oh, don't worry Mr. Mitchell. He's okay. The coat took the brunt of the stabbing, he's already out of surgery and stable." Gregory exhaled.

Lieutenant Hamilton called Gregory when he arrived with the car. Gregory hastily dressed Gracie.

Fully awake and wondering what was going on, Gracie protested. "Daddy, this isn't my school uniform."

"I know Gracie. You're not going to school today; we have to visit someone." As Gregory and Gracie approached the car, the grey-haired middle-aged Lieutenant got out and opened the rear car door for them

"Hi cutie, how old are you?" asked Hamilton.

"I'm six years old," said Gracie. When they entered the car, Gracie whispered, "Daddy, why are we going in a police car?"

"Umm, the nice lieutenant offered to give us a ride to the hospital to check on someone baby, don't worry."

When they arrived at the hospital room, Gregory made Gracie sit outside the room while he and the Lieutenant went in. "Oh Jamal," sighed Gregory as he saw him.

Jamal was asleep with two IV hook ups. Gregory sat by Jamal's bed and clutched his ice-cold hand. There was no response from the teen. Grief stricken, Gregory turned to the lieutenant, "How could someone stab a kid?"

"It looked like a mugging that went bad. Whoever did it took his wallet. He had no ID so we didn't know whom to call. Good thing he had on the peacoat though. I'll be down at the nurse's station. Come and get me if he wakes up. If Jamal can give a good description of the attacker, we can start searching for the perp." The Lieutenant stepped out of the room and bent down to talk to Gracie. "Hey cutie, you wait right here for your daddy, okay?" He patted the top of her head before strolling down the hospital hallway.

Gracie watched the lieutenant leave until he was out of sight. The hospital staff walked by without noticing her. Gracie slowly slid off the chair and peeked inside the room. She observed her dad clutching Jamal's hand as he laid motionless.

Gregory looked behind himself when he heard Gracie crying. "Sweetheart, I told you to wait on the chair," he said as he picked her up and sat her on his lap. She continued to wail uncontrollably. "Gracie, stop crying; Jamal is going to be okay."

She shook her head no before saying, "No, JJ is dead like mommy!"

"No, no he's not dead." Gregory tried to console her, but her wail became louder.

The loud noise caused Jamal to slowly open his eyes. He stared at an unfamiliar ceiling before the memories of what happened came to him. Jamal slowly turned his head to see Gregory trying to console Gracie's hysterical bawl.

"Hey," he said in a hoarse voice. Gracie stopped crying immediately and they both looked up to see Jamal looking at them.

"JJ, you're not dead," Gracie said before she started to climb on the bed. Gregory quickly stopped her.

"Jamal is not feeling well; you can't hug him right now, baby."

Jamal reached out and took one of Gracie's tear dampened hand in his before saying, "Gracie, I'm gonna be okay."

Gregory put his hand over theirs. "You scared us. I didn't know what happened to you when I found out Brandon didn't go to the concert."

Jamal sighed heavily. "I'm sorry I lied. I really wanted to go to the concert, but I knew mom wouldn't let me go alone. Does she know what happened?"

"Your mother's driving back now because we didn't know where you were. I'm going to step out and give her a call now; she needs to know what happened. Gracie, you stay here until I get back." Gregory left the room to find a location in the hospital where he could use his cell phone. He tried to calm Felicia down after he told her what happened. He told Felicia Jamal was awake and talking, however; this event helped her to make up her mind to move Jamal closer. Gregory told her that she was making the decision based on her current emotional state and he encouraged her to talk it through with Jamal first.

Back in the room, Jamal found the automatic bed button and grimaced when he elevated his hospital bed. "Gracie, stop staring at me like that. I'm gonna be fine."

Jamal's words didn't penetrate Gracie's thoughts. She kept staring at him with a serious expression as he dozed back to sleep. Watching Jamal lay under a white sheet brought back bad memories.

The lieutenant was back in the room when Felicia entered. Her eyes were red and puffy and her clothes were disheveled. Looking down at Jamal made her tears start all over again.

Gregory got up to get Felicia some coffee. When he came back, he took Gracie out to get something to eat. They walked to a diner a block away from the hospital. Father and daughter sat in silence as they waited for their platters. Mouthwatering hot plates of food were placed in front of them. Gracie had a stack of pancakes and Gregory had home fries, sunny side up eggs and sausages. "Gracie, eat your pancakes before they get cold," instructed Gregory.

"Sorry daddy, I don't feel hungry right now."

Gregory couldn't argue with his daughter because he

didn't have an appetite either. All he could think of was Jamal. *The boy was stupid for doing what he did, trying to fight thugs over a phone, a replaceable object. And if he'd listened to his mother, he wouldn't have been there in the first place. But all of that doesn't matter, I could have lost him,* he thought.

Gregory considered it a blessing to watch Jamal's talent develop and mature. Jamal was with him and Gracie every week. He remembered the cruise the four of them went on last year. There was a piano in one of the lounges. Jamal instantly went to it and started to play. People heard the music and gathered around the piano with him. A lady walked up to Gregory and told him, "You have a fine son there, he's very talented." Neither Gregory nor Jamal spoke up to say that they weren't father and son. They just smiled at the lady and accepted the compliments.

Gregory looked at the time and decided to head back. Gracie's juice glass was empty, but the food remained untouched. Both walked back to the hospital in silence. He didn't want Gracie in the room again, but she ran ahead of him. When Gregory entered, he saw that Jamal was visibly upset.

"Did my mother tell you what she's going to do?" Jamal asked.

"Yes, she told me, and I told her to think it through."

"Well, she's not taking your advice and she's not listening to me. She's shipping me to 'Mayberry' as soon as I'm well."

Gregory was solemn. He didn't want Jamal to leave, but being a parent, he understood why Felicia felt the need to keep her son closer to her.

"Don't worry, Jamal, we'll work something out if you do move. In the meantime, I believe you should stay with me and Gracie when you're discharged from the hospital."

Gregory did later convince Felicia to let him take care of Jamal at his house since Jamal would be in no condition to travel between homes when Felicia goes back to work. Being that Jamal was so resistant to the move, Felicia agreed. She allowed Jamal to finish out his school year in Brooklyn. This gave her the time she needed to look for a new home. The upstate studio she currently rents wouldn't have been sufficient for her and Jamal.

Gregory re-arranged his work time to stay with Jamal from the day he was released from the hospital. He rented a hospital bed and placed it in the living room area where Jamal could watch TV. Felicia had also arranged for visiting nurse services. Brandon was given the task of picking up Gracie from school. Gregory told the school staff that Brandon was Gracie's cousin.

"Gracie, your cousin is here!" The teaching assistant pulled Brandon aside while Gracie was gathering her things. "Gracie has been very sad in class. When I asked her why, she said she was sad because her brother is sick." Brandon didn't know what to say.

"Ahh, I'll tell her father, maybe he can cheer her up," he said. When Gracie came out to walk home with him, he asked her. "Gracie, why are you so sad in school?"

"I don't know. I guess it's because JJ looks so sad whenever I look at him. I want to cheer him up, but I don't know how," she told him.

"Hmm, let me see what I can come up with to make him happy," said Brandon.

"Brandon, can you pick me up? I'm tired."

"Okay, just this once. You know you're too big for this now, right?" After he picked her up, Gracie laid her head on his shoulder and inserted her thumb in her mouth. "Gracie, you're six years old, take that thumb out your mouth." Gracie turned her head away from Brandon's view, but the thumb stayed.

When they arrived at Gracie's home, Jamal was sitting up in bed on his laptop, checking his YouTube videos.

"Hey Bran. Look, no one's watching our video anymore, it's stale," said Jamal.

"Let me see it again, maybe I can improve it somehow," said Brandon. He sat on the couch with Gracie as he and Jamal discussed the music video until he came up with an idea. He asked Mr. Mitchell if he could put Gracie in a video introducing Jamal's song. Gregory was open to anything that would bring Jamal out of his somber mood. Jamal complained to Gregory everyday about the impending move; he's compared it to a prison sentence.

Brandon told Gracie to keep her plaid school uniform on and put a bow in her hair. He wrote down what he wanted her to say in the video, then he made her put on a sad face. Brandon recorded Gracie stating that she's sad because her brother was attacked after he went to see the John Legend concert and now, he's sad because no one is watching his video. Then, she asks everyone to please watch my brother's video and give it a thumbs up because it would make us both happy.

"That was great, Gracie," said Brandon. He made the video of Gracie the intro to Jamal's video. At the end of the song, Brandon faded in a clip of Jamal sleeping in the hospital bed. After posting the revised video on YouTube, he texted Tasha and some other friends and told them to watch the new video. They all loved it.

"Now what," asked Gracie.

"Now we wait to see what happens. Don't tell Jamal about the video, it'll be a surprise."

****

Within a month after Jamal's release from the hospital, Felicia purchased a spacious three-bedroom home on an acre lot. Her new commute was less than fifteen minutes. The cost of her new home was so low that Felicia didn't have to sell her Brooklyn brownstone to buy it. The brownstone was the only thing of value Jamal's father left for him and she wanted to pass it on to her son when the time was right.

At the time Felicia purchased their new home, Jamal had recovered from his stab wound and returned to school. The revised YouTube video Brandon and Gracie made had gone viral. There were over eight thousand new views after three weeks and the numbers were growing. People commented on how fresh his music was and they loved his cute little sister who did the introduction. Seeing the revised video and the responses it received did lift Jamal's spirits, but then his thoughts would turn back to all those he'd soon leave behind. He dreaded being separated from Tasha. At the youth ministry, Jamal would bring Tasha backstage, just to steal a private kiss. They spent as much time together as they could. When they sat together in church, Jamal would sit next to Tasha on one side while Gracie sat on the other. To Gracie, Tasha was just as beautiful on the inside as she was on the outside. Tasha would stoop down to greet Gracie with a hug and kiss whenever they met in church. Though only six, Gracie could tell by the way Jamal looked at Tasha that he really liked her. Unfortunately for Jamal, Tasha's parents always sat on the same pew to keep an eye on their daughter. The young teens took many chances; sometimes secretly holding hands under a cardigan Tasha would bring and leave on the seat between them. Jamal didn't see how their blossoming relationship could continue after his move, but he was determined to find a way.

CHAPTER THREE

The end of the school year had come and Jamal was miles away in his new home. The spacious split ranch house was located outside of the Utica city center with no forms of public transportation. Felicia purchased a car for Jamal to use, but he couldn't think of any place to drive to that wasn't back in his old neighborhood.

Today was his seventeenth birthday. All his life Jamal woke to the sounds of rush hour traffic and garbage trucks. In Brooklyn, Jamal's second floor bedroom provided a clear view of all the busy avenue activities. The roar of the city bus engine, barking dogs or noisy school kids running down the street; those were his familiar neighborhood sounds. Now, when Jamal pulled back his bedroom curtain, there's not a soul to see. His view was of tall, mature pine and aspen trees. The new sounds were of wind rustling through tree branches and birds chirping cheerfully all day long. Shaking his head, Jamal chastised himself for looking out the window every morning, knowing there was nothing and no one to see. His bedroom was his refuge and Jamal stayed in it as much as possible. The piano and keyboards were his only companions.

As far as he was concerned, there was nothing outside his bedroom walls that was for him. Tasha, his friends, church family, everything and everyone he knew were back in Brooklyn.

Felicia gave him the spacious master suite, which had its own private bathroom, hoping it would incline Jamal's heart to loving their new location, but it didn't work. Every day she came home to a sullen teenager. He even turned her down when she offered to get him a dog. Tired of seeing her son mope around, Felicia devised a plan.

****

Early that morning, Gregory, Brandon and Gracie set out to make the long drive to Utica. Jamal was lounging in his room when the doorbell started ringing continuously. *Who in the world would ring the bell like that,* he thought. Jamal got up from his bed to get the door and give somebody a lesson in manners, but when he opened the door, Gracie ran in and embraced him in a tight hug. Jamal was so shocked he almost fell back. Mr. Mitchell and Brandon stepped in behind Gracie and greeted him with hugs.

"I can't believe you guys are here! Brandon, you couldn't pick up the phone and let me know you were coming?"

"No man, your mother wanted it to be a surprise."

"Hmm, that explains why she's been buying so much food. Gracie, you miss me too?" he asked as he messed her hair.

"Of course I missed you, no one's called me a pest in a long time." Gracie released her embrace and looked past

Jamal into the open living area. "Wow, your house is huge," she said. Jamal gave them a tour that ended at his master suite.

"Jamal, your mother bought you two a really nice home," said Gregory.

"I know, Mr. Mitchell. It's a great house. The school is supposed to be good too and the town's okay, but my home is Brooklyn. Besides, how will anyone in the music industry know I'm up here?"

"What do you mean? That doesn't matter. Have you seen how many hits you received on the revised video?" said Brandon.

"Jamal, you have to do some self-promotion if you want to get anywhere. You're not in the city, but there may be more opportunities to perform in a location like this; the competition is much thinner. Look at Justin Bieber, he came from a small town in Canada. That didn't stop him. Stop sulking and try to make it from where you are. Have you checked out any local venues to see if they would let you perform for free?" said Gregory.

"No, I haven't gone anywhere other than the mall and back to the house."

"I'll tell you what, we'll tighten up your Electronic Press Kit tonight. Tomorrow you and I will go to local venues and try to get you in. Bring your keyboard so they can hear what you have to offer."

"Thanks Mr. Mitchell, I didn't think of doing that."

Felicia came back from the supermarket later than expected. Gregory helped Jamal start the grill on the backyard deck while

Felicia, Brandon and Gracie hung decorations in the living room. That afternoon, they filled up on barbecue and sung happy birthday to Jamal for his 17th birthday. Gracie took pictures of everyone with her tablet.

"Felicia, this is a very nice place and you're surrounded by nature. I wouldn't mind living out here; it's peaceful listening to the birds instead traffic," said Gregory.

"Speaking of traffic, I feel so much better not having to do that long commute every week. It was burning me out and I was so afraid of falling asleep at the wheel one day," said Felicia.

Jamal felt convicted, hearing how hard it was for his mother. He knew he was the sole reason for her having to make those long trips and she kept doing it to accommodate him.

Jamal walked over and gave Felicia a hug while saying, "Thanks for the party mom." That hug made Felicia's day; it was the first warm gesture Jamal made since she moved him to their new home.

That evening, Felicia and Gregory sat on the deck talking while Brandon and Gracie stayed with Jamal in his bedroom. Gracie noticed that Brandon looked upset when he was talking to Jamal. The two had stopped playing their Nintendo game. Whatever Brandon told Jamal made him shake his head sadly. Gracie heard him say, "Why did your dad do that?" When she came closer to listen to what they were saying, they both became quiet.

"Hey Gracie, why don't you play something on my piano?" suggested Jamal. Gracie jumped at this new opportunity. She tried to get the two to pay attention to what she was playing, but their expressions remained solemn.

"Gracie, come over here, I need to tell you something," said Brandon. When she walked over, Brandon sat her down. "You know with Jamal up here and me going to prep school soon, we won't be able to look after you anymore. But I want you to know that you can call us if you have a problem. If anyone bothers you or tries to touch you where they shouldn't, I want you to leave that place immediately, okay? You tell your dad if he's there. If he's not, you call me or Jamal and we'll help you. Do you understand?" Gracie shook her head yes. She didn't fully understand what Brandon was talking about, but his demeanor told her it was serious.

The next morning, Gregory took everyone out for breakfast. Afterwards, everyone but Gregory and Jamal went back to the house. Gregory was determined to get Jamal started on his career path. They scoured the local area, going from venue to venue asking for a performance opportunity. Most of the bars and cafés either didn't allow underaged performers, or they didn't believe their patrons were interested in R&B music. Before the day was over, they managed to get Jamal booked for next weekend. He was to play in Saegertown Square, which was the center open area of the Saegertown Mall. The mall manager recognized Gregory as a member of the GMAC group because he was a huge fan. Performing at the mall wasn't the venue Jamal was hoping for, but Gregory thought it was an even better location than the bars for people to hear him perform. After the booking, they went to a print shop to design business cards for Jamal.

"From this day on, always keep cards with you. It has your social media info and your contact details. When you perform at the mall next week, keep a stack on top of your piano. People may want you for party performances," said Gregory.

"I don't know about performing in people's homes, Mr. Mitchell," said Jamal.

"Listen Jamal, you have to try everything to get discovered. You've got the gift, but if the right people don't hear your talent, you'll never get anywhere. Also, remember to have an easy smile. Try not to look stressed even if you feel that way. Make sure you arrive early to check your sound."

"Wait a minute, Mr. Mitchell, aren't you going to be there with me?"

"No Jamal, there's no need for me to come back here to be with you." Gregory slapped Jamal's shoulders. "You've got this, son. You're better than you think."

****

That Saturday, Jamal walked alone into the atrium of the mall at 11 a.m. He made his mother drop him off one hour before he was set to perform. The mall facility manager had already set up the speakers and amps in front of the piano they provided. Dressed in one of his dark grey church suits, Jamal tried to stay calm. For years he performed gospel songs in front of large church congregations with ease, but now he felt anxious. The mall's frigid air conditioning did nothing to stop beads of sweat from appearing on his forehead. The piano was situated in the middle of the atrium square, about 100 feet away from the mall restaurants and food court. Dim pot lights gently illuminated Jamal and the grand piano as he sat down.

Remembering what Mr. Mitchell told him, Jamal tried his best to appear calm. He checked the sound equipment; everything was set. The facility manager left Jamal to start whenever he was ready. Mall shoppers were going about their business as Jamal quietly began playing the keys. He started with an old Stevie Wonder song that was a favorite of his mom. "Knocks Me Off My Feet" begins with piano music before the vocals kick in. Jamal didn't have to look at the keys, but he did this and frequently closed his eyes to avoid making eye contact with anyone; knowing that doing so would only increase his anxiety. At the end of the first song he segued into the next without looking up. Jamal repeated this for the third song. As his voice warmed and his confidence grew, Jamal raised his volume, singing aloud as the song ended. He exhaled and opened his eyes. The thunderous applause and sight of the crowd standing in front of him made Jamal jolt. His face glowed with astonishment. Jamal had no idea people had stopped and congregated in front of the piano. There were all types of people applauding him, young and old with different ethnicities. Some came over to ask who he was. An elderly gentleman came to shake his hand. Two teen girls were gushing as they spoke to him.

Felicia had promised to drop Jamal off and go home. Jamal told her that knowing she was there would make him nervous. But instead of going home, she re-entered the mall by a different entrance. Felicia concealed herself on the upper balcony where she could secretly video record her baby's first public performance. Jamal's routine and the crowd's reaction brought tears to her eyes. Now she understood that this was what her son was meant to do.

Jamal continued playing the tracks that Gregory selected for him. It was a combination of old and new hits to ensure he attracted all ages. The crowd continued to grow. Some people held their phones up to record his performance. His ninety-minute set was over before he knew it and he'd forgotten to take his break in the middle of the session. Various people came over to ask where he was performing next. Jamal wasn't sure when he would get the opportunity to play again, but he gave them his card and told them to check his Facebook page for his next performance. It was the best day of his life; he couldn't wait to tell Mr. Mitchell all about it.

After the weekend performance, Jamal's YouTube video visits exploded. The mall facility manager called to asked him to perform again the following weekend. This time he offered to pay. News of the teen performer spread throughout the county. Jamal performed in other locations that month and he looked forward to seeing his mother at every performance.

When he attended his new school for his senior year, the students already knew who he was. Many wanted to be his friend. In December, when the other seniors were picking out colleges or figuring out what they were going to do at the end of the school year, Jamal was presented with a recording contract from a Los Angeles record company. It was a surreal experience for him. As a minor, he couldn't sign without his parent and Felicia didn't want to sign anything unless Gregory reviewed the terms of the contract. She also wanted Jamal to go to college like the other students, but Gregory advised her to put college aside. The contract was a precious opportunity that would expire long before Jamal would graduate. Besides, when he becomes successful, colleges will gladly give him honorary degrees.

Felicia and Jamal flew back to NYC to meet with the lawyer Gregory suggested they hire. When the contract was signed, the company flew Jamal to Los Angeles to begin his recording career. Recording company executives immediately handed him over to their Artist Development Department. Jamal was placed on a special diet and made to lift weights to enhance his pectorals. Beauticians removed his slight mustache and changed his haircut. The Development Department groomed him into the artist image they wanted him to portray. Jamal learned how to greet the public and media with a static smile. Choreographers showed him dance moves to use on stage. After his grooming was completed, the execs decided Jamal's name wasn't catchy enough for the public, so they dropped the "J." The up and coming artist was now Amal Bliss. Jamal spent the summer traveling to various venues to promote his music before the release of his debut album. The critics loved Amal Bliss. His music blended R&B, Hip hop and Smooth Jazz in such a way that it appealed to the masses; though some online music streamers found it difficult to categorize his sound. Billboard magazine described Amal's style as a mix of Stevie Wonder, John Legend and Gregory Mitchell rolled into one artist. They marveled at the fact that he wrote most of his own songs. Amal's agent arranged for him to perform on late-night and daytime talk shows to give him more exposure to the media. During every interview, Amal stated he'd never have made it without the mentorship from Gregory Mitchell of GMAC. This statement increased Gregory's royalty payments from MP3 sales and online music streaming companies.

Felicia couldn't be prouder of Jamal's accomplishments. His music career took off so fast that sometimes she had no idea where her son was, so she called him every night. It's ironic, she thought. She moved Jamal upstate to be closer to her, but he'd lived in their new home for only six months before moving 3,000 miles away. The residents in their old Brooklyn neighborhood applauded Jamal's achievements. He couldn't walk into his old church anymore without stealing attention from the pulpit. Of course, he spoke often with his biggest fans, Brandon and Gracie, constantly.

Jamal missed Tasha so much but his career and her parents pulled them in opposite directions. Whenever he was back in Brooklyn, Tasha's parents still gave him a hard time. They were never left alone. Her parents were even more suspicious of Jamal as a musician who sung worldly music. To make matters worse, Jamal's schedule made it extremely difficult to go back to Brooklyn often. Soon, the distance between Jamal and Tasha became too great for them to stay together. Too much time went by before they would see each other. And then, there were the female fans! They didn't have restrictive parents who refused to let them date and they were very, very eager to please.

CHAPTER FOUR

Jamal wiped beads of sweat from his forehead as he exited the stage. He'd just wrapped up his second world tour before his twenty-fourth birthday. The people and venues were all very exciting and he loved the attention. With fans, he had to keep the Amal persona turned on at all times, but playing for the crowd wasn't work for him. Jamal would perform 24/7 if he could, but the energy and motivation he had to put into each show drained him physically and emotionally.

Jamal was proud of the four top ten R&B hits since his debut album. All doubting critics were forced to admit, Amal Bliss was here to stay.

His success also brought loneliness. All of his friends and family were back in New York and he hardly got a chance to see them. So, when 23-year-old Brandon graduated with his bachelors in psychology, Jamal begged him to move to L.A. to pursue his masters. Brandon gladly agreed despite protests from his parents. Jamal had also asked his mother to move to L.A. with his promise to buy Felicia her own house. Since Jamal moved away, Felicia fell in love again and married her new husband, Jonathan, in Utica. The newlyweds politely declined his offer with the promise of re-thinking it for their retirement.

In the middle of his tour, Jamal purchased a 7,000 square foot split ranch in Malibu. The luxurious home came with a recording studio already built into the lower level by the previous musician owner. It was almost perfect. Jamal hired an interior decorator to renovated the home to his specific tastes. His "man cave" held a massive large screen TV, opulent theatre style seating, and the latest technology in surround sound equipment. All bathrooms were decorated with his favorite color. Each contained red onyx slab counters and bamboo flooring. The expansive kitchen included every appliance a person could want, along with a real pizza oven and indoor grill. He made sure all renovations were completed before the end of his tour and upcoming birthday. Jamal arranged for Mr. Mitchell, Gracie, his mother and Jonathan, to spend a week with him in his new home. Since Jamal sent Gracie pictures of his new home upon her request, she couldn't wait to get there. Gracie and Gregory had previously visited Jamal in L.A., but those places were small rentals.

At fourteen, Gracie was no longer the cute little kid with long unruly hair and she didn't like to be treated like one. She stood at 5'9", a height inherited from her tall father. Her curves came from her mother. Gregory's little girl had grown into a beautiful teenager. To Gregory's dismay, boys began asking her out when she was eleven. Remembering what he did with girls when he was a teenager, Gregory kept a strict rein on his daughter's social life. No sleepovers or dating was allowed. He removed Gracie from public school and enrolled her into an all-girls private religious high school. She hated her new school, but her father didn't care about that. Enrolling Gracie in an all-girls school helped him to sleep at night. On her thirteenth birthday, Gregory presented Gracie with a purity ring. She received the ring with a confused expression since it wasn't the new phone she'd been hinting at. Disappointment was written all over her face when he explained that it was her promise to stay pure until she married in the very, very distant future. Gracie nonchalantly agreed. As far as Gregory was concerned, he did everything humanly possible to keep Gracie from turning out like his sister.

Dressed in skinny jeans and a trendy sleeveless tee, Gracie waited impatiently by the baggage carousel. She spotted their luggage and slid in front of a couple, who she perceived as slow-moving tourists, to retrieved both bags. A few men offered to help carry them for her, but she just rolled her eyes and ignored them. Gracie rolled the luggage away from the crowd and sucked her teeth as she waited for her father to catch up.

Gregory arrived a few minutes later. Gracie started rolling her bag toward the automatic exit doors before Gregory grabbed his. Before exiting the airport terminal doors, she turned around to see where her father was.

"Dad, hurry up!" Gracie made an exasperated sigh and rolled her eyes as she watched her father leisurely pull his carry on and checked bags toward her.

"Gracie, you need to calm down. We'll be here a whole week, there's no need to rush."

Gracie exited the automatic door ahead of her father and found the car that Jamal sent for them. The driver stood by the bumper with a sign that said "Mitchell Family." By the time Gregory reached the vehicle, Gracie was enjoying the limo AC with her bags stowed in the trunk.

Gregory handed the driver his bags before he sat in the car next to Gracie. He was breathing rapidly.

Gracie eyed him worriedly before asking, "Dad, did you take your medicine?"

"Yes sweetheart, I took it this morning."

"Please tell me you're not smoking again."

Gregory turned to look at her. "Stop worrying, I'm okay."

The car traveled from the hectic airport to the scenic roads of Malibu. They drove up a spacious curved driveway to Jamal's modern split-level ranch. The driver pulled up in front of the main entrance and removed the bags from the trunk while the car idled. While Gregory tipped the driver, Gracie took the two largest bags and rolled them up to the entryway.

Gracie was shocked to see Jamal open the door himself. She barreled into him with a big hug and kiss before pushing him back. "You see how tall I am? Soon I'll be as tall as you."

"Trust me, that will never happen," said Jamal. Gracie looked around the two-story foyer where they stood.

"JJ, this is sweet! I love it. The ceilings are so high and the moldings are out of this world. Where did you find those sconces?" He turned to look at them.

"My designer had those custom made for the house." As he turned back around, Gregory came through the open door.

"Hey boy, stop chit chatting with that fast-talking teenager and welcome me into your home."

"Hey, Mr. Mitchell," said Jamal as they both hugged.

"You're doing well son, this is a very nice house," said Gregory as he looked around. "Thanks, Mr. Mitchell."

"Auntie Felicia," Gracie said as she ran over to Felicia and gave her a long bear hug. After releasing Felicia, she gave Jonathan a hug. Gregory greeted them with hugs as well. Jamal showed Gracie and Gregory their rooms before giving them a tour of his home. When Jamal brought the two downstairs to show them his renovated studio, Gracie loved it so much she didn't want to leave.

"Come on Gracie, I promise I'll show you how to work it before the end of the week," said Jamal.

"You promise? Wow, I can't wait."

Jamal eyed Gregory. "She's been drinking cola again, hasn't she?"

"Yeah, I made the mistake of taking a nap on the flight. When I woke up, she was on her fourth can." Jamal laughed as they climb the one flight of stairs to get back to the main living area. As they came back into the great room, they heard Gracie talking non-stop with Brandon, who'd just arrived while they were in the studio.

"You know what, let me take a quick nap. Gracie and the flight tired me out," said Gregory.

"Okay, Mr. Mitchell, we'll come and get you when we go out to dinner."

Jamal returned to the great room alone.

"Where's Dad?" asked Gracie.

"Oh, he just went to take a nap."

"I'll be right back," she said as she left the room.

"Wait, where're you going?" he asked as Gracie got up.

"I'm just going to check on him for a minute, I'll be back soon." When Gracie entered the guest room, she saw that her father had removed his shoes and laid down. She went straight for his carry-on bag to take out Gregory's medications. "Dad, you're wheezing, you need to use your inhaler."

"That's okay, Gracie, I just took my pills. I'm waiting for them to kick in."

"Do you need more pillows, dad?"

"No, I'm okay. Go back to the others, I'll be fine." Gracie reluctantly left his side and headed back to the great room.

Jamal approached her when she returned, "Gracie, is everything okay?"

"Yeah, everything is fine, dad's just taking a nap." She walked over to Brandon before he could ask any more questions.

Jamal took everyone out to dinner later that afternoon. They talked about old times and events. Felicia brought up the time when Jamal was stabbed.

Brandon commented, "Man, when you see the women go crazy over that scar, it makes me think about getting one."

"Brandon, that's the dumbest thing I've heard you said yet. Who would get stabbed to become more attractive to women? And I hope the women are just looking and not touching. Boy, I hope you're not sleeping with all those crazy fans," said Felicia. Brandon was about to comment again when Jamal kicked him under the table.

"Ma, I'm just signing autographs and taking pictures with them, that's all," said Jamal. Eager to change the subject, Jamal picked on Gracie. "So Gracie, how're you doing in school now?" said Jamal.

"I was doing fine before dad switched me to an all-girls private school," she said with attitude.

"You'll do better than fine in this school. Without distractions, you'll focus on your work," Gregory said sternly.

"Do you know what dad calls distractions? One boy called the house to ask me on a date; one phone call and dad freaks out."

"No, it wasn't just about one boy. I didn't like the crowd you were hanging out with either. Those girls were too fast, wearing clothes that were too short or too tight, and they were changing you into them."

"Gracie, you're only fourteen, you're too young to date," said Jamal.

"Yeah, you can't just go out with anyone who asks either. You have to let us check him out first," said Brandon.

"How are you two going to check anyone out when you're living on a different coastline?" said Gracie.

"I remember when your Aunt Loretta hung out with a crowd like that ..." Gregory started. Gracie sighed heavily and dramatically rolled her eyes and neck while her father continued to talk. "... Loretta started talking back to my mom, staying out at all hours; she was never the same."

"How is Loretta, Gregory," Felicia asked.

"She's doing okay, now."

"Yeah, she doesn't come to borrow money like she used to," said Gracie sarcastically.

"I'll never understand why you're always hard on your aunt. She always asks about you, but you barely give her the time of day," said Gregory.

The group went back to Jamal's house after dinner. Everyone except Gracie was engrossed in conversation about the old days. Feeling bored, she snuck down to the studio to look over the equipment. The Grand Steinway piano was centered behind the studio glass wall. Separate smaller glass rooms holding other musical instruments were situated on the perimeter of the studio walls. One of the rooms had a set of drums, the other had a bass and guitar. The studio floors were a beautiful honeyed oak while the walls and ceiling were covered with textured, dove grey acoustic panels. Dim lighting illuminated the perimeter of each panel, providing just enough light to see the piano keys.

Gracie brought her tablet with her as she entered the piano room. The studio glass door closed softly behind her, leaving the room in complete silence. She admired the impressive lacquered grand piano. They never had the space for one in their Brooklyn apartment. She delicately traced the curves of the instrument with her hand as she walked to the seat. The expensive piano was Jamal's and Gracie knew better than to play it without asking, but she couldn't help herself. *Besides, what if he said no. Jamal never wants me to touch his stuff and with the door closed, who's going to know,* she told herself.

Gregory started his daughter's piano lessons as soon as

her little fingers were strong enough to hold down the keys, but the songs and poems she wrote on her tablet were self-taught. Gracie practiced her songs whenever her father wasn't around. For years she grew up listening to her father critiquing Jamal's playing and singing. Sometimes she felt sorry for Jamal after he received harsh critiques; she wanted none of that.

Gregory frequently referred to Jamal as gifted. As a young child, Gracie remembered being jealous of Jamal, but as she grew older, the jealousy turned into admiration. Jamal was the full package, a gifted pianist, vocalist and writer.

Now, here she was all alone with this perfect instrument in front of her, begging for someone to play it. It was too hard to resist. The piano had three microphones on stands strategically placed around it. Gracie was careful, she avoided touching anything but the piano as she was determined to not leave any traces of her being in the studio. At first, she played a few simple chords before delving into a song she was working on. The sound created by the Steinway was unbelievably rich and so much better than playing their worn-out baby grand at home. Playing this piano was truly an enjoyable experience. With a smile on her face and closed eyes, Gracie played for the pure enjoyment of hearing the melody she created.

Upstairs, Jamal noticed Gracie was M.I.A. for quite a while before he decided to track her down. *Hmm, if I were Gracie, where would I be now,* he thought. Jamal immediately headed for the stairs. From the bottom of the staircase he spotted Gracie sitting in his seat, playing his brand new mahogany Steinway. Jamal walked over to the control panel. *At least she had the sense not to touch the electronics,* he thought as he checked the panel. Jamal walked to the studio door intending to give Gracie yet another lesson on how to ask before touching his stuff, but with the microphones on, he heard her sing along with the melody she played. The music made him stop. Jamal liked what he heard. The melancholy song was unique and fresh; a mixture of old school acid jazz and pop. Without Gracie realizing it, Jamal turned on the recording equipment to capture the song.

The angle of the piano seat gave Gracie a view of the wall. She was oblivious to Jamal's presence. After finishing the last note of the song, the silence of the studio surrounded her. Gracie jumped when she heard Jamal quickly open the studio door.

"I figured I'd find you here."

"Y-y-yes, sorry; I should have asked before using your piano," she said sheepishly.

"That's okay. Do you mind playing that song through again? I only caught the last half of it."

"Wait, you want to hear my song? The superstar wants to hear my little song?" Gracie said more confidently.

"You know what? Just stop talking and play the song again like I asked," said Jamal.

Gracie sucked her teeth and turned to commence playing the music.

"Wait a minute, I want to re-start and record this in its entirety. Start playing on my mark. You were singing in your natural contralto voice so I'm going to sing after you using my baritone. Let's see how that works."

Gracie was ecstatic that Jamal wanted to record her song, but she didn't want to show it. Jamal brought Brandon downstairs to help with production. The three of them spent many hours working on perfecting the music. Gracie played the song countless number of times and with just as many variations. Jamal and Brandon showed her how to manipulate the sound and tweak the characteristics of the music using the studio control surface. She soaked up every tidbit of recording skill she'd learned from them. The young teen developed a love for the recording process. Jamal had ultimately rearranged the lyrics and sped up the rhythm of the chorus. Brandon added synthesized bass sounds to enhance the song.

Gregory wondered where Gracie, Jamal and Brandon had gone. The studio was in view when he descended the stairs and he saw Gracie and Brandon looking at Jamal for instructions. Gregory walked closer and listened intently to the song being played back. He liked what he heard.

Jamal stopped the music at intervals to adjust the instruments and instructed Gracie and Brandon on what to do differently.

It made Gregory smile to see Jamal taking the time to let Gracie play one of his songs on his Steinway, and he enjoyed the music he was hearing. An idea popped into Gregory's head now that Gracie was occupied. He slowly crept back upstairs, but instead of returning to the great room, he made a beeline for the bedrooms. Once inside, Gregory pulled out his secret stash of cigarettes. He locked his bedroom door and opened the bathroom window. It was his first cigarette in a very long time. He knew Gracie would throw a fit if she caught him.

Earlier in the year, he made the mistake of telling her of his COPD diagnosis and how his smoking caused it. In his case, he had emphysema that was now causing him to have shortness of breath. She broke down, crying and worrying about him so much that he promised her he would never smoke again. But it proved too difficult to leave cigarettes alone. Gregory had been smoking since he was 16 years old and the urge to continue smoking was incredibly strong. When he got the urge back home, Gregory would wait until Gracie was asleep before lightning up. Then one day he couldn't find his stash. He couldn't ask Gracie if she took them because he had promised not to smoke. He smelled them the next day when he was taking out the trash. Gracie took the time to cut each cigarette into tiny pieces before throwing them away. Gregory tried to resurrect them and maybe roll up one cigarette, but as he grabbed the small pieces, he realized that she had poured ammonia over them.

It was difficult to look her in the eye after that event and she watched him like a hawk. He caught her in his bedroom several times searching his things, so Gregory found new hiding spots for his cigarettes. Sometimes he taped them under the kitchen table or behind the refrigerator. She hasn't found those stashes yet, but it was only a matter of time. He hated to see his baby girl worry and Gregory felt tremendous guilt whenever his shortness of breath brought fear to her eyes. Not wanting Jamal to worry too, he decided not to tell him about his illness. The only other person he had confided in was Loretta.

Gracie woke up on the studio plush sectional. Jamal and Brandon were at the controls with the speakers blaring the song they'd worked on.

"What's wrong with you two? You woke me up," she shouted. Jamal turn around with a huge smile on his face, both his head and Brandon's were bobbing to the beat of the song.

"We woke you up so you could hear the finished product, listen. What do you think? It's good right?" said Jamal. The song sounded a whole lot better than what she started with. It was polished and professional. Gracie was disappointed in herself for falling asleep before it was completed.

"I like it a lot, it's a completely new song," said Gracie. Her eyes threatened to close again but the high volume of music prevailed. "I'm going upstairs to put in my retainer and go to bed."

"Okay, but just so you know, this is going on the new album," shouted Jamal.

"Okay, that's great JJ." Gracie was so tired she didn't grasp the significance of what Jamal said. The long flight, caffeine buzz and hours of piano playing had taken its toll.

Jamal and Brandon waved her off as she headed for the stairs, but then Jamal remembered something.

"Wait Gracie," he left Brandon and caught Gracie before her ascent. "Sit down, I want to ask you something."

"JJ, I've been down here all night and you want to ask me something now? This better be good."

"Okay, look, I know you're tired, but I have to ask. Is there anything going on with your dad?" Gracie broke eye contact and sighed.

"You know what, why don't you ask him?" She got up and left before he could ask any more questions.

Though tired, Gracie kept to her nightly routine of checking on her father. At night he slept on a mound of high pillows, but sometimes he turns over in his sleep, making the pillows move to the side. Gracie popped her head in the door and heard her father's labored breath. She walked in quietly and rearranged the pillows before putting them back under his head.

Gregory woke up briefly and said, "Thanks sweetheart."

"Goodnight dad." After a quick shower, Gracie collapsed in bed.

The next day, Jamal took everyone on a charted yacht to Catalina Island. The group stayed at an upscale resort by the beach. Crystal clear water enticed everyone to take a dip in the water. Brandon and Jamal kept an eye on some teen boys admiring Gracie in her bathing suit.

"Poor Mr. Mitchell, Gracie's gonna get a lot of attention from the boys," said Brandon. "Mr. Mitchell is handling the situation with the school change. My mom's going to talk with Gracie before she leaves too; just to see where her head is," said Jamal.

They stayed on the beach for most of the morning. Brandon and Jamal encouraged everyone to take snorkeling lessons.

"You guys go ahead, I don't like water that much. I'm

going back to my room to do some reading," said Gregory.

"Dad, you want me to go back with you?"

"No Gracie, you go and have some fun, I'll be busy with my reading," said Gregory.

Jamal observed Gracie hesitating, as if she couldn't decide if she should stay or go with her father. The earlier excitement she had for snorkeling lessons dissipated as she watched her father return to the hotel.

Something is definitely up, he thought. "Okay, we'll see you later, Mr. Mitchell. Come on Gracie," said Jamal.

Felicia, Gracie and Jonathan took their lessons before joining Brandon and Jamal in the water. Gracie was having the time of her life; she couldn't remember the last time she had so much fun.

The next morning, everyone boarded the yacht for the trip back to Jamal's home. Jonathan and Felicia looked exhausted as they walked stiffly on and off the boat. When everyone arrived back at Jamal's home, Gregory observed the two gingerly make their way to the couch.

"What happened to you guys, why are you moving so slowly?" asked Gregory.

"We had a great time snorkeling yesterday, but we over did it. Getting out of bed was tough; every muscle in my body ached," said Jonathan.

"I could barely sit up straight for breakfast this morning," said Felicia.

"Y'all should know better than to follow those young kids in the water. You're both in your fifties, what were you thinking?" said Gregory jokingly.

"You're right, we should have taken baby steps since it was our first time. I didn't realize how out of shape we were, but I'm definitely doing it again. You should try it too; Gracie had a ball. She's growing up into a beautiful young lady, Gregory; you've done a great job," said Felicia.

"Thanks Felicia, I couldn't have done it without you and Jamal. You have no idea how much you've helped. My job's not done yet though. Can't tell Gracie anything now, she thinks she has all the answers and I know this dating thing will come up again. Luckily, she's not boy crazy yet. I'm keeping her under close watch, though I know there're no guarantees. It's all I can do to keep her from following in Loretta's footsteps."

"I don't believe you have to worry too much, Gregory. I had a talk with Gracie yesterday. She's very mature and sensible for her young age. You're doing all the right things; Jennifer would be proud of you."

"Boy, that was such a stressful period in my life. Being a full-time single dad after Jennifer died. Well, I don't have to tell you how tough it is to be a single parent. You've done a tremendous job with raising Jamal," said Gregory.

"Oh no, Gregory, you're wrong. I did not raise him all by myself, you raised him too. Jamal wouldn't be the man he is today without you. You did so much more than teach him to play the piano; you taught him how to be a man. That's something I could never have done. I know he loves you like a father," said Felicia.

"Well, the feeling is mutual. He's not my flesh, but he's my son in spirit," said Gregory.

"I think both of you did great jobs as single parents. I don't know what I would have done in your place. When my wife passed, my kids were already out the house," said Jonathan.

"Thanks Jonathan, I've made my share of mistakes, but Gracie turned out pretty good in spite of them." Just then, Gracie passed by on her way to the studio stairs. "Gracie, where are you going? I don't want you touching the studio equipment."

"Daaaad, Jamal and Brandon are already down there. They're going to teach me about the electronics. I wouldn't touch that stuff without asking." She then said under her breath, "The Steinway, however, is another issue."

CHAPTER FIVE

TWO YEARS LATER

"Dad, I made some oatmeal for you, it's on the counter. Remember, no milk okay?"

"I'll eat it later sweetheart. You better hurry so you don't miss your bus on your last day of school."

"It's okay Dad. I can catch the next bus if I need to." Gracie washed out her bowl and picked up her bookbag before heading for the door. "I only have a half day of school so I'll be home soon. Don't forget to text me if you have any problems."

"I will honey, have a good day at school."

Gregory stood up from his chair the second he heard the bottom door close. He walked slowly down the one flight of stairs toward the bottom front door. His shortness of breath increased with activity, so he had to be careful to not over exert himself. Gregory had reached a critical stage in his emphysema and he made serious plans to do something about it. He'd struggled to finish his spring semester teachings in May. Getting to and from work on the subway took a lot of energy. Over time, he hated those multiple staircases and the impatient New Yorkers who didn't know how to be kind to those who couldn't walk swiftly. His last doctor was no help. He suggested Gregory carry a small oxygen canister when he travelled to work, but Gregory didn't want anyone to see him with one of those things. He searched around until he came upon a new doctor whose treatment made better sense to him. Gregory submitted his medical leave forms before the end of the spring semester. It allowed him two months off from the fall semester.

As Gregory's illness progressed, Gracie took on more housekeeping roles. She did all the cooking and house cleaning without him having to ask and she still checks on him every night. It's been a struggle for Gregory to look at the worry in her eyes whenever he had an episode. This wasn't the life he wanted for his baby girl. He wanted her to enjoy her summer like the other kids and not worry about every breath he struggled to get out of his damaged lungs.

Gregory reached the bottom of the steps; he rested a bit before walking over to unlock the front door Gracie left out of several minutes ago. It was an excessively warm, sticky June day. The high humidity kept him from going outside, as the heavy moist air wasn't good for him to breathe. Facing the aged stairwell, Gregory closed his eyes and reminisced about the time he carried Jennifer up these very stairs. It was effortless. Jennifer giggled all the way up and he couldn't stop himself from laughing at her. They'd just returned from their honeymoon in Aruba. Gregory opened his eyes and admired the restored stain glass window in the foyer and the reclaimed dentil moldings that framed the ceilings. Jennifer wanted a home with lots of character and the 1905 Brownstone fit the bill. She enjoyed restoring their home and he loved making her happy.

Sighing with regret, Gregory grasped the curved mahogany handrail to assist in his climb to the second floor. The ascent took more effort and required a mid-stairway rest period. *This situation is only temporary,* he thought. Next week, he planned to move downstairs. His tenant had already agreed to move upstairs and Loretta was coming over to assist the moving company with packing. When he reached the second floor landing, Gregory sat down in his overstuffed recliner. His cellphone rested on top of papers he had requested from his attorney.

Two hours went by before the phone rang. "Hello? Yes, I'm here. I left the door open so you can come on up when you get here," said Gregory. About an hour later, he heard the front door on the lower level open and close before footsteps quickly climbed up to the second floor. Gregory stood up to greet Jamal as he came through the open door. Jamal had to hide his shock when he saw Mr. Mitchell, <u>as</u> he hugged a much thinner version of his mentor. The strong six foot two, broad shouldered man must have lost at least fifty pounds.

Gregory called Jamal a month ago and asked for his help. The news of Mr. Mitchell's illness overwhelmed him. The man who taught him all he knew had a chronic lung disease for several years and he knew nothing of it. Jamal felt guilty for not asking him about his health when he visited two years ago, but Jamal knew Mr. Mitchell well enough. If the man didn't tell you something, he didn't want you to know. His decision was to respect his mentor's privacy.

Gracie used to call and text so often he had to ignore her at times; but he'd hardly heard from her in the past year. He actually missed hearing from the pest. Jamal and Brandon texted her several times about their song burning up the charts. It was becoming one of his biggest hits and he owed it all to his little sister. With Mr. Mitchell's permission, Jamal set up a royalty account for Gracie that she will have access to once she turns 21. Looking at Mr. Mitchell now made Jamal realize why Gracie didn't express the excitement he expected from her. Taking care of her father must have been overwhelming, and she kept it a secret.

"It doesn't feel right, Mr. Mitchell; Gracie should know about the surgery you have planned. When she finds out that I kept it from her, she'll never speak to me again."

"Don't worry about Gracie, she never stays mad for long. Besides, when she comes back home, I'll tell her that I made you promise not to say anything. Loretta will contact you guys if there are any problems. In the meantime, Loretta's moving in until I recover. I wrote down her number somewhere in these documents." Gregory picked up the stack of documents and added them to a folder. "Gracie's passport, birth certificate, school information; it's all in here along with the temporary guardianship papers. If all goes as planned, and it will, I'll be recovering at home long before she's ready to go back to school. If the recovery takes longer than that, Loretta will continue to stay with us," said Gregory.

"Well, you'll have to tell her that one, I'm not going to argue with her about living with her aunt."

"Jamal, I really appreciate your doing this for me. I know you're busy with your career and don't need a teenager following you around. We'll lay down some ground rules for her to follow."

"Mr. Mitchell, this is me you're talking to. You don't have to worry about a thing, I could always handle Gracie. I know how she thinks."

"Well, that was when she was a little girl; she thinks she's grown now. She can be sneaky when she doesn't get her way," said Gregory.

"Trust me, Mr. Mitchell, I know her better than she knows herself. Besides, it would be nice to have more family around my camp. There're so many phony people in L.A. Sometimes I have to pretend to like them and they're pretending to like me. I can't be myself around them, but I know that I can be myself with Gracie and Brandon. And she won't be the only female around either. My girlfriend stops by sometimes and my father's daughter may visit before my tour."

"Your sister? Hey, that's great Jamal; how did you find her?"

"I didn't. My deadbeat dad, or should I say, the sperm donor, decided to track me down. He called mom and she told him how to get access to me. I'd just finished a show in Dallas when he showed up backstage with my sister. He suddenly realized I existed and wanted to have a relationship. Imagine that, he waits until I'm 25 years old to have a father/son relationship. I'm certain my fame and fortune had nothing to do with his sudden interest," Jamal said sarcastically.

"Don't let the bitterness get to you, son. Your dad isn't a bad man, he's just selfish. I'm sure he loved you and your mom, but Malcolm likes to do whatever makes him happy. Some people don't realize what's important in life until it's too late. I ruined my marriage with my selfishness so I can't say that I'm better than anyone else," said Gregory regretfully. "How did your meeting go with your father and sister, what did you say?"

"Oh, I was cool. I said I was surprise to see him. He called me son, but I set him straight. I told him, I'm too old to start calling someone dad, so I'll just refer to you as Malcolm. He had the nerve to get upset and storm off when I said that. My sister Sofia on the other hand introduced herself and said she wanted to get to know me because I was her only sibling; so, I invited her to come for the week before my tour," said Jamal.

"It's good to have a sibling. I wished Gracie had other siblings, but I guess it just wasn't in God's plan," said Gregory.

"Don't worry, Mr. Mitchell, Gracie will always have a brother in me." Jamal and Gregory spent the rest of the morning together catching up.

Gracie waved goodbye to one of her school friends before exiting the city bus. It was the last day of a hectic school year. This year she had taken over all of the household duties. It was tiring at times balancing her chores with school work, but it's what she had to do. The only plans she had for the summer was to relax and take care of her dad without the distraction of school.

Gracie watched her father slowly deteriorate, losing more

weight and having more episodes of breathlessness. In the beginning, he said he'd get better and she believed him at first. When she did her own research, Gracie realized that he wasn't taking good care of his condition. That's when she decided to take an active role in his recovery, whether he liked it or not. Gregory didn't like it. Gracie wanted to accompany her father to his doctor appointments because she had questions she wanted to ask about his health, but Gregory wouldn't let her skip school.

When Gracie turned the corner onto her block, she noticed the shiny black limo double parked outside of her home. Her casual lazy walk became a sprint to her front door. Gracie ran up the stairs two at a time and rushed through the front door.

"JJ, you didn't tell me you were coming? What did you get me?" she said as she rushed to hugged him.

"Whatever happened to hello or it's nice to see you? Do I have to buy you something every time I see you? Can't my presence be your gift?" Gracie sucked her teeth and shoved away from Jamal before turning to close the door.

"JJ, you need to stop smelling yourself. Those fans made your head swell too big. Let some of that hot air out so you can stay grounded." Gregory started laughing as he looked at Jamal's facial expression.

"I don't believe this; I fly here all the way from L.A. to ask you to stay with me for the summer, and this is the greeting you give me?"

Gracie's head snapped to attention before saying, "Wait, what did you say?"

Jamal continued, "Maybe I need to rethink this. I thought it was a good idea to bring my little sister over to hang out with me and Brandon for the summer, but people will hear that mouth of yours and believe you have no manners and that will reflect on me."

"Wait … wait, JJ don't be hasty; I have manners." Gracie curtsied and bowed gracefully before stating in an exaggerated formal voice, "Good afternoon, my dearest brother. My heart is overwhelmed with joy to be in your presence. How art thou?" Both Gregory and Jamal began to laugh.

"Alright, that's over the top. Give me something in between those two extremes and you can come," said Jamal.

"Really, I can come? Yes," she said while jumping up and down. "Trust me, you won't regret it." Gracie hugged him again.

When she turned around, the smile left Gracie's face. "Wait, I can't go, I have to stay home."

"No Gracie, it's okay. I want you to go and have a good time. This is a great opportunity for you to learn more about music production," said Gregory.

"Dad, I can't leave you alone."

"It's okay, Gracie. I told Jamal all about my illness and Loretta is going to stay with me while you're gone."

Gracie sighed as she turned to Jamal, "I'm glad you know now, it's been so hard keeping it a secret. You have no idea what it was like not being able to tell anyone."

"I'm sorry, Gracie, I didn't realize how hard it was for you," said Gregory.

"It's okay, pest. I know Mr. Mitchell made you promise

not to say anything." *I hope you remember this day and forgive me when you find out about the surgery,* Jamal thought. "You should start packing, we're flying back to my house tomorrow. Oh, and make sure you pack everything you need," said Jamal.

"Everything? Are we taking a trip to the moon? Why would I need to pack everything?" asked Gracie. "I'm just staying for a week or two, right?"

"Hmmm, there's that mouth again; I thought we had that under control," said Jamal.

"Alright, alright; it'll be tough but I'll learn to hold my tongue," said Gracie.

Chronicles II

CHAPTER SIX

"Oooh, this car is NICE! You know, I'm at the legal driving age now," said Gracie as she admired the custom burgundy leather interior.

Jamal laughs before saying, "You don't know how to drive?"

"No, but if you give me this car I will be inspired to learn quickly."

"Keep dreaming pest. By the way, you don't learn to drive with a Jaguar, but if it's okay with your dad, I'll get you lessons before you go home."

"Okay, I'm going to hold you to that."

"I know you will," said Jamal.

The warm dry California winds blew through the convertible as Jamal drove up the scenic Pacific Coast highway. Gracie admired the vibrant orange poppies that grew along the highway while breathtaking views of the surf were on the other side of the road.

"I like driving in a convertible. You get a better view of the sights and smells. If you're thinking of what to get me for my next birthday, make it a convertible."

Jamal laughs, "You never give up, do you."

"I like this weather too. It's warm, but there's no humidity; it would be great for dad. I wonder if he misses me yet."

"Gracie, we just left this morning. Don't tell me you're already homesick?"

"No, I'm fine; it's just that dad depends on me for stuff. He tries hard not to show it, but sometimes he needs help. Aunt Loretta better know how to take care of him."

"Gracie, what is it with you and your aunt?"

"I don't know, I just get the creeps whenever she's around. When I was younger, she would come to visit, but it was never to spend time with dad or me. She only came when she needed money. Once she got it, that was it. We wouldn't see her again until she was broke. She's much better now, though. Dad said she took care of me after my mother died, but I don't remember that at all."

"Hey, you should be glad you have an aunt. I don't have any aunts or uncles; well I don't have any on my mother's side. I wouldn't know my father's family because I don't know him."

"I never thought of your father having family. No one talks about your dad, but it's possible you have aunts and uncles somewhere. I definitely know I don't have any uncles, cousins or siblings."

"What are you talking about? You have me. That's better than ten siblings. I'm the greatest brother anyone can have; you are blessed and highly favored!"

"Oh, my goodness, you are so full of yourself. There

must be something in the air out here that makes celebrities loopy. Please don't go crazy on us like Kanye." Jamal just laughed.

"JJ?"

"Yeah?"

"Do you still pray and stuff like you used to?"

Jamal exhaled, "Honestly, I don't do that much anymore. Why do you ask?"

"Well, it's just that so much of your music has explicit lyrics now. The youth minister at church told us not to listen to music with explicit lyrics. So, technically, I'm not supposed to play your songs unless you have a clean version. Why do you add curses to your songs anyway? You never did that in the beginning."

"Hmm, that's a tough question. I didn't want to add them, but the record company said it's the only way to expand my market. They said my image was too clean."

"Oh, I didn't know they asked for stuff like that. At least you don't do all that crazy stuff the other celebrities are doing. It's a good thing you have Brandon to keep you grounded."

"What? Brandon keep me grounded? You're confused, it's the other way around. Brandon doesn't have to do anything to me, I'm the one who keeps him grounded. He's the one who's drinking and going out with any woman he meets in the club."

"That doesn't sound like the Brandon I know; he would never do anything to bring shame to his father's ministry."

"Well, there are things you don't know. After he had a

bad argument with his dad, he decided to live the way he really wanted to. Remember, he's a preacher kid, they always rebel when they leave home."

Gracie shook her head, "No, I don't believe that. Brandon has always been the level headed one."

"Gracie, you don't know Brandon like I do. He's been going wild out here, doing everything he couldn't at home."

"No, you're just trying to make yourself look better. I'll check him out for myself."

"Okay, you do that; check him out for yourself."

"Now, if you're not trying to be a player too, tell me who you're dating."

"Listen Gracie, you're a kid, you don't need to be in my business like that. I like to keep that stuff private."

"Oh, in other words, you're not dating anyone right now. Maybe you should give Tasha a call," said Gracie teasingly.

"You know what, let's change the subject," Jamal said sternly. "Your dad told me you liked working in the studio with me and Bran so much that you're interested in becoming a sound engineer or music producer. I think you're selling yourself short. I've been telling my agent about you and he knows you wrote the lyrics to our song. He's interested in promoting you as a new artist. What do you think about that? I know you have more songs than the one we worked on; you can play one of them during your interview."

"I don't know JJ, performing doesn't interest me."

"Listen to me. There's nothing like the feeling you get when people scream your name and you have the look and the skills agents want. Why don't you just try it? A lot of people would kill for an opportunity like this. Do you want to talk to my agent?"

"No, not now, but thanks for asking."

"I don't believe this. You copy everything I do. I offer you an opportunity to be a recording artist like me, but you choose now to be different?" Jamal said incredulously.

"That's not true, I don't copy you."

"Yes, you do. Think about it, you always want to eat the same food I eat, play the same video games I play, and now you want a convertible too. You might as well be a performer like me."

"Well, I don't know. I can't be a performer like you because I don't like standing in front of an audience."

"How do you know that if you never tried it?"

"Umm, I don't know. When I watch you on stage, you're like a different person. You become Amal! They love everything you do and I can tell that you love performing. I just can't envision myself doing what you do on stage."

"Hmm, that sounds like you're complementing me," Jamal said with a smirk.

"Oh, would you get over yourself already! Please stop reading your fan mail."

"Alright, alright I'll stop. But seriously, everything you see me do on stage was learned. They taught me how to perform. You can be taught too."

"JJ, it's not just your performance. Dad's always talking about how gifted you are, so I know you can do what you do. He never said those things about me."

Jamal sighed. "Listen, you're his baby girl. I know Mr. Mitchell. He doesn't want you on stage gyrating or doing sexy dances for the audience, so I can see him discouraging you from being a performer. Don't get me wrong, this industry and the people in it are tough and two-faced. Everyone will want to put their hands in your pockets too. You'd be surprised of how many people try to hustle me for money. If you can't handle being around those types of people, then no, you shouldn't be a performer. I just don't want you to think that you can't make it if it's what you want. I know you can sing, write music and play the keyboards. There are artists out here with recording contracts who can't sing as well as you do and they can't write or play. I can teach you how to watch your back in this industry, so if you ever change your mind about being a recording artist, just let me know, alright?"

"Okay, thanks, JJ. You know, I really liked working in the studio. I want to learn all that I can while I'm here."

"Of course, I've already got some things for you to work on. Maybe we can do another song together. Have you been following our song? It was number one on the Billboard R&B chart in March."

"JJ, that's your song. I just contributed the lyrics, everything else was from you and Brandon."

"Gracie, it's our song; it wouldn't be anything without your lyrics. Remind me to show you your royalties account."

"I have royalties?"

"Yes, but you can't access it until you're 21, so don't get too excited."

"But I could use the money now to buy one of these,"

said Gracie with a smile as she slapped the dashboard.

Jamal rolled his eyes, "You see, you want this because I have it. You always want what I have. Even when you were little you were always touching my stuff with those grubby little fingers; and now I have to polish your prints off my dashboard."

At Jamal's remark, Gracie put both hands on the dash, making as many fingerprints as possible. Jamal sighed, "You ever wondered why we call you pest?" They drove a few more minutes before Jamal pulled off the highway onto a narrow road that led to his home. After he put Gracie's bags in the spare bedroom, the two walked downstairs to the studio. They found Brandon at the controls with headphones on, nodding his head to music. Gracie called out to him, but he was oblivious to their arrival until Jamal snatched the headphones off.

Brandon quickly turned around. "Hey, you guys are here already?" Brandon grew up into a football coach's dream. Standing at six foot four and built like a linebacker, he made Jamal's six-foot narrow frame appear petite. He stood up and embraced Gracie in a tight bear hug while she muffled, "I can't breathe," into his chest. Brandon put Gracie back on the ground, saying, "The Pest is in the house! What do you want to do while you're here? Do you want to go to the theme parks?"

"No, that's okay, we've been to all of them already. I'd rather hang out with you guys and do what you do."

"Hmm, I don't know, Gracie. We're adults, you can't go to most of the places that we go for fun," said Brandon.

"Gracie, you just got here, why don't you go to your room and take a nap or go out by the pool. Bran and I have to work on something in the studio right now."

"Alright, I might as well start unpacking now."

Gracie went to the room Jamal showed her earlier. She unpacked and took a quick shower. Feeling hungry and not wanting to take the guys away from their work, she rummaged through the massive open concept kitchen to see what was available to eat. There were tons of prepared meals and frozen entrée's in the commercial sized refrigerator, but none of them interested her, so she decided to make her own dish. She chose to cook a dish that her dad could no longer eat because of the amount of cheese it contained. Gregory stopped eating cheese and dairy because of the excessive mucus it created. Gracie found ground beef and mozzarella in the fridge. Sixty minutes later, she was taking her baked Ziti dish out of the oven. The refrigerator contained several prepared salads. She found a Caesar salad and placed it on the table with warm garlic bread. Jamal and Brandon were concentrating heavily on the track they were working on when she invited them to have dinner with her.

"Gracie, you didn't have to cook, I would have ordered whatever you wanted," said Jamal.

"That's okay. I'm used to cooking dinner now." She served them heaping portions of the cheesy pasta dish. It looked good, but the two hesitated and looked at each other before sticking their forks in. "It's okay to eat, I cooked this many times with non-dairy cheese for dad."

"Yeah, but your dad loves you so much he would eat it

even if it tasted nasty," said Brandon. Jamal laughed until he saw Gracie giving him an angry stare. Both men took small sample bites before digging in.

"This actually tastes good," said Jamal.

"Why are you so surprised that I can cook? I've been taking care of a lot of things at home; I'm not a little kid anymore."

"I know, I know; we just have to get used to you being older. Give us some time," said Jamal.

CHAPTER SEVEN

"Who is it? It's too early to wake up," Gracie mumbled to herself. There was non-stop knocking on her door. She yelled, "Why are you knocking so much, is there a fire?"

"Well, somebody's grouchy in the morning. I'm just letting you know that I'm leaving in a few minutes for a radio interview this morning. I should be back before noon, so you can go back to sleep," Jamal said before closing the door.

"Wait, wait! I'm coming with you," said Gracie before jumping out of bed.

"Oh no, you're not coming with me. It's not a kid friendly show. I don't want you around these people."

"JJ, I'm not a kid anymore and I'm going whether you like it or not. I didn't come here to sit in the house every day."

"Look, I'll take you somewhere when I get back. I don't want you coming to this."

Gracie ran in the bathroom. In five minutes, she was running out of the house, trying desperately to catch up with Jamal's long strides to his car. She rushed into the passenger side of the Jag before Jamal could lock the door.

"Gracie, go back to bed. Look at your hair, it's a mess."

"Don't worry about my hair, I have a scrunchie, see." Jamal kept staring her down with his arms folded. "You might as well drive because I'm not getting out of the car," said Gracie as she fastened her seat belt.

Jamal sighed before turning the engine on. He drove back to the highway and took the exit for downtown Los Angeles. They entered through the back of the building to avoid any fans that may have staked out the front entrance. Security ushered the two of them into a freight elevator that took them to the station floor. Fearing that he would ditch her somehow, Gracie stuck to Jamal like glue. Jamal was recognized as he entered the studio office. The receptionist escorted them to a lounge room with a huge flat screen and comfortable seating. The table in front of the couch held a basket of baked pastries, juice and water. Gracie's stomach growled as she viewed the refreshments.

"Go ahead, eat and stay out of my way," said Jamal. He was dressed in a fitted black leather Versace jacket, ripped designer jeans and a printed tee. One of the workers came to escort him into the studio, leaving Gracie behind.

The famous DJ Drey of L.A. waited for him in the studio. The live show was broadcasted on the radio and Internet. All the rooms in the station were installed with speakers so everyone could hear the broadcast. Gracie heard DJ Drey introduce Amal Bliss to the fans as the man who had the current #1 R&B song in the country. It was the second #1 song from his latest album. They gossiped a bit and told a few jokes before the talk became raunchy. DJ Drey asked Amal who he was dating these days.

Jamal: "I've been dating around until recently. Now I have a new special lady in my life."

DJ Drey: "Yeah, I know what you mean. Sometimes you have to do some sampling at the buffet before you find out which dish you like. One time I had seven different entrees on my plate before I dove in (background laughter in the studio).

DJ Drey: "Tell me Amal, what's the highest number of entrees you sampled at one time?"

Jamal: "Oh well, I like to be in control of what's going on, so the most I've had at one time was maybe four."

DJ Drey: "Man, with all the chicks chasing you down, four is your max?"

Jamal: "Yeah, well if you have more than four it just gets out of hand, you know what I mean," (more background laughter in the studio).

Gracie choked on her orange juice. She clasped her hand over her mouth at first, and then she put fingers in her ears to block out the rest of the sordid sexually explicit interview conversation.

"Hey sweetie, can I help you with something? Are you waiting for someone?" An obviously affluent middle-aged black man stepped into the room and approached Gracie with questions as his eyes briefly rested on her chest. He was tall and slender, wearing a wonderful cologne and dressed in an expensive fitted grey suit.

Gracie felt awkwardly underdressed. She'd gotten dressed in a hurry and threw on what she usually wore in the house, a sleeveless fitted black top with the word "Brooklyn" printed in hot pink on the chest area, a faded jean mini skirt and red espadrille wedges. The outfit enhanced her curves and contrasted with her light toffee complexion. She smiled back bashfully as she told the man that she was waiting for her brother to finish his interview.

"Your brother is Amal Bliss? I never knew he had such a gorgeous sister, and you're from Brooklyn too of course? My name is Ron Winter, but everyone calls me Ronnie. I used to head a group called The Sangster's. What's your name?"

"My name is Grace."

"Oh my, that's a sweet name. Here, why don't you take my card. I would be happy to show you around town if your brother is busy." Gracie noticed his title on the card said Station Manager and Broadcast Engineer, this caught her interest.

"Excuse me, Ronnie, do you give station tours? I'm interested in sound engineering so learning about radio equipment would be very helpful."

"I would be happy to give you a private tour of the station whenever you're ready, sweetie." Ronnie sat down and asked Gracie more personal questions before he stood to leave. He reached out his manicured hand to shake hers. After shaking her hand, he turned it over and kissed the back of it before leaving. More time went by before Jamal said his goodbyes and exited the studio. Gracie was beyond ready to leave. They got back into the car and drove off.

"Did you hear? The second song I released is the #1 R&B song in the country right now! What do you think of that, composer?"

"JJ, that's great, but I'm not surprised, you always have several hits on your albums."

"I still don't understand why you're not excited about our song," said Jamal.

"I don't know, guess my mind is so focused on dad that I never thought about it."

"Gracie, your dad wanted you to take a break from worrying while you're out here, so stop worrying. Hey, do you want to have more breakfast? I'm starving," said Jamal.

"No, I don't think I can eat anything after hearing your interview. It was sooo disgusting," said Grace.

"You see, that's why I told you not to come; you should have stayed in bed like I told you. I knew I should have locked the doors to the car to keep you out."

"JJ, you're not really like what you told them, right?"

"Of course not, I don't have orgies, I'm not a freak."

"Oh, then why did you tell them those things on the radio?"

"I didn't have a choice. If I told them that I'm a one woman at a time guy, they would say I'm boring or gay, and neither of those labels sell music."

"I didn't know you had to make up things like that to be famous," said Gracie.

"Unfortunately, there are a lot of things you have to do to sell your music. Making music is the fun part in the scheme of things. The adoring fans who claim to love you will steal your songs by downloading them illegally. You make the real money touring when you sell out the venues. The only way to sell out the venues is to keep your face and name in the media. That means you must do interviews wherever you can. There are many talented artists out there who have a hard time filling concert venues because either not enough people have heard of them, or they just don't seem interesting. The public is drawn to drama first, talent is a distant second."

"What do you mean?"

"Let me put it this way, if I was arrested for a DWI or for beating up a girlfriend, more people would talk about me on Twitter, Facebook, etc. That would generate more interest in me as an artist. Suddenly, I would get more TV interview offers, and more people would come to the concert. New fans would listen to my music or watch my performance only because they recently heard or saw something about me in the media."

"That's messed up JJ."

"Yes it is, but there's nothing anyone can do about it. Just like there's not much an artist can do about people stealing their music instead of buying it."

"Wow, now I know why concert tickets are so expensive."

"Yeah, it's the artists' bread and butter; without it we're starving artists."

"Oh, I forgot to tell you something. When you were being interviewed, I met this man called Ron Winters. He said he was the lead singer in a group called The Sangster's. Apparently, it made him rich and he owns several radio stations now. Look, I have a card from him. He's the Station Manager and Broadcast Engineer. He said he'll give me a private tour of the station and show me the equipment."

"Oh really? Let me see that card," said Jamal. After

Gracie hands Jamal the card, he sticks his hand up though the convertible top opening, allowing the rushing air to blow the card away.

Gracie looks back frantically. "JJ, why did you do that? Ronnie's number was on that card."

Jamal calmly replied, "Gracie, are you crazy? Do you think I'd let that old pervert take you on a 'private tour' of the station?"

"I don't think he's a pervert, he didn't say anything nasty. Besides, I can handle myself."

"Oh, you're funny. How's a sixteen-year-old going to handle a lecherous middle-aged pervert? You don't know his reputation with girls or how he runs the station. Think about it, Gracie, he's the station manager, who do you think makes the DJs ask those dirty questions? Look, some men don't care that you're not of age yet. Some like Ronnie prefer relationships with minors. They're just looking at your body. There's no care or concern for who you are. They would say or do whatever they can to trick you into a situation where they can take advantage of you. Don't worry about learning the business. Brandon and I will teach you what we know and you'll learn the rest when you go to college. You don't need to hang around the wrong types of people to get an education."

"Ugh, you and dad always treat me like a little kid! I told you already, I can handle myself. I take the bus to school every day, don't you think I've been approached by men before?"

"You have? How do you handle them?"

"I either ignore them or tell them to get out of my face before I call the police."

"Have you told your father about this?"

"Are you kidding? He's already placed me in an all-girls school to keep me away from boys. He'll freak out and send me to a nunnery if I tell him about men looking at me. Dad doesn't acknowledge the fact that I'm almost an adult."

"Your dad's just looking out for you, Gracie."

"I understand that, but he takes it too far; he tries to protect me from the world but that's wrong. If I don't learn how to deal with situations, I won't be prepared to live as an adult when I become one."

"Hmm, I never thought about it like that, but please don't be growing up too much out here. I want to bring you back the way I found you." Gracie and Jamal returned to the house after having breakfast. Brandon was already in the studio working on the same track from yesterday. Jamal pulled him aside after Gracie went to her room.

"Bran, you know that old radio station manager with the cheesy grin on his face all the time?"

"Yeah, what about him?"

"That old fool was hitting on Gracie while I was being interviewed."

"Nooo, you kidding me, right? Can't he tell she's under age, is his eyesight going?"

"I'm sure he knew she was under age. That old dog told Gracie he could give her a private tour of the station and show her his equipment."

"Are you serious? He's lucky I wasn't there."

"That's not all, guess who took his card with plans to go on the tour? Yet, she explained to me in the car that she's not a little kid and she can handle men."

"Handle men? No, this can't be true. The pest can't handle men."

"She thinks that since she talks back to some perverts on the bus, she has experience with handling men. This is the same girl who packed Mr. Pockets in her suitcase."

Brandon laughed and shook his head. "She still has that raggedy old teddy bear? Man, what are we going to do?"

"We'll have to watch her like hawks and keep her in the house where it's safe because this town is full of Ronnies."

Later that afternoon, Gracie came down to the studio. "Brandon?"

"Yeah pest, what's up?"

"What church do you go to out here? Can I go with you tomorrow?"

Jamal started laughing, "Yeah, tell her how you 'do church' out here, Brandon."

"Jamal, you ain't no good," said Brandon. "Gracie listen, I don't go to church out here, I'm just living the free life, if you know what I mean."

"In other words, Gracie, Brandon spends his weekends going to parties and keeping company with wild women," said Jamal.

"They are not all wild women. Sometime I have meaningful relationships. One day I will surprise you when I get married," said Brandon. This makes Jamal laugh even harder.

"Tomorrow's not good for church anyway because we're

going out tonight," said Brandon.

"We are?" said Gracie enthusiastically.

"Ahhh no, just me and Bran; you'll have to stay home because you're too young to go to the club."

"I can't believe you're just going to leave me here while you two go out and have a good time. Maybe I want to have a good time too."

"Oh no, like I said before, I want to bring you back to Brooklyn the way I found you. I can't have Mr. Mitchell yelling at me for letting you have a 'good time.' Anyway, you'll go out when I take you with me to the American Music Awards in two weeks."

"Are you serious? You're really taking me? That would be sooo great! I've never been anywhere fancy like that. I have to buy a dress and get my hair done. I wish Aunt Felicia was here to help me."

"Don't worry about that, I'll get Serena to hook you up."

"Who's Serena?"

"That's his on again, off again girlfriend," said Brandon.

"At least I only have one on again, off again girlfriend; do you even remember the

names of the women you sleep with?" asked Jamal.

"Oh Brandon, are you really like that?" Gracie asked.

"You know what, I'm just gonna leave now before I'm insulted further," said Brandon. Unfortunately for Brandon, Gracie wasn't letting the topic go, she stood in his path before he could exit the studio.

"What happened Brandon? Your dad is a Pastor and you're saved. Now you don't go to church and you're sleeping around? What happened to all the praying and bible school classes? You practically lived at the church," said Gracie.

"That's part of the problem; I lived church every day. There was no freedom. Out here I can do what I want to do without those nosy saints telling me what I'm doing wrong. By the way, some of those saints are hypocrites. There're people in the church doing things that will make a sinner cringe and those same people will turn around and judge you. You know, I didn't ask to be a preacher kid. I was born into it. I got tired of being good all the time when everyone else does whatever they want to do. I want to live my life without anyone preaching to me," said Brandon.

"Oh, I think you've done a lot of living and then some; you've sure done a lot more than

me," said Jamal.

Gracie just shook her head. "I'm gonna text dad. I can't believe he shipped me over here

to stay with you two heathens. Tomorrow's Sunday and I want to go to church. Who's coming with me? Both of you could do with some spiritual cleansing."

"Hey, I'm okay. It's Bran who needs the cleansing and maybe some penicillin while you're at it," said Jamal as he laughed.

"Are you serious? You're no saint; you're the first one who was dogging women. I started by picking up your leftovers. You were just like me until Tasha found out who you really were and stopped talking to you," said Brandon.

At the mention of Tasha's name, all the laughter left Jamal. Losing Tasha was his biggest mistake. Jamal was so caught up trying to please everyone that he neglected his biggest fan and first love. Tasha loved him and his music. Whenever he played the piano in church, there were never any nerves playing in front of an audience. All he had to do was look at her smiling face to realize, all was well.

Jamal changed more than he intended to fit into his new life. From the beginning, his producer and agent told him that the good church boy image had to go. They said he spent too much time with his mama and he needed to be manly. The memories of their criticisms came to him like it happened yesterday. *Don't you want women to come to your <u>concerts</u> screaming your name? They won't throw panties at you if you don't look like the type of man who appreciates them. You can't be soft; these women want to see a real man. They're your audience and it's up to you to make them happy. If they're not satisfied, they're not buying your concert tickets.*

Jamal made drastic changes to every aspect of his character because of their suggestions. He went out with as many girls as he could, believing it would roughen his squeaky-clean image. They told him, *"Virgins don't sell records."* The sex wasn't a sacrifice, but there were regrets and risks. The sad part was that the first woman he gave his virginity to was more interested in the fact that he was to become famous than she was interested in him. She wanted to make a video of them having sex, but he drew the line there. His groomers showed him how to drink. They made him work out to make his biceps bulge and they gave him dancing classes. Jamal obtained several tattoos at their recommendation. It was all part of the work required to create the image needed to sell his music; and he was willing to do whatever it took.

Phone calls to Tasha became infrequent. It wasn't that he didn't love her anymore; he was loving his new life. The tabloids didn't help. They portrayed him as a hot lascivious celebrity. Tasha wanted no part of this new life and he let her go without a fight. She found a new boyfriend at church and moved on. Since then, Jamal had many women, though he had no love for any of them.

He has an understanding with Serena. She loves his lifestyle; he loves the sex. Being seen with him also helps her career as a model. It wasn't a serious, 'come meet the parents,' type of relationship.

Gracie noticed how solemn Jamal became after hearing Tasha's name. She always thought they would have married as soon as they were able to. Remembering the way they looked at each other in church, she knew that was love. Everyone knew those two were into each other. To Gracie, it looked like Tasha's parents got their wish. Jamal is over here looking sad and lost, while Tasha was back in New York dating someone else.

****

The next morning Jamal wrapped loudly on Gracie's door before sticking his head in the room.

"Wake up Gracie!"

"I'm up, I'm up; why are you waking me up now," she whined.

"You still want church?"

"Sure I do. I'll get ready now," said Gracie as she rolled back the covers.

"No need to change, just follow me," said Jamal. Perplexed, Gracie put on her robe and rubbed her eyes. *What is he up to,* she thought. She followed Jamal to the media room where there was a 90" flat screen TV on the wall in front of theater-like seating. He sat her down in the front chair and pressed the remote to a channel that showed Pastor Joel Osteen.

"You told your dad that me and Bran wouldn't take you to church, so he texted my mom. I just got a lecture from her about moral degradation. So here you go, enjoy your services!" Jamal tossed the remote in Gracie's lap. Gracie's mouth hung open in disbelief.

"JJ, you are so wrong," she said as he laughed while exiting the room. She did stay to watch Osteen and TD Jakes until she got hungry. The media room was next to the studio so Gracie decided to pop her head in the door before going back to her room. As she peered into the darkened studio, she noticed someone lying on the floor in front of the overstuffed sectional. Walking into the studio, she saw that the person who apparently rolled off the couch onto the floor was Brandon. Gracie ran to him quickly.

"Brandon, what's wrong? Are you okay?" She shook his large frame repeatedly until he moved on his own.

"Ohhhhhh," he moaned. "P-Please stop that shouting," Brandon whispered. Gracie scrunched her face and pinched her nostrils.

"Ugggh, your breath smells like vomit. Bran, are you drunk?"

"Hmmm, maybe just a little. Can you get me some water please?" Gracie ran to the kitchen and pushed Jamal away from the refrigerator before grabbing several bottles of water.

"What are you up to now, Gracie, are you going to baptize yourself?" said Jamal as he laughed.

"Is everything a joke to you; don't you care that Brandon is sick?" said Gracie.

Jamal sucked his tooth. "He ain't sick, he's drunk. And he's drunk because he wants to be that way."

"JJ, don't you think there's something wrong with a person who wants to be drunk? Don't you care?"

"Listen, I don't want Brandon sick and vomiting all over the place, but I can't control what he does. He's a grown man who doesn't listen to anyone. I just make sure I'm there to keep an eye on him so he doesn't drive drunk."

"I don't understand why you guys have to go to clubs anyway."

"We go because it's fun and it makes us happy."

"Humph, you could've fooled me. You're your usual mean self and Brandon is far from having fun." Gracie ran back downstairs and gave Brandon the water. "How's your stomach Bran? Do you want me to make you some breakfast?"

"Sure, that sounds good, thanks Gracie," Brandon whispered.

"Well, I'm going to wash up quickly first, why don't you do the same and we'll have breakfast together." Gracie freshened up before heading back to the kitchen. Walking quickly, she bumped into a tall strikingly beautiful woman. The woman was barefoot and wearing one of Jamal's robes. "Hey, who are you?" Gracie asked her.

"Oh, you must be Gracie. Hi, I'm Serena. I'm sure Jamal told you all about me."

"Oh … yes," said Gracie awkwardly. She vaguely remembered Jamal mentioning Serena's name. Gracie surmised that Serena must have spent the night with Jamal since she smelled like his cologne. *Uggh, there's too much going on in this house,* she thought.

"Umm, I'm going to make some breakfast for Brandon, would you like some too?"

"You can cook? Wow, that's so domestic. Sure, I'll have some breakfast. I'll eat anything but carbs, thank you," said Serena before she walked out of the kitchen with a bottle of spring water.

Gracie went to the refrigerator to see what was available. She pulled out some bacon and a fillet of salmon to go along with the scrambled eggs and toast she'd planned to make.

Later that morning, the four of them sat around the marble kitchen island, eating breakfast and drinking coffee. Everyone was dressed except for Serena, who was still wearing Jamal's robe.

Brandon had several helpings of food before pushing away from the table. "Thanks Gracie, that really hit the spot. I'm gonna take some Tylenol and rest for a bit."

"That sounds like a good idea. I think I'll rest by the pool for a while, staying out all night can be really tiring," said Serena as she left.

Gracie watched her leave before whispering to Jamal, "Is Serena a model?"

"Yeah, she's a model, we've been going out for a while now."

"Hmm, is this a serious relationship? Could there be a wedding in the future?"

"Hold up, slow your roll. No one said anything about that. We're just seeing each other exclusively for now. You know, I think I'll lie by the pool too. Thanks for breakfast," Jamal said before leaving.

Gracie exhaled and looked at the time. She placed all the dishes in the dishwasher and exited the kitchen. Bored with staying in the house, she called an Uber to take her to a local mall. She changed into a fitted orange sundress and tan gladiator sandals. With her hair gathered into a ponytail, she applied a little makeup before grabbing her bag. Gracie left a note on the refrigerator that read *I'll be back in the afternoon,* before leaving for her pick up.

She went to the closest mall she could find on her google map of Malibu. It was an outside mall with many upscale shops. After two hours of walking in and out of stores into the searing dry heat, Gracie decided to look for cover. She headed for Starbucks and ordered a peach ice tea before taking out her tablet. She had accumulated close to a hundred files containing mostly songs and poems in various stages of completion; these were her treasures. Her father came to mind as she altered the lyrics on one of her songs. She'd promised her father that she'd stop calling him every day. Gregory told her he was enjoying spending time with his sister. He encouraged her to spend her time learning as much as she could from Jamal and Brandon.

Gracie initially believed her trip would be for a couple of weeks, but her dad told her to stay the summer and spend time with Jamal before he started his next tour. He kept telling her to enjoy herself, but Gracie was ready to go home. She enjoyed spending time with Jamal and Brandon in the studio, but there was nothing for her to do when they weren't working on something. *Maybe I'll tell JJ to book my flight home after the awards*, she thought. Grace had to admit to herself that she really missed her father. For as long as she could remember, her dad's hugs smelled of nicotine mixed with cologne. It was part of who he was; his smell, the scratchy beard and million-dollar smile. Whenever she was upset about something, just seeing her dad's easy smile would tell her, it's not that serious.

Determined to enjoy her day out, Gracie pushed thoughts of her father out of her mind and started working on one of her unfinished poems. A few hours went by before she decided to take a break. She heard her phone vibrating in her bag. Picking up the phone revealed that she missed many calls and text messages from JJ, so she quickly texted him back.

"Where are you!!!" read one of the messages.

She texted back her location and told him of the note she left. *"I'm coming to get you now!"*

"Why?" she answered, but there was no reply. Gracie was waiting in the parking lot when Jamal's Jag rolled in front of her. She walked quickly to the car and got in.

Without looking at her, Jamal said, "Don't ever do that again!"

"JJ, I don't understand why you are so upset; I left a note."

"Yes, you left a note but you didn't say where you were going. That was irresponsible of you."

"JJ, why are you tripping? I'm sixteen and I am responsible; I have been taking care of my dad and myself for the past two years. I just wanted to get out of the house so I decided to go to the mall."

Jamal seemed to calm down. "Okay, you're right. I may have overreacted a bit, but I'm not used to you leaving the house by yourself. So next time, speak to me before you leave, okay?"

"Okay, JJ, but you have to loosen up. I'm not the little kid you used to babysit; I'm grown now."

"What were you doing all that time anyway, you only have one small shopping bag?"

"I've been writing. I keep all of my information on my tablet. My journal, my songs and

poems, my whole life is on this tablet. I take it wherever I go."

"You have more completed songs? Maybe I should take a look at your tablet."

"Over my dead body! It contains my personal journal, it's my heart and soul," Gracie said dramatically.

Jamal chuckled, "Alright, alright; give me a break. There's enough drama out here without you adding to the mix. I'll just wait until you're asleep and then I'll take it," Jamal teased.

"Really? I'll leave it on the table for you and I will sleep like a log because I know you could never crack my password."

"We'll just have to see about that."

When they got back to the house, Serena and Brandon were waiting in the great room. "She looks fine to me, I don't know why you worry so much," said Serena.

"That's fine for you to say, I had to make sure she didn't go to Ronnie the pervert for his special tour. I'd never be able to explain that to her father."

"JJ, you're overreacting; I told you I can take care of myself. I've been doing it for a while now," said Gracie.

"I'm sure that's what all the kids say before their picture ends up on the back of a milk carton," said Brandon.

"You two are ridiculous," said Gracie.

"Why do you call Ronnie Winters a pervert," asked Serena.

"You don't keep up with what's going on out here?" Jamal asked her.

"I've heard of Ronnie Winters, he's an extremely rich man who owns some of the top radio and Internet stations in the L.A. area," Serena replied.

"Yeah, he's rich but he's also a known pedophile. The man has been in court multiple times for committing sodomy or sexual assault on minors, but somehow his lawyers manage to keep him out of jail," said Jamal.

"Yeah, he's the original virgin slayer. I had my dog fixed but I still wouldn't leave her alone with him," said Brandon.

"Brandon, you have a dog?" Gracie asked him.

"Yeah, she's at my apartment."

"You have an apartment, I thought you lived here?"

"Yes, he has an apartment because I don't allow him to bring all those strange chicks into my home," said Jamal.

"Brandon, I still don't understand why you of all people

are living like that. You're the pastor's son, I can understand a little rebellion, but you've taken it too far," said Gracie.

"Wow, you know you're not living right when a 16-year-old tells it," said Jamal.

"Hey, this is one of the reasons why I left Brooklyn. Everyone looks at you under the microscope when you're the pastor's kid. I think it's time for me to go home, I gotta check on Fergie anyway," said Brandon.

"Wait up, I'm coming with you; I want to see Fergie. I couldn't get a dog because the hair could make dad sick."

"Well, I haven't cleaned up lately, but sure, you can come. Bring your PJs because I'm not driving back tonight."

"Great, I'll get my stuff," said Gracie. On her way out of the room she saw a strange expression on Jamal's face. "Umm, it's okay for me to sleep over, right?" she asked as she was walking out.

"Sure, it's fine," said Jamal with a smirk.

The next morning Gracie stepped over shoes Brandon left in the hallway of his condo. Brandon's kitchen sink was filled with dirty dishes. Hardened food encrusted pans were left on the stove. Gracie was going to put the dishes in the dishwasher, but the putrid smell that offended her nostrils as she opened the appliance door made her slam it shut. There was no dish liquid by the sink so she compromised by using some laundry detergent she found in the bathroom. Gracie plugged the drain before filling the sing with hot sudsy water so that the plates with the hard crust could soak until the food could be removed.

When they arrived last night, Gracie played with Fergie

and didn't notice just how filthy the apartment was. Remembering the smirk she had seen on JJ's face, Gracie decided to give him a call to get answers.

"Hey Gracie, what's up?"

"JJ, why didn't you tell me Brandon's place was a dump."

"Good morning to you too," said Jamal.

"Oh sorry, good morning. Now, why didn't you tell me this place was a dump? Luckily Bran doesn't use the second bedroom. It's the only room in the house that wasn't filthy. The spare bathroom looked like it was never used. It was filled with cobwebs and a humongous spider that did not like visitors. His kitchen sink had old dirty plates yet he has a dishwasher so I don't understand. What's wrong with him?"

Jamal laughed. "I couldn't tell you his place was a dump and embarrass him in front of everyone. Besides, you're sixteen; you've had all your shots," said Jamal as he laughed again.

"How does he entertain all the ladies you say he goes out with? I've seen his room. The floor is covered with old laundry and there are empty liquor bottles everywhere."

"Umm, I think he uses the second bedroom to entertain his lady friends."

"Ewwwww, I slept in that bed!"

"Oh, don't worry. He always changes the sheets in that one because one time, one of his lady friends smelled someone else's perfume."

"Oh, that's still so gross. I've got to get out of here, but I don't want to leave poor little Fergie. I could tell she misses being around people; she was jumpy when I took her out for a walk. Bran doesn't spend enough time with her and she's all alone. Would it be okay if I—"

"No, Gracie," Jamal stopped her before she finished the sentence. "I don't want any pets in this house."

"Wow JJ, you're still just as mean as ever."

"No, you don't understand. Bran and I need to keep our separate spaces to stay friends. If I let you bring the dog this time, he'll think it's okay to bring him again. Besides, my crib is not dog proof."

"Okay, I think I understand. So, when are you going to pick me up?"

"Isn't Brandon driving you back?"

"I don't know, he's still asleep and it's already 10 a.m."

"Did he go out drinking last night?"

"No, but he did go to bed early, around 9:30. He's been sleeping for over twelve hours; that's not normal. I stayed up and played with Fergie some more before going to bed later."

Jamal sighed, "Gracie, I think you need to know that Bran has a drinking problem. I don't know how serious it is, but he does drink before he goes to sleep."

"I don't understand, why is he drinking and doing all these things that he never did in the past, what happened to him?"

"Well, he's had some problems, but you'll have to ask him for details on that. Brandon hasn't been back to Brooklyn to see his family for a long time. I think cutting himself off from them makes him drink more."

"That's sad, I never knew any of this; guess I was too focused on my own problems."

"Gracie, how are you going to know; you're just a kid and this happened years ago."

"Ugh, when are you going to stop calling me a kid!"

"Okay, okay; I'll call you a teenager. Is that better?"

"It's a move in the right direction. So, are you going to pick me up?"

"Yeah sure, be outside in ten minutes."

CHAPTER EIGHT

"**G**racie, Serena's here."

"I'm ready, aren't you coming with us?"

"Nope, I'll drop you off and pick you up. Can't let my fans see me shopping for cocktail dresses."

"Jamal, you don't have to come, I'm taking Gracie in my car," said Serena.

"Well that's even better. You have my card so have fun."

Gracie was excited to go shopping with a model. It's been a few years since she went shopping with anyone since her father didn't allow her to "hang out" with her old friends. The most she could do was meet someone at the library. In Gracie's mind, Serena was gorgeous. Serena had high cheekbones, a Barbie doll figure, large almond shaped eyes and a smooth honey complexion. Her hair and makeup were flawless. When Gracie got dressed this morning, she looked in the mirror and nodded in approval at her outfit; but now, sitting next to Serena, she felt frumpy in her loose-fitting peasant blouse and acid washed skinny jeans.

They visited many exclusive shops where Serena had already made appointments. The attendants knew her well.

Gracie couldn't believe the prices they would give for the dresses she tried on.

"Serena, are you sure this is okay with JJ?"

"Girl don't worry. Photographers take pictures when everyone enters, so you have to look good when you walk in with us."

Serena approved of a sleeveless, full-length light grey sequined gown that hugged Gracie's curves and accentuated her narrow waist. The front high split made Gracie anxious. She had never worn anything that was sexy before. They went on to purchase matching stiletto heels and new makeup. When their shopping was complete, Serena drove them to Marney's for lunch.

"Marney's makes the best shakes in L.A. I think you'll like the food, too," said Serena. Gracie ordered a mocha cashew butter shake and a bacon wrapped lobster burger. It was the best shake she had ever tasted.

"I have to come back to this place. This shake is out of this world. Thanks for bringing me here, Serena."

"You are very welcome, sweetie. So, tell me about life in Brooklyn. A pretty girl like you must have left a boyfriend behind, what's his name?"

"I don't have a boyfriend; I haven't kissed a boy since I was 14 and my father made sure I'll never kiss another until I'm an adult. He enrolled me into an all-girls school."

"Surely you must have sneaked a date in here and there; I can't believe your father is that strict."

"You don't know my dad; he is beyond strict and JJ does whatever he says, so there's no chance in my dating anyone out here."

"Don't worry, once you're seen in that dress with the makeup, you'll get plenty of interest. I can help you meet some guys when you're ready. For now, you have to practice walking in your heels so you can get used to them. Have you thought of a style for your hair yet? I'll tell you what, take this card. This is the shop I go to. Give them a call and make an appointment in advance with Andre for the morning of the show. He'll know what to do with your hair." When they were done, Serena dropped Gracie off at Jamal's house before continuing on her way.

****

On awards night, the four exited their limousine and posed for photographers before entering the venue. Fans shouted for Amal as they walked toward the entrance. Gracie was amazed at Jamal's fixed smile and graciousness with the media. She lost all anxiety over her high split dress when she saw what the celebrities and Serena were wearing. Serena's dress looked like it was painted on. The cut of the dress was so low in front, Gracie didn't understand how her breasts didn't just pop out. She was tempted to reach over and touch the fabric, just to confirm that it was actually there, but Jamal had already lectured her on how to behave because he did not want Gracie to embarrass him.

Their group of four casually walked by well-known artists from every genre of music. Whenever Jamal stopped to talk to a few celebrity friends, a camera would appear out of nowhere to take a shot of them. He received many impromptu mini interviews as they walked toward their seats. Brandon and Gracie made sure to step outside the camera range as the media took pictures or videoed him, but Serena was asked several times to unlatch from Jamal so only he would be seen in the shots. Being exposed to the lights, media people and celebrities made Gracie excited and nervous at the same time. She held onto Brandon's arm so tightly that he complained she was cutting off his blood flow. They were seated under theater lights so bright that Gracie wished she wore shades. She couldn't believe the four of them were sitting so close to the front, surrounded by so many popular artists. When Jamal told Gracie he was taking her to the awards, she thought he would sit up front and her seat would be way in the back with the other peons who watched on. Brandon, Jamal and Serena were watching her again. Gracie was determined to get a grip, just so Serena would stop laughing at her and Brandon would stop telling her not to gawk at people.

Brandon nonchalantly pointed out Ariana Grande talking to Taylor Swift; they were surrounded by their entourage. Many of the celebrities were out of their seats, conversing with one another like regular people. Gracie spotted two of her favorite artists talking and laughing together; she wished she was included in the conversation. The two, Gregory Porter and Esperanza Spalding, were standing less than 20 feet away. She felt like running over there and giving them a big hug. Her mouth must have been hanging open because Jamal told her to stop drooling and staring at people. Gracie did as she was told. She admired Jamal's calmness, though it wasn't a surprise to her. She rarely saw Jamal expressing excitement about anything. He was an emotional rock and she was proud to be here sitting with her brother. Gracie surmised Jamal will never know how much this night meant to her. She'd never tell him how she felt because she knew his ego would explode.

The awards seem to go on forever. They included categories Gracie had never heard or thought of, but now they were announcing the nominees for best male artists soul/R&B. Gracie was so excited, she bounced up and down in her seat when they announced Amal Bliss. Again, Jamal told her she was embarrassing him so she toned it down. Brandon's been laughing at her reaction all night. Like Jamal, he was also relaxed and calm.

They took a long time to announce the winner. Unfortunately, Jamal didn't get the award. To his credit, he didn't flinch, though Gracie thought he was robbed. Not because he was her brother, but in her mind, the person who won wasn't half as good. Now they were announcing the best soul/R&B album. Gracie stayed calm when they mentioned Amal Bliss as one of the nominees because she didn't want him to feel bad if someone else won.

To her surprise, and maybe Jamal's too, he won the best album award. Gracie was so proud of him that she clapped until her hands ached. The camera panned to Amal after they displayed his album cover onstage. The audience applauded as Jamal stood up and signaled for Brandon to follow him. Gracie liked the way JJ included Brandon in everything he did; she loved that they were so close. Brandon did co-produce a few of the songs on the album, but many artists don't acknowledge co-producers. As she was applauding, Jamal turned around and grabbed her arm to make her stand up.

"JJ, what are you doing? You're embarrassing me now and you are out of your mind if you think I'm going up there on stage in front of the whole country."

But Jamal didn't stop pulling. Gracie vigorously shook her head "no" as she tried to shrink back into her seat.

"Gracie, if you don't stand up, everyone watching TV is going to see me pick you up and drag you on stage; now get up," said Jamal. His threat got her up and walking, though she kept between Jamal and Brandon.

On stage she stood behind Brandon so no one could see her shaking. When Jamal accepted his award, he went on to speak. At that moment, Brandon grasped Gracie's shoulders and positioned her in front of him, in full view of the audience. Gracie smiled on the outside, but she fumed inside. *They probably thought it was funny to drag me on stage so that I could embarrass myself,* she thought. The hot stage lights were even brighter than they looked. In the midst of thinking of ways to pay Jamal and Brandon back for dragging her onstage, she heard Jamal speak of the song she wrote; then he reached back and pulled Gracie to the podium. Jamal introduced Gracie as the daughter of his mentor, Gregory Mitchell. He then told everyone to give her a hand for composing their hit song that was on the album. Gracie was overwhelmed and couldn't believe the audience was clapping for her! Never have she felt so full of joy. Her heart was pounding out of control as she smiled at the audience. Jamal motioned for her to say something, but the only words she could say were, "thank you." Gracie then stepped back out of the spotlight. This was the happiest moment of her life. Brandon stepped up after Gracie and said a few words as the co-producer on the album. When Brandon finished, Jamal placed the award in Gracie's trembling hands as they walked back to their seats.

Brandon and JJ looked at Gracie with grins on their faces. She knew they planned this together. Gracie wanted to say something. She wanted to thank and scream at them at the same time, but no words came out.

"Bran, can you believe this? She's speechless! Let's enjoy this rare moment because it will never take place again." The two started laughing at their joke, but uncontrollable tears streamed down Gracie's face.

"Gracie, what's wrong, are you mad at us?" asked Brandon as he put his arm around her shoulders. She could only shake her head no. "Are those happy tears then?" he said. When she nodded her head, they both seemed relieved.

The next few hours went by quickly. Billboard and other media photographers took pictures of the three of them. Serena tried to get in a few frames, but the photographers asked if she could step aside. After the photographers left, Jamal and Serena got up separately to talk to other attendees. Gracie's head was pounding so she got up to take a break from the bright overhead lights.

Gracie didn't get far before Ronnie literally bumped into her. He seemed to come out of nowhere.

"Hey sweetheart, sorry about that," he said as he bent

down to hug her as if they were close buddies. "You looked fabulous on stage. Love that dress by the way. I had no idea you were a composer; you must come to the station for an interview. You are a really talented young lady and you have music in your blood. I had no idea your father was Gregory Mitchell, and here I thought Amal was your real brother."

"No, we're not blood related, but we grew up together. He's the only brother I know."

"Hmm, that's interesting; so, this means that you're just living with two guys right now, right?" Gracie thought something was wrong with the way Ronnie said that, but she couldn't figure it out. A camera person walked up to take a picture of them. She posed next to Ronnie, but just before the camera flashed, Ronnie put his arm around Gracie's waist and pulled her close. After the photographer left, Gracie excused herself to go to the restroom. She didn't need to go, but she wanted an excuse to get away from Ronnie; he was creeping her out.

The opulent bathroom was a massive lavender decorated lounge with grey shag carpeting. It was the swankiest bathroom she'd ever seen. Long crystal chandeliers lit up the merlot velvet couches. The toilet stalls were located on the other side of the mirrored lounge wall. Each toilet was enclosed in a spacious water closet. They were mini rooms with floor to ceiling mirrored doors trimmed with strip lighting. All the stalls were empty and open. Gracie entered the stall farthest from the entrance. Her head was spinning. She sat down and massaged her temples. With her eyes closed, she recapped everything that took place tonight.

A few minutes went by before the restroom door opened to a group of noisy women. They were laughing and talking loudly. Gracie sighed, "Guess it's time for me to get back anyway." She stood up and stretched. Gracie's hand was on the stall doorknob when she heard one of the women talking about Amal. The ladies were no longer speaking loudly, but she could still make out what they were saying.

"Hey Serena, when are you going to get your man to make your situation permanent? I mean, you guys have been dating for almost a year, right?"

"It hasn't been a year yet, but I brought the subject up several times. He always says the same thing, 'What we have is alright.' To shut me up, he gives me more money to go shopping. So, I don't argue with him. What else can I do?"

"Hmph, you know what that means? It means he has no intention of making your relationship permanent."

"Girl, sometimes you have to fight dirty to get what you want. You're a few years older than him, and you're not getting any younger," another woman added her advice.

"Yeah girl, better put your boo on lockdown before another woman snatch that up."

"Nicole, he knows better than to look at another woman. I've invested too much of my time in our situation for him to kick me to the curb."

"Honey, you know what to do right? Just take a pin and stick tiny holes all over those condoms. When the baby gets here, he'll have only two choices, marry you or give you a generous monthly check. Either way, you get the money. What's better is that since you're a model, he'll have to support you because the baby may ruin your figure."

"I don't know Nicole, do you think that will work?" asked Serena.

"Sure, it worked for my girlfriend. She gets a nice check every month for herself and the baby; it's like hitting the lottery. You better not wait too long though. He just won another award, so a new wave of skanks will be coming onto him. You better get your award, girl."

"You know what? You're right. Jamal has to take care of me; these little shopping sprees aren't enough," said Serena.

"That's right, you go get yours, Serena. Don't just play house, own the house!" The ladies continued to talk about the details of the baby scam.

Gracie's ears were burning. She couldn't believe Serena would do something so dirty to Jamal. After Serena and the other women left, Gracie waited a few minutes before exiting the restroom. The last thing she wanted was for Serena to see her leave the bathroom.

It was a long walk back to the seating area for Gracie. Serena was already seated next to Jamal with her arm around his shoulder. Gracie was fuming, but she kept her mouth shut because she didn't want to ruin Jamal's night. She observed his behavior long enough to know he was still pumped about the award. Gracie was happy too, until Serena killed her joy.

When Brandon decided to get up and walk around, Gracie tagged along with him. They entered a large crowded foyer. It was filled with reporters and celebrities. Photographers dipped in and out of the mass, taking pictures of various groups. Gracie felt out of place, standing in the midst of people she considered real artists. Just when she was going to unload her info to Brandon, she felt a tap on her shoulder. She turned around and was face to face with one of her favorite Jazz Artist. It was Esperanza Spalding, the artist whom she believed was the greatest Grammy award winning female jazz artist of this century. Gracie snapped out of her starstruck haze when Brandon called her name.

"…I just wanted to come over and tell you that I loved the song you composed with Amal. I play it all the time," said Esperanza.

All Gracie could get out was a star struck "Thank you." Brandon saved the moment by asking Esperanza if she would take a picture with her. One of the photographers happily snapped the photo for them before Esperanza left.

"Brandon, you are so my favorite person right now," said Gracie.

"Come on, pest. I'll take you home now. Think you've had more excitement than you could handle for one night," said Brandon.

Gracie bolted out of bed in the morning with Serena's plan on her mind. She called her father and as usual received his voice message. Waking Brandon was an ordeal, but she had to tell someone. She shook his shoulder for several minutes before Brandon opened his eyes.

"Gracie, why are you waking me up?"

"I need to tell you something important." Gracie made Brandon come to the kitchen. Brandon guzzled half a mug of the fresh coffee Gracie made before she began. As she explained what she heard, Brandon's only response was an occasional blink of his bloodshot eyes.

"Gracie, I've been telling Jamal Serena was a gold digger from day one, but he never listened to me. Maybe with this new information coming from you, he'll believe it."

"Great, let's go tell him now."

"Gracie, we can't bust into his bedroom with this info."

"So, what are we going to do?" she asked. Brandon thought for a minute, then he took out his cellphone and called Jamal. It rang for a while, but Jamal did answer the call. Brandon walked away from Gracie to talk to him. When he was done, Brandon hung up and started taking food out the refrigerator.

"Umm, is that it? What did JJ say?"

"Gracie, don't worry. This is adult stuff. It's got to be handled delicately."

"Brandon, I'm not a kid, why can't you just tell me what he's going to do?"

"He's handling his business. We delivered the message, now it's up to him to check it out. Let's wash up and meet back here. I'll make you some breakfast when you come back." Gracie rolled her eyes as they exited the kitchen.

Later that morning, Brandon and Gracie were eating omelets when they heard loud shouting coming from Jamal's suite. It was Serena cursing Jamal out. She stormed into the kitchen with tangled hair, holding a hastily packed knapsack. Gracie thought about running to her room before Serena saw her, but it was too late.

Serena walked swiftly to Gracie, who was unconsciously backing up.

"I promise I'm going to get you for this!" she screamed while pointing her finger.

"You need to leave now," said Brandon as he stepped between them. Brandon put a protective arm around Gracie's shoulders as the two watched Serena stormed out the door.

"You think she's really going to do something to me?"

"Pest, don't stress about Serena; she's just shooting off steam. Besides, there's nothing she can do to you with me and Jamal around."

"I feel bad now. Do you think JJ loved her?"

Branson sighed, "I wouldn't call what they had love. Don't worry about Jamal, he'll be alright."

Jamal didn't leave his suite that day. Brandon coerced him into watching a game that night, but it was clear that Jamal's mind was elsewhere. Gracie hoped things would go back to normal, but then things got worse.

Ronnie's radio station started talking trash about the three of them. They said that Jamal, Brandon, and Gracie were involved in a perverted love triangle. Jamal's agent called Jamal to let him know what was being said. To Gracie, this was ten times worse than Jamal's dirty radio interview. She was going to call her father, who she expected would suggest she'd come home now, but Jamal told her he'd already explained everything to him.

The next day, Jamal's agent came to the house. Gracie was able to listen to their conversation from the top of the stairs.

"Jamal, we have to do damage control so these lies won't

hurt your career. Why do you call her your sister anyway?"

"She's the only sister I know at this point, we grew up together. Her father is like a father to me. We are brother and sister," said Jamal.

"Hmm. Well, I'll explain to the record company that these are slanderous lies. The legal department will get to work on it. It'd be a good idea to have your usual birthday party and invite the media this time. In the meantime, you should send your sister home."

"Look, I'm okay with your plan, except I'm not sending Gracie home until she goes back to school. That pervert is not going to control my life," said Jamal.

****

Gracie's heart sank when she saw the same story in the gossip magazines. They displayed photos of the three of them receiving their award onstage. They also had the photo Gracie took with Ronnie. Jamal's lawyer made the magazines retract the story in their next edition, but the damage had already been done. Some daytime television celebrities were already discussing the Amal Bliss rumors. Fed up, Gracie called her dad several times, but his message box was full.

Since the day the radio station aired those rumors, more people recognized the three when they went out in public. During dinner at a restaurant, people would point their fingers in their direction. Jamal and Brandon told Gracie not to worry about it because no one believes those stories anyway. They carried on as if it was no big deal. There were some positives; Jamal's agent received more interview requests for Amal, and MTV wanted him to perform at their awards show.

"Things are turning around for us, you'll see," said Jamal. Sadly, that was not the case.

CHAPTER NINE

GRACIE

"**G**racie, wake up!" JJ was yelling and shaking me at the same time.

"I'm up, I'm up," I said, though my eyes were still closed.

"I just booked a flight for us to New York. We leave in an hour."

"Why, what's going on??"

"Gracie, your dad is in the hospital. He's asking for us and it doesn't look good."

"Why is he in the hospital, what happen?" I asked.

"Please Gracie, hurry up. We can talk on the plane."

I didn't understand why my dad didn't call me if he was entering the hospital. It wouldn't be the first time he had an episode. Sometimes his medicine doesn't work well and he has to go to the hospital for tests. I'm hoping JJ's overreacting, but something just didn't feel right.

During the flight, JJ confessed to me that dad was having experimental lung surgery and he didn't want me to worry about it. It all made sense now. I haven't heard from dad in over a week, but still; JJ knew everything. It felt like someone punched me in the stomach. JJ didn't say much more on the plane. That really scared me because it told me he was worried.

We arrived at JFK airport at noon and took a car directly to the hospital that daddy was staying in. JJ knew exactly which room dad was in. JJ and I went in together while Brandon stayed in the hallway.

Nothing could have prepared me for what I saw. I'll never forget the image of my father lying in the hospital bed with tubes and IVs attached to his frail body. They had an oxygen mask over his face yet his breaths were very labored. My tall and broad father seemed small and shrunken. His skin was pale and his eyes were open, but unfocused. Dad's been sick before, but never like this. He couldn't speak. When I touched his arm, his head slowly turned in my direction. Dad attempted to raise his hand to wipe away my tears, but the IV prevented him from reaching that far. I held on to his arm. He looked so tired and worn out. JJ came and stood next to me; he took dad's hand. We stayed in the same position until dad closed his eyes. It was then that I noticed Aunt Loretta sitting behind us. She got up and hugged us. No words were spoken, but we knew dad was dying. Questions flooded my mind but I couldn't focus on them. I knew dad was getting worse each year, but he didn't look like this when I left.

Suddenly the machines went berserk. There were alarms and loud beeping noises, yet dad didn't move. The hospital staff rushed in and pushed us out the door. We were led to the waiting room. I closed my eyes and prayed, yet at the same time, I felt my prayers was futile.

One of the doctors came out of my dad's room sometime later. I knew what he was going to say before he opened his mouth. JJ fell apart. I was numb. I watched JJ and Aunt Loretta cry together. They hugged me, but my eyes were strangely dry.

I was ready to go home and sleep in my own bed. I must have said this out loud because Aunt Loretta and JJ were looking at me funny. Aunt Loretta had to talk to the nurses. JJ and I waited around until she was ready to go.

When we got to my house, I took my bag from the driver and headed for my second-floor home, but Aunt Loretta stopped me. She ushered me to the lower level door. *Why was she taking me to our tenant's door,* I thought. Did they move out? When we walked in, I saw that our furniture was down stairs. Before I could ask anything, she explained that dad moved to the lower level so that he wouldn't have to climb the stairs anymore. It made sense to me. I just wished someone thought to tell me about it.

"Which bedroom did dad stay in?" I asked casually. Aunt Loretta pointed to the back bedroom. I took my bag and rolled it to my dad's room. Well, it's my room now.

"Why don't you take a nap Grace, you must be tired," said my aunt.

"Okay, that sounds like a good idea; I'm beat." Again, both JJ and Aunt Loretta gave me a strange look. My eyes drooped; I actually did feel extremely tired now that I was sitting on the bed. I must have passed out because I still had my shoes on when I woke up. I had the strangest dream. In the dream, I was lying on the floor and looking at a slit of dim light coming from under a door. Someone was on the other side of the door calling my name in a low voice. It was an eerie feeling. Somehow, I knew not to open the door, but the person didn't go away. The knob on the door started to jiggle and I felt so afraid I crawled away from the door as far as I could. There were other things in the room, but it was so dark I couldn't see what they were. I bolted out of bed with that same feeling of fear and dread. My heart and my head were pounding. Then reality hit me. My father was dead! I started crying uncontrollably. Both of my parents were dead, now where do I go from here?

It was night now and I didn't know how long I slept. I reach my hand out for the cell phone on the night table when it brushed against one of my dad's pill bottles. I picked it up and read the back. This one said it helped with sleep, so I took one tablet and went back to bed.

The smell of bacon frying woke me up. Bacon was one of my favorite foods. It smelled great this morning, but I had no appetite. Getting out of bed was hard and my movements were sluggish. When I walked to the kitchen, Aunt Loretta was there making breakfast. I could tell she'd been crying because her eyes were puffy and bloodshot. She told me JJ went to his house last night, but he was coming back this morning. Aunt Loretta said she was waiting for him to come back because she had a lot to tell us. She wanted both of us to hear it at the same time. I'm not sure what that meant, but I do know that I want to stay in my house.

When JJ came back, the three of us sat down to eat. I'm certain the food tasted great; it was just that my mouth couldn't taste anything. I ate just to keep from getting hungry. Aunt Loretta started telling us that dad planned to have lung reduction surgery to help with his breathing. He expected to be fully recovered by the end of August, but when the doctors opened up dad's chest, they saw advanced cancer that had spread throughout his abdomen. I listened to the rest with my head in my hands.

"Gregory's medical insurance didn't approve of the surgery, but your father wanted to have the surgery anyway. He took out a loan against the house with the intention of paying it off when he was better, but he spoke with his lawyer before the surgery just in case. If he didn't survive, the house would be sold to settle the loan and the remaining money would be put away in a trust fund for you, Gracie. You will have access to it at age 21. He also said you had a separate college fund and he wanted you to live with me if anything happened to him," said Aunt Loretta.

"I don't want to live with anyone, I can take care of myself," I said.

"Gracie, you are a minor, you're not allowed to live by yourself," said JJ.

"I can't believe 'you' are telling me a minor can't live alone."

"I wasn't exactly alone; mom came home every weekend and your dad looked after me during the week."

"I would argue with you, but I don't have the strength now, this is too much to deal with," I said. I got up and went back to bed, but my mind was racing with thoughts. I was panicking about what to do. Why did my father plan surgery without telling me? Falling to sleep was difficult this time so I took another pill just to relax.

It was 8 p.m. when I woke up, vaguely remembering that I experienced the same nightmare again. Why am I having these bad dreams now on top of everything else that's happening? I walked around the apartment, but everyone had left. There was a note on the refrigerator door. JJ and Aunt Loretta went to make arrangements for the funeral.

****

All of dad's old band mates were at the burial service. They spoke to Aunt Loretta and me. Some gave words of encouragement, but I don't remember any of the conversations. My mind was fixed on my dad's body lying in the coffin. Pastor Maddock came and quoted some scripture before the gravediggers lowered dad into the ground. Gravediggers, is that what they call those guys? I can't imagine having their job. Aunt Loretta was sitting to my left, bawling her eyes out. I didn't want to end up like that so I took a pill before we left for the wake this morning. JJ was crying silently. I switched back and forth between the two, holding onto Aunt Loretta or JJ. They were really distraught. Brandon kept looking at me as if I had something on my face, so I kept my distance from him.

At home, or should I say, my soon to be ex-home, people kept talking to me. Dad's old band mates told me what a great and talented man my dad was. They didn't realize I wasn't interested in hearing any of that. He didn't respect me enough to tell me what he was doing, why should I care about what he did in the past? They couldn't leave fast enough for me. After the crowd left, there was tons of food left behind. Aunt Loretta and Aunt Felicia kept offering food to me, but I haven't been hungry for a while. Aunt Felicia stuffed a plate in my hand and told me I had to eat it, so I headed for the kitchen to toss it out secretly.

The kitchen was occupied. Peering in from the entrance, I saw Brandon and his dad, Pastor Maddock, having an animated conversation. Curiosity made me stay in earshot. I wanted to know what made Brandon change from a straight A preacher kid to the philandering alcoholic he was today. In the past he'd always answer his father with, "yes sir or no sir." Now, he was speaking disrespectfully to his dad. Something must have broken in him because I never saw this side of Brandon before.

"Son, what do want me to say? I'm so sorry. My heart is full of sorrow for the hurt I caused you. I was wrong about everything. Please, we need you back in our lives. Can't you ever forgive me?" asked Pastor Maddock.

"Look dad, that time has passed and this isn't the time or place to discuss this," said Brandon. He stalked out of the kitchen and walked right by me, as if I wasn't there. The expression on his face was of pure anger and sadness. I wish I could help him, but it's all still a mystery to me.

The next day Aunt Loretta and I packed away items to put in storage. Looking around the living room, I noticed dad's Grammy award on the shelf. Aunt Loretta took it down and carefully cleaned it. I wrapped it in packaging material before putting it in a large box. I didn't want this to sit in a storage unit though. I heard Johnny Cash's Grammy was auctioned for $187K. Of course, my dad wasn't as popular, but this dust catcher should get me a few thousand if I need the money. When JJ arrived, he told me he'd arranged secured storage for dad's piano. I asked if he could secure the Grammy too. He decided to take a look. JJ delicately picked up the award and hugged it to his chest like it was the Holy Grail or something. He definitely appreciated it more than me.

"JJ, why don't you take it to your house? I have no use for it," I said.

"Are you sure, Gracie? You know what, I'll hold onto it for now, but I'm sure you'll want to display it one day."

A realtor came this afternoon to assess the value of my home while we were packing. Brandon was with me helping to move the boxes we had packed. He was trying so hard to cheer me up, so I faked a few smiles just to put him at ease. We had a lot of stuff and everything couldn't fit in storage, so the leftover furniture was sent to charity. Aunt Loretta took some of my things to her house as she assumed that I was moving there, but JJ wanted me to stay with him until it was time for me to go back to school. I wanted to stay in my home.

Thinking about being homeless was draining, so in the midst of their discussion, I said I was tired and was going to take a nap.

"Gracie, it's only three in the afternoon. Why don't we go for a walk or something?" said Brandon. There he goes again! He was looking at me as if he wanted to say something, but couldn't remember what it was. I declined his offer as I kept walking to my destination. The bed was calling me. I crawled in and took one of my pills before sinking into darkness, yet again.

There was more to my dream this time. Someone picked me up off the floor and took me into a bright room. I knew it was a woman, but then I woke up. The clock said 4:10 a.m. I got myself up and started looking through dad's papers. Dad had showed me the account he had for my college fund. I gathered all the fund documents and placed them in my luggage because I didn't want these to get lost in storage. By the time Aunt Loretta woke up, I had sorted through all of dad's documents. The important ones were packed away. I'd also packed away dad's clothing for the Salvation Army pick up.

JJ, Brandon and I were flying back to L.A. tonight and I wanted to have everything I needed before we left. My dad's suitcase was in the closet. I filled it with some of my things, along with the remaining pills I'd emptied into a baggie. With the empty prescription bottle in tow, I made a quick trip to the drugstore. When dad was alive, he gave me authorization to pick up medication for him, so the pharmacy gave no problems getting a refill on the pills. These are temporary, my plans are to stop taking them when everything is settled. That night, we said our goodbyes to Aunt Loretta. She doesn't seem like a bad person; I'm sorry that I gave her such a hard time when I was younger. The three of us flew back to JJ's house.

Since we came back, Brandon kept fussing over me,

telling me stuff like "get out of your room and go outside to get fresh air," but I didn't see the point. My days were spent in my room. JJ was taking my dad's death hard too, but he was planning this party that the agent set up. It took all of his free time.

One day I searched the house but there was no sign of him. His office was empty except for a large envelope on his desk. I was on my way out when the writing caught my eye. I know my dad's handwriting. The envelope read "Authorization for temporary guardianship of a minor." I knew this had to be about me so I opened it up. There were several documents in the envelope, including my birth certificate and passport. There was also some sort of contract that had both my dad's and JJ's signature. The details in the contract stated that Jamal would have temporary guardianship of me until September 1, or when my father recovered from the surgery.

Reading it made me angry. If only JJ had told me what was going on, I could have spent time with my dad before he died. Instead of telling me the truth, JJ let me sit around his house, wasting time while he knew dad was dying in the hospital. I missed my father's last days and it's all his fault. Dad told him to take me. JJ always did whatever my dad told him, so who knows if he even wants me here. I kept reading but my tears were making the documents wet. Using the sleeve of my robe, I dried the papers and tried my best to put them back in the envelope neatly. I went back to my room and locked the door. All these questions came rushing to my mind. What should I do? Where could I go? How could God be so cruel to take away both of my parents? Could I trust anything JJ says? He doesn't care about me; he's just fulfilling a promise. What will he do when he's tired of me hanging around? What am I going to do about school since I don't have a home anymore? My head started to hurt so I took two pills before lying down and drifting off into sleep.

The dream was vivid this time. Aunt Loretta and a man were talking, but then Aunt Loretta left the room. The man kept staring at me after Aunt Loretta walked away. Suddenly, Aunt Loretta came back and yanked me by the arm. We went into the dark room and she laid me down on a blanket-covered cushion on the floor of a large closet. I started crying, but she closed the door anyway; I heard a key locking the door. With my thumb in my mouth, I cried while I laid on the floor in the dark.

"Gracie, open the door!"

The sound of JJ yelling my name and the loud knocking woke me up. I heard both JJ and Brandon calling my name. I sat up and quickly and put the pill bottle under my pillow before rushing to the door to open it. My steps were wobbly but I made it in what I thought was good time. As soon as I opened the door, Brandon and JJ rushed in.

"Didn't you hear us? We were knocking and calling your name for at least ten minutes. What were you doing?" asked Brandon.

"I was sleeping until you woke me up."

"Do you know how long you were you sleeping?"

"What's the big fuss, I slept a few hours."

"Gracie, when was the last time you ate?" Brandon asked. I exhaled and scratched my head but couldn't remember if I ate yesterday or the day before. My head was feeling fuzzy and my throat was extremely dry. "Okay, you're taking too long to answer that question. I want you to wash up and meet us in the kitchen," said Brandon.

They left me alone, but I knew they weren't letting me off the hook. I could tell that Brandon suspects something, so I moved the pills from the pillow and placed it between the mattress and box spring.

The shower washed away the fuzziness that I was feeling. Trying to appear normal, I nonchalantly walked into the kitchen and poured myself some orange juice. They stood together, watching my every move. Pretending to be hungry, I grabbed two blueberry muffins from the basket on the counter. Brandon started as I sat down at the kitchen island to eat.

"Gracie, we know the past week has been very hard on you. We're all grieving the loss of your father and we know that you feel it the most. Look, you know we love you and if you need to talk about anything at all, we're here for you, alright?" I shook my head up and down and hoped that was the end of it, but he continued. "Gracie, is there anything you want to tell us?" I shook my head no. Brandon gave me a disappointed shake of his head and continued. "Okay, so my next question is this, what are you taking?"

I choked on my muffin before replying, "What are you talking about?"

"Listen, I'm no dummy. I've been around lots of women

who take stuff. Those are the ones I stay away from because their inebriated conditions can put me in trouble. I know the symptoms of drug use, especially the dull look of the eyes. Now tell me, why do your eyes look like that?" Brandon brought his face close to mine as they waited for an answer. I had to think quickly about what to say.

"Well, I don't know, I mean, I have been crying a lot. Guess that makes my eyes look strange."

JJ exhaled as if he was holding his breath. Turning to Brandon, he said, "You see, it's nothing. Gracie is too smart for that." Turning to me he said, "Listen, there's no need for you to lock your door though; I don't let strange people upstairs so keep it unlocked so we can reach you." Being fully satisfied with my reply, JJ walked away, but Brandon wasn't convinced. He left us in the kitchen and went to my room. In the past, I heard him tell JJ stories about his dad. His father used to search his and his older brother's room once a month. He would make them stand there while he searched. Brandon's father was one of those pastors who was always afraid the devil would come after his children to get to him. Drug searches were just one method Pastor Maddock used to keep his boys on the straight and narrow path. Apparently, Brandon drew on this knowledge when he searched my room. In the meantime, I started on my second muffin because my body began craving the calories I missed while sleeping. Suddenly, the bottle of pills was slammed on the counter in front of me. The movement made me jump back. I knew I was in trouble now.

Brandon shouted out, "Explain to us why your father's

pills were found under your mattress!" Jamal swiveled my stool around so that I could face them. He was fuming with his arms folded while Brandon stood over me, waiting for an answer. I had to think fast again.

"It . . . it's . . . not what you think. I took them because I remember when dad couldn't sleep, he would take them. When I slept in his room, I had trouble sleeping so I took one. I kept them with me just in case I had trouble sleeping again. It's not like I'm abusing drugs or something."

"Well if you're not abusing these pills, why didn't you tell us you were taking them when I said your eyes looked funny?"

"I don't know, guess I was afraid you would overreact," I said in the meekest voice possible.

"Gracie, I can't believe you would think of taking your father's medication. Don't you know that's dangerous? Now we're going to flush these because you're not supposed to take them. If you have trouble sleeping, drink some warm milk," said JJ.

"Okay, I'm sorry I scared you guys. I didn't mean too." I lowered my forehead into my hands to shield my eyes.

"It's okay, just don't do it again," said JJ as he patted the top of my head. "And please, do something with this hair and stop skipping meals."

"Okay, JJ." I said this as I gave him a hug. I made my exit out of the kitchen, but I stopped in the hallway when I heard them talking.

"Jamal, we can't just dismiss this; I think she's lying."

"Bran, you worry too much. She's not addicted to

anything, she's just grieving hard. Gracie and Mr. Mitchell were inseparable; he was her life and she was his. We're both grieving."

"Well, I hope your right," said Brandon.

That night, I tossed and turned but couldn't sleep. If I had just one pill, I know it would help me sleep. The clock said 1:12 a.m. when I got up. I couldn't lie down anymore. I went to the kitchen and warmed some milk. After I drank it, I sat with my head on the counter, waiting for sleep to come. Nothing happened. It was 2:30 in the morning now. I had to find something to help me sleep. One by one I searched the medicine cabinets in the house, but there was nothing of interest. Jamal wasn't in his room so I snuck into his master bathroom medicine cabinet. There wasn't anything in there worth taking. He had some old cough medicine, but it boasted of a non-drowsy formula. My desperation increased. There was liquor downstairs at the bar near the studio; it was Brandon's stash. I tiptoed downstairs to the bar and peered into the studio. Brandon wasn't there; they must have gone out together again. I found an opened case of his favorite vodka behind the bar and pilfered a full bottle. After taking one sip, my eyes watered and I coughed as the clear liquid burned down my throat. How in the world could someone drink this every day was beyond me. The second sip wasn't as bad so I continued to sip until I started feeling how I imagined Brandon feels when he's drunk. By the time I reached my room, my mind had a comforting numbness similar to the feel I'd gotten from the pills. The bottle and I went back to sleep in my room.

That same dream came back except this time I realized it wasn't a dream; these were memories. This time Aunt Loretta carried me to the closet, but I didn't want to go in there. I was crying but she put me in there anyway. She laid me down on a comforter, but I jumped up and tried to leave. Aunt Loretta grabbed me and put me back on the comforter again. This time she held me down. I was trying to pry her fingers up but her grip was too strong for me. I said, "I don't like you, auntie! You mean." Then the strangest thing happened. Aunt Loretta started to cry. That made me stop struggling, guess I was confused. Eventually she got up and went out, locking the door behind her. I woke up with a massive headache and mixed feelings about Aunt Loretta. What was she doing to me when I was little? Why lock me in a closet? I made up my mind. No matter what, there's no way I was going to live with my aunt; but what else can I do? JJ's going on tour soon. He doesn't want me here, he's just the one who got stuck with me. I can't stay at Brandon's, even he doesn't want to stay in his home.

Ewwwww, something smelled really bad! I looked down at my Disney pajamas and realized I'd vomited on myself while I slept. I don't remember doing that. It was early in the morning and I needed to get up. Standing in front of the bathroom mirror was scary. There were bags under my bloodshot eyes and dried vomit on my chin. After showering, I dressed and bundled the bed linen and PJ's under my arm to take downstairs to the laundry. Unfortunately, the perfume smell of the detergent intensified the pounding in my head. There were no signs of Brandon or JJ, so I just sat on the laundry room floor and waited for the laundry to finish.

My thoughts were on my future. Brandon and JJ are tight friends who're always close. Now that they know about the pills, they probably can't wait until I'm gone. Thanks to dad switching my school, I don't have any close friends. My only family is an aunt who used to lock me in a closet. What am I going to do? My tears started again and I couldn't get them under control, yet somehow, I drifted off to sleep.

"Gracie, what are you doing on the floor? Come on, get up," said JJ while he shook my shoulder. I got up slowly, the hangover headache was still with me.

"Oh, you found her," said Brandon when he came into the laundry.

"Where were you guys?" I said, anxious to take the focus off of me.

"We went out like we normally do; what have you been up to?" said Brandon suspiciously.

"Nothing much, was just doing some laundry."

"Gracie, listen, I know it's been boring for you here with no other females in the place, but that's going to change. I've asked my sister to come here earlier than we planned so you'll see her in a few weeks…"

"What do you mean, your sister is coming…I'm your sister; you're not making sense."

"Oh, umm, I don't really know her. She was the baby my dad had with some woman in…."

"I never knew you had a real sister, you never told me that. Brandon, did you know?"

"Um, sort of," said Brandon. This situation was making

me angry. How could Jamal

have a real sister and not tell me?

"Am I the only idiot who believed I was your only sister?" Guess Brandon could see my

anger because he decided to lie.

"Gracie, I only found out recently about Jamal's other sister."

"Jamal, are there any more secrets you're keeping from me?" Jamal looked uncomfortable answering me.

"No Gracie, there are no secrets."

"You're a liar!" I yelled louder than I intended too, but it felt good to yell it out. "You didn't bring me here because you wanted to. You were doing my father a favor. I found out dad gave you temporary guardianship of me. Why didn't you tell me?" My tears started again, I tried in vain to stop them. "You keep everything from me, even the fact that you had a real sister." Jamal grabbed my shoulders to calm me down, but I shoved him away.

"Gracie, calm yourself down, there's no reason to yell at Jamal in his house. He was only doing what he thought was best." Brandon's statement made me feel betrayed and alone. Why couldn't he stand up for me sometimes?

"You know what, I'm done, and you're right. I have no business yelling at Jamal when I'm a guest at his house. By the way, you sound a lot like your father right now." Brandon winced as if I slapped him, but it was the truth. Pastor Maddock always instructed Brandon on how he was supposed to behave and Brandon never liked it, but now he's acting just like his dad.

I pushed past Jamal and took the linen out of the dryer.

"What are you doing now," asked Brandon.

"I'm going to put everything back the way I found it before I leave." Confused by my statement, they looked at each other before following me upstairs. I put the linen back on the bed, making it as neat as possible. Then I pulled out my trunk and dad's luggage from the closet. With the trunk opened on the floor, I started for the armoire to retrieve my clothing.

"Stop it, Gracie, you can't leave when you want to. I'm still your guardian and I say you're staying until it's time for you to go back to school. Then, you will move back to Brooklyn to live with your aunt. This is what your father wanted, so that's what's going to happen," said Jamal. He still thinks I'm the little kid he used to boss around.

"Newsflash, my father's dead so any CONTRACT he made with you is void. You are no longer my TEMPORARY guardian!" I screamed. "And FYI, I'm not staying with any aunt who made me sleep in her closet."

"Listen Gracie, I don't know what you're saying about your aunt, but you are not leaving this house until I say so! Now put your clothes back before I do it for you," yelled Jamal. He turned his back and angrily slammed my door on his way out, leaving me with Brandon.

"Gracie, what's gotten into you? You know Jamal has nothing but love for you. I know you're hurting because you miss your father, but taking your hurt out on someone else is not right. Your father wanted you to enjoy your summer before you had to come back and watch him recover from lung surgery. Jamal was just helping him to make you happy." I know Brandon meant well, but I didn't want to listen to anyone right now. Everyone has lied to me.

"Brandon, please leave me alone," I pleaded while rubbing my temples. Shaking his head, Brandon did as I asked. All these weird thoughts were coming in my head. I felt silly and stupid for acting like JJ was my real brother and Brandon my real cousin. Did they allow me to think like this because they felt sorry for me? Did JJ take me to the awards to please my father? Why did my aunt lock me in the closet? Does she really want me to live with her or is she just following instructions from dad? I wish I could wake up from this nightmare and go home to my father, but he's not there anymore and my home is no longer mine.

Now I feel bad for arguing with Jamal; I really should apologize. He was only doing what he thought was right. I'm staying out of his way for a while since his big birthday party is tomorrow. I'll apologize afterwards; maybe if we have a calm conversation, he'll be okay with me leaving. It's strange how Brandon has good advice for everyone but himself. One day I hope to find out why he changed. Maybe I can give him some good advice.

****

The night was rough. With no more pills to help me sleep, I resorted to the pilfered bottle of vodka. Just in case Brandon decides to search my room again, I stashed it in a bag and placed it in the bathroom at the bottom of the garbage pail. Dad taught me a lot about hiding places in the past two years. The man would do anything to smoke a cigarette, even give up his life and leave me an orphan. "This is for you dad," I said before chugging the bottle of vodka. After drinking my fill, I secured the bottle back in its hiding place before crawling into bed.

The next morning, party planners and other strange people were setting up in the house. They transformed the recording studio into a club-like atmosphere. Jamal was usually upbeat for parties, but this time he was somber. I attributed it to his recent breakup with Serena. I'm still disgusted by what she planned to do. Serena was no angel, but she was his girlfriend and I'm responsible for destroying that relationship. Wish I could cheer him up, but mine is probably the last face he wants to see. The timing of this party was too close to dad's death for me. I told JJ and Brandon that I'm staying in my room during the celebration. They were okay with that. JJ tried to talk to me about our argument, but I told him to hold it until after the party because there was too much going on in the house. We need time to have a serious discussion without interruptions; he agreed. I did give him a hug and his birthday present to show that I'm not angry with him anymore. First thing tomorrow, I'll apologize properly.

It was early in the evening. JJ's party was in motion while I stayed in my room watching TV in my pjs. My window faced the driveway. I could see the valets parking guest cars. A few interesting celebrities showed up. I think I saw Dr. Dre and Robin Thicke. One of these days I'll ask if he really know these people. I'd planned to catch up on some writing this night, but my mind wasn't focused. My desire for the bottle of vodka kept interrupting my thoughts. My hands have been shaky since I stopped the pills. I know I should leave the vodka alone, especially with Brandon snooping around, but then I start thinking of how bleak my future looks. JJ will leave for his tour in a few weeks and I have to live somewhere else. Nothing took my mind off of my situation. I'm alone and no one alive really cared about me. How did I end up with parents who cared more for drugs and cigarettes than their only child? What does Aunt Loretta have planned for me? Is she one of those secret crazy people who lock kids in the closet, or does she just not like me?

My hand was on the bottle in the bathroom before I realized I'd walked there. Unfortunately, there wasn't much left to help me sleep. After draining the remnants, I threw my robe on over my pajamas and went downstairs to retrieve another bottle. I could hear the music coming from the studio when I entered the small bar area. There were only three vodka bottles left in the case. Will Brandon notice one of the bottles is missing? I didn't care at this point, so I took a bottle and stashed it into the deep pocket of my robe. The neck of the bottle was still visible, so I walked with my hand covering the top pocket, just in case someone saw me.

With a few steps left before I enter my bedroom, I heard Brandon call my name. He must have some type of radar or maybe he's psychic. I don't know what he's got, but I knew I was busted. Still trying to hide the vodka, I turned my body to the side, keeping the bottle out of sight.

"Gracie, what are you doing? It's 8 p.m. and you're dressed for bed already? Are you feeling okay?"

"No, I'm not feeling well so I'm going to bed early."

"What's wrong? Is it your stomach or a headache?"

"Yeah, it's both, so I'm just going to stay in my room where it's quiet. Don't worry about me. Go and enjoy the party." I really hate lying to him. Brandon had such a worried look on his face when I told him about my fake illness.

"Wait, you haven't eaten anything today have you? Stay in your room, I'll bring you something later, okay?"

Ugh! I was so mad I wanted to kick something. All I wanted was to drink his vodka in peace. Was that too much to ask? Now I have to wait because "nosy" Brandon would definitely smell the vodka on my breath. I walked back to my room and pulled out the suitcase to hide the bottle. Then I waited. Brandon came back about 40 minutes later. He brought me some chicken soup and Melba toast, which was nice. Unfortunately, he stayed with me until I finished half of the soup. I drank from the bowl instead of using a spoon because my hands were shaking and I didn't want him to notice that. He did notice me sweating though. I convinced him that I was coming down with the flu or something. When I put down the soup, he turned off my TV and made me lie down to rest before he left. The soup was comforting. I wished it did help me sleep, but my restlessness never left. I needed the vodka, so I kicked off the damp sheets and retrieved the bottle from the suitcase. On the first chug, the vodka went down the wrong way and I had a coughing fit. It was too much too fast, but then the warmth was spreading through me, calming me down. My body was relaxing as I continued drinking. I took a nap right there next to my suitcase.

It was late when I woke up. Took me a while to remember why I was on the floor. The clock showed 11:22 p.m. The party below must be really raging now; guess no one will be checking on me. I don't know why, but that made me sad. I took more gulps of the vodka; this stuff was becoming easier to tolerate. The suitcase blocked the path to my bed so I kicked it aside. It was then that I noticed the plastic bag sticking out from the bottom corner of the suitcase. I tugged on it and to my surprise, it was the bag of sleeping pills I placed in my suitcase at the house. How did I forget about them? Immediately, I put several in my mouth and washed them down with the vodka. There were enough pills left for many, many nights. Now I can really sleep. Just in case Brandon returned, I went to the bathroom to brush my teeth and washed the vodka smell from my mouth.

On the way out the bathroom, my body became extremely fatigued. It took forever for me to walk back into the bedroom. My legs refused to move. The room kept moving even when I stood still. My head was straight, but somehow I was looking at the ceiling. How can this be? The walls felt furry, but when my head moved to the side, I realized I was on the floor feeling the carpet. How did I get down here? Everything in the room was spinning and my heart was pounding like crazy. Something was wrong. Maybe I took too many pills. I started to panic. My legs didn't want to stand up so I dragged my body toward the hallway outside of my bedroom. There was no one around so I kept dragging myself forward. I can see the stairs now, but the urge to sleep was so strong. Someone was walking up the stairs. I opened my mouth to yell for help, but the sound that came out was strange. It doesn't matter, I know that Brandon must be the one on the stairs. He will help me.

CHAPTER TEN

RONNIE

Ronnie whistled to himself as he carried the mocha cashew butter shake from his car. His new friend told him that his secret date loved these. If it weren't for her encouragement and keys to Amal's house, he would never take this risk. He couldn't afford any more mistakes, but at this time of night his date should be in bed. After all, young ladies need their sleep to stay healthy. Just thinking about who was waiting for him made his body react in anticipation. *That idiot Amal and his friends are in the studio having a party with loud music, so this should be easy.* Gracie had been on his mind since they first met. Ronnie remembered the outfit she was wearing, that worn, short jean mini skirt. *It'd be real nice if she wore that for me now.*

Jamal's driveway was filled with expensive vehicles and valet parking workers. Ronnie stayed behind the shrubs as he walked to the side entrance of the home. The keys gave him entrance to a foyer near the laundry room. Ronnie quietly walked up the circular stairs. He was overjoyed to find his friend moaning on the floor several feet from the him. One look at her eyes told him that he wasted precious time adding the crushed roofies to the cashew butter shake.

CHAPTER ELEVEN

Gracie watched through half opened eyes as the person who came up the stairs put a Marney's shake cup down on the floor next to her. They were saying something, but she didn't recognize the voice. Turning her head, she saw Mr. Winters with a huge smile on his face. *Why is he here and why is he smiling,* she thought. When he picked her up she relaxed, thinking that he was going to get help, but instead of going downstairs, he was taking her back into her room. Through her haze she felt something on her chest. As she looked down, she saw Ronnie's fingers pulling the robe away from her breasts as he was carrying her. Alarmed, Gracie began to struggle as best she could to get out of his grip, but the pills and vodka combination made her attempt futile. She screamed no, no over and over, but even she didn't recognize her voice. Ronnie entered her bedroom, turned off the light and closed the door behind them. He dropped her on her bed and immediately began to remove the rest of her robe. Her hands were not strong enough to fight him off. Gracie was crying now, but Ronnie's smile never left his face. After removing the robe, he stopped and stood up, but it was only to hurriedly remove his shoes and clothes, exposing his gray-haired chest. He was about to remove his underwear when Grace tried to dash out of bed. Her body betrayed her, the movements were slow and lethargic. She only managed to roll off the bed. This made Ronnie laugh as he picked her up and threw her back on the bed. He was pulling off her pajama top. Again, she tried fighting, but Ronnie was becoming impatient. The top was yanked off. He pushed her shoulders down on the bed and placed his mouth on one of her breasts.

The realization of what he was doing made Gracie gag. Suddenly, sleeping pills and vodka laced vomit spewed out her mouth, covering his head and her chest. Ronnie cursed her and got up. He dragged her with him to the bathroom. Ronnie threw Gracie in the shower and turned it on while he cleaned the vomit off his face and hair. The cold water immobilized Gracie as she cried out, "God please help me!" Ronnie dried his face and hair carefully with one of her towels before retrieving Gracie from the shower. He dragged her, soaking wet, back into the bedroom as she struggled to get loose from his grip. The cold water from the shower seemed to give her more energy and her struggling was harder for him to control. Ronnie's smile was replaced with a grimace. He threw her on the bed, but Gracie quickly grabbed the comforter and wrapped it around her body. She was holding onto the comforter as tightly as she could. This infuriated Ronnie. He smacked her with the back of his hand. Gracie cried out from the pain and her hand left the comforter to cradle her cheek. Ronnie quickly yanked the comforter off. He then pulled her pajama bottom down to her ankles. Gracie closed her legs and pulled her knees up, but Ronnie smacked her harder this time. The sting from this slap was worse than before. Naked, Gracie started crying again.

"Aww, don't worry baby, there's no reason to cry," he said in a mock soothing voice. "If you make me happy, I can keep you supplied with whatever you're on."

"No, no please don't do this," she cried out.

Ignoring her cries, Ronnie was in the process of pulling his underwear off when a sliver of light came into the room.

Brandon stood in the doorway with another cup of chicken soup in his hand. He flicked on the light to get a better view of what he thought he was seeing.

Before the cup of soup hit the floor, Brandon was on top of Ronnie, tackling him to the ground before pummeling his face repeatedly. Ronnie fell unconscious after receiving several blows to the head. Brandon then began kicking the motionless body with all his might while it laid on the floor. Gracie wrapped herself in the vomit stained comforter and started to shake.

CHAPTER TWELVE

The police arrived with an ambulance for Gracie when Brandon called 911. When the authorities saw the state Ronnie's body was in, they called for another ambulance. They questioned Brandon about the life threatening beating he'd given the naked middle-aged man. Ronnie lay on the floor bleeding with a misshaped face. Bits of his teeth and blood were taken as evidence in case he didn't make it. Among Ronnie's many injuries was a broken jaw, broken ribs and a ruptured spleen. Paramedics rushed him to the hospital for immediate surgery.

The police were still questioning Brandon while Jamal rode in the ambulance with Gracie. The medics couldn't make sense of Gracie's slurred speech. They pumped her stomach and took the cashew shake to try and determine what drug she was on. Vomit samples were also taken from the comforter for testing. They told Jamal that her vomiting was a good thing and probably brought out much of the toxins in her system. Gracie was still spaced out of her mind during the ambulance ride, but she was cognizant enough to remember the sight of Jamal crying.

At the hospital, Jamal was relieved when the nurse confirmed there was no sign of rape. He thanked God that Brandon had arrived when he did.

Gracie woke up the next morning with a pounding headache. Though memories of the previous night were fuzzy, she knew they were real. Her cheeks were still swollen from the blows Ronnie gave her. A nurse came in and asked how she was feeling. She informed Gracie that she had not been physically raped. Her toxicology report revealed the lethal combination of sleeping pills and alcohol in her system, which could have ended her life. Gracie was embarrassed that someone else knew what she'd ingested. She felt dirty and ashamed of what happened.

There were more visitors that morning. The police wanted Gracie's version of what happened. They wanted to know if she was attempting suicide or if Mr. Winters forced her to drink the alcohol and take the pills. He was facing multiple charges, including sexual assault and aggravated sexual battery. Later that morning, the resident psychologist asked a series of questions to confirm that Gracie was not suicidal. The hospital Social Worker seemed genuinely concerned. She left her card with Gracie to call if she needed someone to talk to.

Jamal knocked on the door and entered. He'd just hired a lawyer to help Brandon fight the attempted murder charge. Now he had to face Gracie and help her any way he could. Seeing her swollen cheeks made him want to kill Ronnie.

Gracie wasn't sure if Jamal was angry with her for taking the pills and alcohol, or for messing up his party. She searched his face, but he just looked sad. Jamal came over and kissed the top of her head. "I'm not going to ask how you feel because it's a stupid question at this point. What I do want to tell you is that I'm sorry. When I went over everything in my mind, I realized that I failed you. Whenever I looked in your eyes, I knew you hadn't recovered from your father's death, but I didn't know how to deal with that. Brandon warned me that you weren't behaving right. I didn't listen because I was afraid he was right."

"JJ, I'm ..." Gracie tried to interrupt him.

"No, wait. Please let me finish. Your father's surgery shouldn't have been a secret. I should have convinced him to let you come back. You would have handled his death better if you were there from the beginning. What happened last night, that was my fault, too. The police showed me the keys Ronnie had. They were the ones I gave to Serena. She walked out with my keys and I never changed the locks. On top of that, I told you to keep your door unlocked because I always thought you were safe in my home." Jamal sat on Gracie's, bed but she turned her head away from him.

"JJ, I don't want you to see me like this."

Jamal removed one of her hands from her face. "Look at me, Gracie. I'm going to help you get through this, but I need you to answer one question honestly." Gracie turned around as instructed. "Gracie, were you trying to kill yourself last night?"

"No, I didn't know what I was doing. After you guys took away the pills, I realized I couldn't sleep without them. When no one was around, I took Brandon's vodka. I've been drinking it every night. Last night when I found the pills, I took them without thinking. None of this is your fault, I'm the one who messed up. If I'd listened to you that day and stayed out of the car, Ronnie wouldn't have known who I was."

"Listen, that's not your fault. Ronnie's a rich pedophile that believes he can rape whoever he wants. Brandon was so glad he came to your room when he did. He knew you took the vodka you know. He was angry with himself because he believes you got the idea of drinking from him. He wanted me to tell you not to worry about him."

"Please tell Brandon I'm sorry and I hope he can forgive me for getting him in trouble."

"Gracie, he's going to be alright. I've got him a great lawyer who's doing everything he can to get him out. Ronnie's upset because he'll need plastic surgery to fix his face, but he deserves every broken bone and more for what he tried to do to you. I don't want you to think about it anymore, no one is going to hurt you again, okay?" A tearful Gracie sat up and embraced Jamal. "I want you to get some rest. When you're better, I'll bring you home and everything will be okay." Jamal kissed her head again and made Gracie lie down to rest.

Sleep evaded Gracie for the next few days. The doctor told her the sleeplessness came from her dependency on the pills and they weren't going to release her until her addiction withdrawal was over. During her stay, Gracie requested more visits from the social worker and the two worked out a plan for Gracie's future after her hospital release.

****

Gracie's release day was tomorrow and she was ready to go home, her real home, not Jamal's house. She wanted to release him from the burden he felt obligated to carry. With help from the social worker, Gracie received her Emancipated Minor papers. The document allows her to legally live without a guardian. With both of her parents being deceased, the papers weren't difficult to obtain. The difficult part would be telling Jamal and Aunt Loretta.

With her tablet, Gracie checked the Internet. The media reported different versions of Ronnie's attack on her. Some said Ronnie did rape her while other's reported that she and Ronnie had an ongoing clandestine relationship. They showed the picture she took with him at the awards. It seemed most of the media didn't care to get their facts straight. They were more concerned with talking about Amal Bliss, who up to this point had no controversies in his life.

Ronnie Winters' face was plastered on the front cover of every L.A. newspaper. In his testimony, Ronnie threw Serena under the bus. He told the police that Serena set up a secret date between him and Gracie and he accepted the date not knowing that Gracie was under age. Who could prove him wrong? Serena was the one who gave him the keys to Amal's house and she told him which bedroom Gracie would be waiting for him in. The police searched for Serena, but she was nowhere to be found. Faced with bad press, her modeling agency promptly disposed of their contract with her.

Because Ronnie didn't succeed in his goal of rape, his sexual assault and battery charges were reduced to a six months prison sentence. His expensive lawyers had the charges reduced to two months house arrest, arguing that Ronnie needed immediate facial surgery and couldn't recover properly in prison.

To Gracie, it felt like he was getting away with what he did but the situation quickly changed. His wife filed for a divorce, stating that this incident was the last straw. Other past victims recognized his picture in the newspapers. One by one they were coming forward with their stories of sexual assaults and rape committed by Ronnie Winters. Sadly, the youngest victim was thirteen when he raped her.

Loretta flew in to be with Gracie during her release. Gracie was dressed and ready to leave when Jamal and Loretta arrived. She was certain they'd already planned out all aspects of her living arrangements and she dreaded the confrontation she knew was coming.

Their voices were raised and they looked at Gracie incredulously, but there was nothing they could do to change her status. Gracie's emancipation documents were legal. Both Jamal and Loretta spoke to the hospital social worker demanding that the status be reversed, but it was too late. Obtaining the status meant she needed financial means to support herself, so she used the generous college fund that her father left for her use.

"Gracie, I don't like this. It's not what your father wanted," said Loretta. "Why don't you want to live with me? Is my apartment too small?"

"No, Aunt Loretta, this has nothing to do with that."

"Then please tell me what the problem is. I'm not leaving you until I know."

"It's not important, Auntie."

"You're wrong, this is very important and we have a right to know," she said with Jamal nodding yes to her statement. They stared at her, waiting for an answer.

"I remember what you did," said Gracie.

"Remember what?" Jamal asked impatiently. He looked at Loretta who closed her eyes and lowered her head. She knew exactly what Gracie was talking about. It was a memory she'd believed her niece had buried and left in her past.

"Gracie, sweetheart," Loretta began with a somber tone. "I can explain. There's a lot that you don't know."

Jamal looked back and forth between the two before asking, "What happened?"

"She remembers when I used to lock her in the closet at night and make her sleep on the floor," said Loretta. Jamal sat down and placed his head in his hands. "Gracie, I know it sounds terrible, but I did it to protect you. I had to protect you from… someone."

"Okay, where are you going to live, how can you pay bills? You don't have any money," said Jamal.

"When I go back to Brooklyn, I'll find a place to live, but I plan to live in my house temporarily until it's sold. Dad left me a huge college fund so I'll live off of it until I get my GED, then I'll start college early."

"Gracie, that's not how your father planned for you to attend college," said Aunt Loretta.

"I know it's not what we planned, but he's not here to see the plan through, so I'm changing it. I don't have a home, but I'm sorry, I'm not ready to move in with you,

Auntie. And JJ, I don't want to be your burden. You have a tour coming up and a real sister to get acquainted with."

"Where's this coming from? No one said that you were a burden," said Jamal.

"Look, I appreciate the fact that you want to take care of me, but I need to take care of myself from now on. I want to be on my own."

"Well, that's not acceptable to me. Look at what almost happened to you. It's dangerous out there and you're not an adult yet. I don't want to get a call in the middle of the night to find out you're in trouble 3,000 miles away. You know this is not what your father would have approved of."

"Jamal, let's just get out of here for now. We can discuss this at your house," said Loretta.

When they walked into Jamal's house, he went directly to his suite, leaving Loretta and Gracie alone to talk.

"Gracie, I want to explain everything to you," said Loretta.

"What do you mean Auntie?"

"I mean everything that happened in the past, including the reason why I had to lock you in the closet."

"This doesn't make sense; did someone make you lock me in that dark closet?"

"In a way, yes. Let me start from the beginning."

CHAPTER THIRTEEN

LORETTA

"Your grandparents were a happy couple. Your father was their first child and they loved him, but my dad always wanted a daughter. Anyway, they weren't expecting me when I came because many years went by after Gregory was born. So, when I was born, dad spoiled me rotten. He gave me whatever I pouted for. I had the latest clothes, the best they could offer. My dad called me his little princess and I loved him so much. Don't get me wrong, I loved my mom too, but I could do no wrong in my dad's eyes. If I came home with a bad grade he would say, maybe the teacher didn't do a good job with teaching you.

"When I was fourteen, dad's doctor told him he needed surgery on his heart valve. He told us not to worry because it was routine surgery, so we expected the best; but then he died. Daddy's death ruined my world in so many ways. Mom was never the same after that. She lived in a fog most of the time and didn't pay much attention to me anymore. She didn't ask about my grades or how my day went.

Looking back on it, I guess she was depressed. Your dad was busy touring the world at that time. He stayed home for a few weeks after the funeral and then left me alone with mom.

"I was a spoiled brat who was starving for attention. So, I looked for attention elsewhere. After school I would hang out with the other kids who didn't go straight home after school. We would hang out at this burger grill restaurant, wasting time and playing pranks on each other. My grades were suffering, but I didn't care. That's where I met Terrance. He hung out at the same grill that we high school students went to after school.

"At 21, Terrance was a high school dropout who was determined to make his own way. Terrance had ambition and he was making money with his business ventures. I never knew what work he did, but he had a car while the other boys were still learning to drive. All the girls liked the way he looked. Terrance was fine and he kept his body in good shape. When he asked me out, I was on top of the world. We had a few dates before it started getting serious.

"Terrance never came to my house because I knew my mother wouldn't approve of me dating an older guy. I was in the 10th grade at the time. He would pick me up from the bus stop in the morning and take me to school. He would also pick me up after school and dropped me off a few blocks from my house after having sex with me in the car.

"This went on for several months before a ninth grader confronted me about stealing her boyfriend. When I confronted Terrance about the other girl, he got upset and drove off. I tried to contact him, but he'd blocked me from his phone and never called me again. I cried for weeks but I couldn't talk to my mother about it because I kept it from her.

"During my first semester in college, mom got sick. We found out she had cancer in the spring and she passed away right after my 20th birthday. I was devastated. By then, your dad had his own place in the city. He would check on me and take care of the house bills, but I spent most of the time in that huge 3,000 square foot home by myself. It was too much for me to manage so we sold it and purchased a small house just for me. I'd stopped going to school and was just hanging out at clubs. Your father wanted me to go back to school, but I protested, I wanted to enjoy life. Your father gave me the remaining money from the sale of our family home and I spent it all without thinking. I was in and out of jobs because I was still spoiled and self-centered. Sometimes I showed up late to work or I would talk back to a customer or quit when the boss would discipline me. Your father sent money every month and I looked forward to his checks. But when your dad married your mom, he cut me off financially for good. I was furious and I blamed your mother for messing up my funding, though it wasn't her fault. Cutting me off was your father's decision; yet I still referred to your mother as a gold digger. Jennifer tried to have a relationship with me, but I was the reason why that never happened.

"My life of fun was over; financially, I'd hit rock bottom. I used to be a snob. There were certain jobs that I refused to work at but now I had to take whatever I could find just to pay the utility bills and buy food. I thought I was too cute for the retail job I was working at. I was what men would call high maintenance. Lots of money was spent on my hair, nails and anything else I thought I couldn't live without. One of my old friends put Terrance in touch with me. We met up. He apologized for dropping me like he did and made up some story about not being involved with the 9th grader. I believed him because I was still in love, so we got back together. It was the worse decision in my life. Terrance knew me well. He said all the things he knew I wanted to hear. He sweet-talked me into letting him move into my home to keep me company. He swore that I was the only woman he ever wanted. We instantly renewed our sexual relationship.

"The bills were piling up and I needed to make more money to pay them off. That was when Terrance told me about his new business venture that he wanted me to be a part of. He told me we didn't have to worry about money because with a body like mine, we could make a sex video and sell it for money. At first I refused, but Terrance said people did it all the time. It was no big deal. It turned out that we weren't just making a sex video, we were making a porn movie. I didn't like doing the things he made me do; it made me feel really dirty afterwards. Terrance did the editing himself and he completed the movie in three weeks. It was obvious to me that he'd done this before, but I never questioned him about his skills. Terence marketed the film for months but there weren't many sales. In the meantime, he helped me to get a temporary job as a stripper. It brought in some money, but my tips were low. Some of the men at the strip club were just too grubby for me to let them touch me. I didn't like it either, it made me feel just as dirty as when we made the movie. I kept all of this from your father. Money got tight and silly me, I just realized that I was the only one paying the bills. That's when we started arguing. I wanted Terrance to get a job. He was living in my house and eating my food. Terrance became extremely angry. This was the first time I saw that side of him and it was the first time I became afraid.

"Your father called me when your mother died, he was heartbroken. Though your parents were divorced, Gregory never thought your mother would turn back to heroin, especially since she had you in her life. Jennifer took good care of you, you know. Guess she made a bad decision in a moment of weakness.

"It's funny how you could perceive a person to be so strong emotionally that you'd never think they'd crack. Your father changed when your mother died. He never got over her death. Though he would still smile when we saw each other, I could see the sadness behind it. Gregory was in the middle of a tour when your mother died. He asked me to babysit you until he got back. You were about three years old when he turned you over to me. I didn't have a strong relationship with you prior to this because I didn't want to deal with your mother. Anyway, your dad paid me $1,000 a week, which was very good money. I still remember how hard you cried when he left. He looked so sad when he left you.

"To be honest, I wasn't as caring towards you as I should have been. The only thing on my mind was finding a job to make money. Most of the time, I turned the TV to cartoons and left you in front of it until you needed to be fed or something. Occasionally, you would wander over to the bedroom where Terrance and I were. I didn't mind at first until I saw the way Terrance started looking at you. I don't know what it was, but I had a feeling that he was thinking of doing something to you. Suddenly, he was interested in playing with you whereas before he would say keep that rug rat away from me.

"One day when I was cooking in the kitchen, I heard you screaming. When I checked to see what was going on, Terrance was taking your clothes off. He had the video equipment set up with the lights. I screamed at him, what are you doing? He told me he had a new idea for us to make money. He was going to take naked pictures of you and sell them on the Internet. I screamed at him and took you out of the room. He protested that he wasn't going to hurt you, he was just going to take pictures. I was so disgusted with what he tried to do. I wanted to kick him out of the house right then, but I was afraid he would get violent. I didn't know what to do, your father wasn't coming back for nine days. Those were the longest nine days of my life. I had to make sure that nothing happened to you, but I worried that Terrance would wait until I was asleep and get to you. There was no one else I could leave you with. Most of the friends I had left worked during the day. The other friends stopped talking to me because I owed them money. The only way I could think of to protect you was to lock you in the walk-in closet. It sounds terrible, but it was the only way I knew of to keep you safe. Sometimes when I took you out of the closet in the morning, you would say, 'I don't like auntie.' It broke my heart every time I heard that. You don't know how low I felt.

"Before your father came back, I threatened you not to say that I put you in the closet. I remember the day Gregory arrived. When you saw him at the door, you ran into his arms. You screamed whenever he tried to put you down. I was so afraid that you would tell him everything. Later, he called to ask if anything had happened because you changed so much. Gregory told me you had regressed in some of your behavior; you ate with your hands instead of using the utensils, and you had potty accidents. You already had sessions with the child psychologist after your mother's death, so your therapist also noticed the change in you. I didn't say anything because I was afraid that if I told him what I did, he'd kick me out of his life. I had to make up a lie. I told him that you were frequently asking for your mommy. From that day, I carried that lie and fear with me every day, fear that you would remember and tell your father everything.

When you were back in your home, sometimes I would come over to ask your father for money. You would look at me strangely, as if you didn't trust me. That look made me want to leave your house as soon as I received the money. Did you remember back then? Did you ever recall what I did?"

"No, it's only recently when I was stressed that I remembered that time. I had no idea of what happened when I was younger. I didn't trust you when I was younger, but I couldn't figure out why though," said Gracie.

"I wanted to get rid of Terrance, but I didn't know how. He rarely left the house at this point. After I saw what he tried to do with you, I stopped having sex with him and used the spare bedroom to sleep in. He would argue with me for doing that. The arguments grew worse over time. I got a second job and worked long hours just to stay away from him. When I came home from work, he would accuse me of being with someone else. Sometimes he followed me to work. Every move I made was tracked. When he called me, I had to call back right away or face his anger when I got home. One day, I was fed up with everything. When we argued this time, things got worse. He became physically abusive and then he forced himself on me. When I screamed that I would go to the police if he didn't stop, he said, 'Go ahead and call. Once the police see the porn movie we made, they'll arrest you for calling them. And what do you think your brother will say when I send him a copy of the movie we made? I couldn't have done it without your approval, sweetheart. Sorry, you're stuck with me.'

"It was a crazy situation. I was trapped in my own hell, forced to live with someone who could be a pedophile for all I knew. My mind was stressed out. Every day I was afraid of him and ashamed of myself. One day, I couldn't take it anymore. I walked away from everything. My job, my home; I let it all go."

"Where did you go?" asked Gracie.

"I stayed in a seedy hotel for the first two weeks before I had to resort to sleeping in the back seat of my SUV. Even with the blankets I stored in my trunk, some nights were freezing. I used my gym every day to take showers and change clothes. I snuck back after a few weeks and watched the house at night. I peeked through the window hoping that he'd left, but he was still there. The place was so unkept inside and the mail was overflowing in my mailbox. I was furious, so the next day I had the lights turned off. That must have made him really mad because he came to your house looking for me. I didn't count on that. I had been keeping in touch with your dad, pretending that nothing had changed. Terrance told your dad that I was missing for days and the electricity was cut off. Your dad never liked Terrance, but he was worried about me. When he called, I had to lie to him again. I told him we had a fight and I'm staying at a friend's place for a while. Your father wanted to go to the house and physically kick Terrance out, but I told him that I would go back soon. I didn't want Terrance to show him the video. Your father hated Terence and he didn't know the things Terrance was putting me through."

"So what happened in the end, did he leave?"

"Yes, he left after that, but he completely destroyed the house. He must have used a sledgehammer and busted the walls and the plumbing. When I saw the state of the house, I cried because I knew it would take too much money to repair. That was the price I paid to get rid of him. I had to get financial help from your father again. He helped me to sell it though the money I received wasn't enough to buy another home. That's when he bought the condo for me and added your name to the deed. So, you see, if you move in with me, you'd be living in your home. I promise not to interfere with your life.

"My life has changed for the better since then. I got therapy, went to school and trained as an administrator. Now I work in an elementary school with the principal. I'm happier now and I don't date, so you won't have to worry about any strange men coming in our home. Please Gracie, why don't you stay with me? Honey, you've been through too much this summer, you shouldn't be alone."

"Look Auntie, I appreciate you're telling me about what happened, but I still think it's best for me to be on my own."

Loretta sighed loudly. "Well, okay, but will you at least call me and Jamal regularly to let us know you're okay?" Gracie nodded her head that she would. Neither of them noticed when Jamal came back to the kitchen.

"It's not okay with me. It's not what your father wanted and it's not what I want."

"JJ, I don't want to stay here, besides, you're going on a long tour in a few weeks."

"That doesn't matter. I can figure something out, but you can't live alone, that would be a disaster."

"JJ, you can't be serious, I'm perfectly capable of taking care of myself."

"Yes, I'm very serious. Look, your father left you in my care, I'm responsible for you. If you leave, I'm done. I don't want to get a phone call in the middle of the night because you're in trouble or end up pregnant," said Jamal.

"Is that how you really see my future? If you believe I can't make it in life unless I'm under your control, you really have gone crazy. Look, I'm going back to Brooklyn whether you like it or not, and I'll make it without you, you'll see.

You can go ahead and block my phone number because I won't be calling you. You never wanted me here anyway."

"What are you talking about now?" said Jamal.

"Oh, just forget it."

"Gracie, Jamal, please don't part like this."

"Too late Auntie, it's settled."

"Excuse me, Mr. Bliss, can you take me to Brandon? I want to see him and let him know I'm leaving."

"I've already asked Brandon if I could bring you down there. He told me that he didn't want you to see him in prison. He also said he doesn't want you to worry about him. The police charged him with aggravated battery. The lawyer's trying to reduce his sentence to thirty days, but nothing's finalized."

"What? How can that be? Brandon protected me when Ronnie tried to rape me. Serena should be the one in prison. What woman sets up another woman to be raped? Now Brandon is suffering for her crime," said Gracie.

"Gracie, I'm so sorry about that. I never imagined she was the kind of person who would set up a crime for revenge. The police are still searching for Serena. If they can't find her, I promise I'll hire a private detective to track her down. She has to pay for what she did to you."

****

Loretta returned to New York that evening. Before leaving, she pleaded with Jamal and Gracie to drop their fight before Gracie left, but both were too stubborn to listen. Still angry with Gracie's decision, Jamal barely said a word to her the rest of the evening. He'd taken her bag to her former room earlier. After the police completed the investigation, he had the room professionally cleaned. It was getting late and Jamal was busy in the studio. Gracie walked upstairs to get ready for bed, but found that she was unable to walk through the door of her room. Suddenly, all the memories of what happened flooded her mind. Her heart raced as she ran back downstairs to get Jamal, but she stopped herself. *There's no way I'm sleeping in that room again, but how can I prove to JJ that I can live on my own if I run for help whenever I'm afraid?*

Gracie went back upstairs. She ran into the bedroom to gather her things and her suitcase and headed for the downstairs spare bedroom. With her luggage banging down each step, she had made her way to the lower level when Jamal came out to investigate the noise.

"What's going on, where are you going?"

"I'm going to sleep downstairs tonight." She saw Jamal's expression changed from indignation to sympathy.

He asked, "Do you need my help?"

"Thanks, but I've got this."

In the morning, Gracie made breakfast for herself and Jamal with hopes that he had calmed down since yesterday. With her flight booked before she left the hospital, she planned to leave within a few hours. They had an easy conversation over breakfast, discussing everything except her pending departure to Brooklyn. Time had dwindled. Gracie got up and cleared the table. She placed the cookware and plates in the dishwasher.

"JJ, could you bring my luggage upstairs please?"

"No, if you're going to live on your own, you have to start doing things for yourself."

"Really JJ? Do you think the thought of carrying my own bags will make me not want to go home? You're ridiculous." Gracie exhaled loudly before going downstairs to bring up her luggage. Jamal stayed in the kitchen and continued reading his magazine.

Gracie had to make two trips downstairs for both bags. After pulling her second bag to the main door next to the first, she turned to go into the kitchen. Determined to have a truce before leaving, Gracie said goodbye and embraced Jamal's seated figure in a hug, but he was unmoved.

"I meant what I said, Gracie, if you leave, that's it, I won't be calling you because I'm against what you're doing." Gracie dropped her arms and walked away. Jamal only looked up when he heard his front door close.

Chronicles III

CHAPTER FOURTEEN

GRACE

Flying on a plane by myself, this was a first. There'll be many first from now on, but I can't think about that now. Aunt Loretta texted me before I got on the plane. The real estate agent sold my home. How did that happen so fast? The new owners are moving into the house in thirty days. That doesn't leave me much time to find a place to live, especially with my budget. I have to make this work. I know JJ, he's just waiting for me to fall on my face and beg him for help. It's never going to happen though. I'll sleep on a park bench before I do that.

I have to focus on more important things now. The first thing I need to do when I get off this plane is buy an air mattress and some linen. I am not sleeping on the floor tonight. The next thing I must do is look for a job. My college fund is fairly large, but I want my funds to last as long as possible. Thankfully, my credit card account still works. I used it for the Uber ride home and for shopping. The social worker gave me a list of things I should do immediately. The first thing to do is enroll in a GED program to get access to my education fund.

It's strange walking into my home now, strange and lonely. So many things have been removed that my voice echoes in the apartment. My air mattress wasn't the most comfortable bed, but it did the job. Just before I went to sleep that night, I texted JJ and Aunt Loretta to let them know that I made it home okay. I've been checking my phone constantly, but JJ hasn't replied back, guess he's still mad. I did get a welcoming response from Aunt Loretta. She was genuinely happy to receive my text. I'm grateful for the opportunity to live on my own, but it is nice to know that someone cares about me.

Sunday morning was great. I got dressed up and made my way to my church. It was a beautiful August day and I was looking forward to seeing familiar faces to make me feel at home. There was a crowd standing on the church steps. That meant Reverend Maddock's previous service was going overtime and the ushers were keeping the doors closed until the early congregants exited. I saw a familiar family. They recognized me, smiled and waved hello. That made me feel good, but then I noticed a few of the men looking at me in a certain way. It wasn't a "hello, nice to see you" look. One man was looking me up and down. I looked at my outfit to see if something was wrong, but that wasn't it. He was staring at my body. Guess they believed those nasty stories the media made up about Ronnie and me. Just like that, my good feelings disappeared and I felt out of place. So, as the doors opened and the early congregants exited the church, I turned around and walked back to my home.

I called Aunt Loretta and told her what happened. She was angry that those men were staring at me. She wanted to come with me next Sunday and speak to Reverend Maddock about them, but I said it didn't matter. The next morning, I scoured the rental ads. The apartments were out of my price range. Even the studio apartments in my neighborhood were out of reach for me financially. I visited several places for rent in other neighborhoods. Some of those places just weren't for me. One was a room for rent where I would have to share the bathroom and kitchen with three men. The way the men leered at me told me this wasn't a good idea. I made my way home with no success. Some of my neighbors were outside. A few were genuinely sympathetic and expressed their sorrow over my father's passing while others looked at me as If I had a bad disease they didn't want to catch. Those fake news stories were causing a lot of problems for me. I decided to focus my home search in other neighborhoods and start fresh with new neighbors. Tomorrow, I'll search the 'not so nice' areas for a home with no roommates. It'll take more of my college fund than I planned to spend, but I need to feel safe.

My electricity was still on, but I had no television. It's funny, a month ago I was eating prime rib with JJ and Brandon at one of those famous L.A. restaurants. Now, I'm sitting on my airbed eating Chinese takeout, watching YouTube shows on my laptop. Still, I don't regret leaving California, I only regret how I did it. I'm praying that JJ will stop being angry with me so we can talk again.

In the morning Ms. Evans, the real estate lady, used her key to open my door. She didn't seem too startled to see me come out of the bathroom. Apparently, she knocked but I didn't hear anything. She came to ask if I could move out five days before the 30-day period because the new owners wanted to walk through the house prior to signing their contract. So, now I have only three weeks to find a home. I told her of my dilemma, but I promised to be out by that date. How I was going to do it was beyond me. Ms. Evans surprised me with a suggestion. She knew of a landlady with a basement studio apartment for rent. I asked how much was the rent, but Ms. Evans told me not to worry about it right now. She wanted me to see the lady today though. I was extremely happy to oblige. I called the landlady right away and asked if I could see the studio today, and she told me to come ASAP.

On my way to visit the studio, I thought, *maybe my luck is turning around*. Then I walked to the building. It was a gorgeous brownstone with two steps down to the lower level. My heart sank because I knew this place was way out of my budget. I knocked on the door anyway, hoping for a miracle. I'm not picky, maybe there's a small space behind the boiler that I can call home.

Mrs. Rivas walked carefully down the stone steps of her brownstone. A black and brown Dachshund ran out in front of the elderly lady to sniff me. As I bent down to rub his head, I thought about Brandon's dog. Who's taking care of Fergie now that Brandon's in prison? I can't see JJ taking her in.

"Sorry for taking so long, these arthritic knees give me problems sometimes," said Mrs. Rivas.

"Oh, I'm sorry your knees are hurting. Please don't rush on my account," I said. Mrs. Rivas was a petite elderly lady. She wore a faded housecoat and worn moccasins. I followed her as she walked down the two steps to the bottom cellar door. Mrs. Rivas opened the door to the studio and stepped aside to let me in first.

The studio was so quaint and beautiful. The walls were white painted brick and the floor appeared to be laminate wood look, but it was just what I needed. It was an open space with a small bathroom. A two-burner cooktop was next to the sink and small fridge. This place was spacious and well maintained; I couldn't imagine that it would be in my budget though.

"Mrs. Rivas, this place is exactly what I need. Can you tell me what the rent is?" The price she gave me was so ridiculously low that I had to ask her again just to make sure I heard her correctly. Mrs. Rivas repeated the same price. I signed the lease ASAP and she gave me the keys just like that. She told me I could move in at any time. It seemed too easy, but I'm not complaining. She did have rules about no sleepovers or loud parties. That wasn't a problem for me.

Finding a home took a huge weight off my shoulders. I went directly to my bank for first month's rent. From there I went to my storage unit and made arrangements for my things to be delivered tomorrow morning. Once that's done, I'll get some boxes from the grocery store and pack up the things I have at home. When I'm done, I'll cleaned up for the new owners. I hope they take good care of it. This old house was my world. I grew up here, but now I have to leave it and the worst summer of my life behind me. Tomorrow I'll sign up to study for the GED exam. Next on my list is getting a job. It's not a necessity to pay the rent, but it will keep me from total dependence on my fund.

****

The first two months of my emancipation were brutal, but it all worked out in the end. I have a home, a job, and I'm in school. Now my biggest issue is loneliness. I missed having people around who cared about me. My 17th birthday was the saddest day of my emancipation. I thought for certain JJ and Brandon would call as usual, but I got nothing, not even a text. Aunt Loretta and Aunt Felicia called to wish me a happy birthday, so it wasn't too bad. My co-workers at my grocery store job were surprised when I worked on my birthday. They didn't understand, there's no point in my staying home to celebrate. Aunt Loretta was working and there's no other family to celebrate with.

I've kept up with JJ's career. Amal Bliss' popularity increased tremendously and he's been touring more than ever. Wish dad could see him now, he'd be so proud. JJ's made good changes on his new album too. It included two gospel tracks, one was a duo performance with Kirk Franklin. None of his new songs contained explicit lyrics. I was so impressed with the new album I immediately picked up my phone to text him before remembering he doesn't speak to me anymore. I really miss Brandon, too. He was always there for me when I had a problem. I've searched the background of every Amal Bliss media photo, but Brandon wasn't in any of them. Brandon's Facebook page is closed and his phone number's no longer valid. I'm praying nothing bad happened to him in prison. Brandon's big on the outside, but he's such a gentleman on the inside. He's too nice to be in prison with criminals.

Aunt Loretta and I spent Christmas together. It was nice to spend Christmas with someone. Since then, we speak on the phone several times a week. We've become close, like friends. When I need advice, she's always willing to help me. She helped a lot with obtaining my school records to apply to college. My classes start in January and I'm gonna ace them all, for dad and me.

I haven't seen Aunt Felicia since the funeral. She and her husband retired to Maine to be closer to Jonathan's kids. She asked if I wanted to stay with them. I appreciated the offer, but my mind's focused on getting my education in New York. Besides, who knows if I'd somehow mess up their lives too. I doubt Aunt Felicia knew that JJ had written me off. I didn't bring it up because I don't want her to force him to call me.

CHAPTER FIFTEEN

Grace looked herself over once more before grabbing her handbag and keys. Her unruly highlighted curls were meticulously flat ironed into a smoothed neatly shaped bun and the new makeup she purchased gave her the more mature look that she desired. Grace's interview outfit, a charcoal grey blazer and skirt suit, may have been too conservative to wear for a Gym Reception position, but she didn't know what else she had that would work. What she did know was that she's ready to move on to something better. The hours at her supermarket job kept increasing, leaving less time for her studies. She'd asked her supervisor several times to reduce her work time, but instead of working with her, he suggested she drop college and become an assistant supervisor at the store. This was Grace's final semester at the community college. Her fall semester acceptance to the prestigious NYU Steinhardt School required top grades. Grace was determined to not let her job take precious time from her studies.

Going to work and school left little time for a social life. Her closest friend was her new dog Cujo. That's how she wanted it in the beginning, but now, with Aunt Loretta's urging, she was ready to live more. No more turning down date requests or lying about having a boyfriend when she didn't.

Grace fell in love with Cujo at the shelter. The Animal Rescue Association found Cujo lying next to two other pups that had succumbed to the cold New York winter. The mother was never found and they didn't know how long he was left on his own. The young pup was emaciated and filthy. He survived physically, but the experience left him distrustful with a bad attitude. Despite the rescue staff's best efforts, he remained unfriendly and was deemed inappropriate for family adoption. The attendants gave him the name Cujo because he'd snarl at anyone when approached. Before releasing him into her care, they asked Grace several times if she really wanted "this" dog, but hearing Cujo's story further convinced her that this was the dog for her. Being an orphan herself, Grace related to Cujo's pain. She was determined to make him understand her credo. Life's not fair, but you can't let that stop you from living. He snapped at her at first, but she took him home anyway. Using a fleece comforter, Grace made a bed for the camel colored Chihuahua mix next to the covered radiator. The first thing she did every morning was feed Cujo. By the time she was dressed, he'd be waiting by the door, ready for their walk. The early walks were difficult. Cujo would chew on his leash and snarl, but Grace stuck to her discipline routine. They went on walks three times a day until Cujo gave no resistance to the leash. He grew fond of the small kibble treats she gave give him after each successful walk. The treats along with a good rub after the walk converted Cujo into the happy playful dog Grace knew he could be.

This was their first spring together. Grace had packed away Cujo's doggie sweaters for the next winter. The two enjoyed their early spring walks through Fort Greene Park. Gracie loved the greenery and Cujo loved sniffing anything that moved. The distrustful, anxiety-ridden dog now trotted with confidence.

It was time to go. She nudged her four-legged apartment mate back into their home before locking the door.

When Aunt Loretta spotted the new job posting at her gym, she called Grace immediately.

"I know the owner from church. I observe everything; he treats his workers with respect. His son started his physical therapy practice six months ago and it's booming. They need someone to assist the gym members and make physical therapy appointments. I know you can handle this, Gracie, I've seen how hard you work at the market. This is a better job with fewer hours," she said. The bus commute was twenty-five minutes from her home and if she gets the job, her commute to her new college would only take twelve minutes.

One of the principles Gregory Mitchell instilled in Grace and Jamal was to never be late to a gig. Doing so tells the person that you do not respect their time. So, when the bus left Grace three blocks farther away from her destination than she expected, she walked casually to her facility because she'd left her home earlier than needed.

Reed Fitness & Physical Therapy Center was located in the downtown Brooklyn business district. Their entry was bright and welcoming. A waiting area with plush burgundy seating was to the right of the entry; the reception area was to the left of the entry. It held a long-elevated counter in front with sports apparel displayed behind glass underneath. A tall refrigerated unit containing various brands of water and health drinks was behind the counter area. A muscular middle-aged bald man stood behind the counter joking with a customer. Grace waited patiently until he finished his joke and turned around.

"Hello, you must be Miss Stewart," he said.

"Oh, sorry, no I'm Miss Mitchell. I hope I didn't arrive too early?"

"Don't worry about that, I like early. Lateness is what I can't stand. Please come up and have a seat." Fifteen minutes into the interview, Miss Stewart arrived through the entry door slightly out of breath. Mr. Reed instructed Miss Stewart to have a seat in the waiting area. Being pleased with what he heard so far, Mr. Reed asked Grace to wait to be interviewed by his son. He walked past the exercise equipment to the physical therapy department in the rear of the building. Grace thought the interview was going well so far. On the inside she was overjoyed. Mr. Reed spoke as if she already had the job, but then she overheard some of the conversation between the owners.

"Dad, she looks very young. You really think she's mature enough to handle your members and my patients?"

"Eric, she's nineteen, with two years of solid retail experience. I imagine she has experience dealing with many different customers. Ms. Mitchell recommended her and she came early to the interview. And how are you calling someone else young? Twenty-seven doesn't make you Methuselah."

They must have heard Grace chuckle at the joke because their heads turned toward Grace before they lowered their voices. A few minutes passed before Eric Reed walked over and introduced himself. Grace thought his stern look was too serious for someone his age. Eric was muscular like his father, but much taller. He wore thick-rimmed glasses and a thin mustache, but he still looked like a young college student. During the interview, Eric suggested several scenarios and asked what Grace would do in each situation. After each reply he entered notes into his tablet.

"The hours would be part-time only from 6 to 11 a.m., Monday through Friday. We've had problems with employees getting to work that early in the past. Would you be able to get here on time?" said Eric sternly.

"Yes sir, I'm always on time," said Grace. They talked for a few more minutes before Eric shook her hand and told her that they would be in touch when they made a decision.

Grace's confidence deflated after Eric Reed walked away. She thought for certain that Mr. Reed was ready to give her the job. On her way out she passed by Miss. Stewart, who looked as if she was in her late 20s. *Just what the son wants,* Grace thought dejectedly. Someone pushed the door open just as she reached for it, making her handbag and the contents spill on the floor.

"I'm sorry, miss, I shouldn't have been rushing," the man said as they both stooped down to retrieve her handbag. "Are you a new member here? My name is Kenneth."

"Nice to meet you, Kenneth, my name is Grace. No, I'm not a member, I came for an interview."

"Well, it's very nice to meet you and I hope you get the job," said Kenneth as he held the door open for her.

"Thank you," said Grace as she exited. She thought Kenneth was cute. He was tall, lean and muscular with an attractive smile. Grace could tell that he was attracted to her, but she didn't have the courage to return the eye contact she knew he was waiting for. *It's so crazy. Here I am living in a time when women are encouraged to be fearless, yet I don't have the guts to start a relationship,* she thought. Her phone rang. Grace knew who was calling her before she looked at the cellphone. "Hi Auntie."

"Well, how did it go?" said Loretta.

"Auntie, I can't get a hello, how was your day, out of you?"

"Gracie, stop toying with me, you know I called to get the details. How did the interview go with Mr. Reed?"

"Which Mr. Reed are you referring to? The nice one or the stuck-up black Clark Kent?"

Loretta laughed, "I take it you're referring to Eric. He's a good-looking black man, but those glasses are over the top, aren't they? Clayton told me he wears them because he wants his patients to take him seriously. It's a good sign that both owners interviewed you. You may already have the job, but don't call Eric names, he's a nice guy."

"Nice? Okay, I wouldn't call him mean, but 'Nice' is a stretch. I would say he's stoic or apathetic. By the way, junior told his father that I was too young, so don't count on me getting this job, Auntie."

"I can't believe Eric said that, he's young himself."

"You could have fooled me. He doesn't act young. He was so serious and cold when he interviewed me. The only warm thing about him was his handshake."

"Gracie, I know Eric. He may not make good first impressions, but he's a good guy and he's a great gym manager."

"Gym manager? I thought that was his father's job."

"His father is very busy, he runs a boxing gym at another location. You know Mr. Reed use to be a professional boxer, he competed in the Olympics."

"Oh, I did not know that."

"Eric's parents divorced when he was young. Eric travelled back and forth between his parents throughout his childhood."

"Oh, that must have been tough, no wonder he's so uptight."

"Gracie, you are too much," said Loretta as she laughed. "Don't worry, I'm sure Mr. Reed will convince his son that you're the right person for the job."

"I hope so, I'm beyond ready to quit the job at the market. Just in case, I'll apply for a few more positions."

"Gracie, remember you don't have to work. You can still move in with me you know."

"I know Auntie, and I appreciate the offer, but I like my independence. At first it was tough living on my own, but I like where I live and I have Cujo to keep my company. I know some people wouldn't go for Mrs. Rivas' rules, but I wasn't planning on inviting anyone to my small place anyway. Also, the rent is so cheap, I'd be a fool to give it up. You never know though, one day I may get tired of my independence and show up at your door with Cujo."

"Oh, I keep forgetting about him. Is he still chewing your shoes?"

"No, you won't have to worry about that, he doesn't do that anymore. Cujo's perfectly trained."

****

Two days later, Gracie received the call from Snr. Mr. Reed. "Auntie, I got the job!" Grace yelled into the phone.

"You see, didn't I tell you that you were getting the job?"

"Yes, Senior Mr. Reed must have had the final word. I can't wait to show Clark Kent that young people can be great employees."

CHAPTER SIXTEEN

At 5:45 a.m., Grace stood outside the doors of Reed Fitness & Physical Therapy Center, waiting for one of the owners to open the door. Snr. Mr. Reed popped out from a side entrance and motioned for her to follow him in. After Grace got settled, he started training her immediately on how to greet the members and use the electronic member card machine. Part of her job included wiping down the exercise equipment with sanitizing solution first thing every morning. He then showed her how to operate the phones. Mr. Reed made her feel welcomed. Gracie was sitting behind the raised counter laughing heartily at Mr. Reed's jokes when Eric and Kenneth walked in together.

"Well hello there. It's good to see you again and congratulations on your new job," said Kenneth.

"Thank you, Kenneth, it's good to see you again, too," said Gracie with a smile.

"Good morning, Miss Mitchell, do you two know each other?" asked Eric.

"We bumped into each other when she was leaving a few

weeks ago. I'll be seeing you around Grace," said Kenneth as he left.

"Watch out for that one, he loves the ladies," Snr. Mr. Reed said to Grace under his breath. "Well, I think you've got the hang of things here. Eric, why don't you show Grace around the back and give her some of our staff tee shirts."

"Sure dad. Grace, follow me." Eric gave her the tour of the physical therapy area and the separated rooms they have for fitness classes. The center was much larger than Grace originally thought. He showed her the equipment that was stored under the therapy tables and in the storage room.

"Here are the tee shirts, you can take what you need. I've got to get ready for my patients soon, but let me know if you need anything. I'll be in my office."

Before Grace could respond, the front door buzzer was heard. They both walked swiftly to the front entrance. Standing near the counter was a tall blond woman and a little boy with his arm in a sling. He appeared to be about five years old.

"Good morning, are you Mrs. Bassati," Eric asked.

"Yes, and this is my son Max." The woman continued speaking to Eric while the little boy walked closer to the exit.

Grace saw that little Max was afraid so she stooped down to engage him in conversation. She introduced herself and asked him some questions. At first, he looked at the floor and gave her one-word answers, but then he opened up.

"Are you afraid, Max?" she asked. He shook his head yes.

"Max, there's nothing to be afraid of. Mr. Reed is going to make you better, but if you're afraid of anything he's doing, you can tell him how you feel, okay?" Max shook his head yes.

"Hi, Max, I'm Mr. Reed. Why don't you follow me to the back." Max reluctantly followed Eric while Mrs. Bassati told Grace that she would be back to pick Max up after his appointment.

Grace returned to the counter with Snr Mr. Reed, who introduced her to the members as they arrived. Suddenly, Max came running from the physical therapy area without Eric. He was headed for the door when Gracie intercepted him.

"Max sweetie, where are you going? Your mom is not back yet."

"I want to go home, Ms. Grace." Eric came running out afterwards, but he stopped when he saw Gracie had Max.

"I'll tell you what, why don't I come back with you for a few minutes. Would that be okay?" Max shook his head yes. Grace picked him up and brought him to the back, with Eric leading the way. She sat him down on the table where his coat was.

"Thanks Grace, I'm so sorry about that. My assistant was supposed to be here, but she's running late again," said Eric.

"It's not a problem, Mr. Reed."

Eric continued administering therapy to Max. After a few minutes, Grace got up. "Max, I'll bring your mother to you when she's back, okay?" As she turned to leave, Grace tried to untangle herself from Max, but he wouldn't let go of her shirt.

"Please stay," he said in a small voice. Grace looked at

Eric, who nodded yes. He brought over a chair so Grace could sit while holding Max's good arm. Eric continued to give Max's other arm gentle exercises. Grace told Max how brave he was and he rewarded her with a huge smile.

"I like your smile, Max, you need to smile more often," she said. This made him smile even more.

Eric's assistant Laura came in walking swiftly to Eric before saying, "I'm sorry, Mr. Reed, my train was delayed again."

Eric didn't change his expression. "Laura, we'll talk later. Max, this is Ms. Laura. She will take good care of you."

"Bye Max, I'll let you know when your mom is here, okay?" said Grace.

"Laura, Grace is the new receptionist, she's been helping out," said Eric.

"It's good to meet you," said Laura.

"It's nice to meet you too, Laura," said Grace.

The morning went by quickly. Snr Mr. Reed stayed behind the counter with Grace as more members and therapy patients came in. Kenneth came by the counter to talk to her before he left. He told her that he and Eric met in college. They shared a dorm room in their freshman year and have been friends ever since. Kenneth majored in dentistry and currently interns at his father's practice. He was so charming and he made Grace feel comfortable.

"You have a great smile Grace, did you have dental work done?" asked Kenneth.

"Ahem, Kenneth, stop flirting with my new employee and let her do her job," said Snr Mr. Reed. Kenneth said a quick goodbye before leaving. Before the door closed, an overweight elderly lady with a walker came through the door, aided by a young man.

As she approached a chair, the young man said, "I'll pick you up later grandma." He turned and walked out the door. The lady looked around at the seating. Using her walker to steady herself, she attempted to slowly lowered herself to a seat. Grace left from behind the counter to assist her.

"Good morning, are you here for a physical therapy appointment?" she asked.

"Yes, you must be new, what happened to Natasha?" asked the woman.

"Sorry, I don't know who that is. This is my first day. My name is Grace. May I have your name? I'll tell the PT staff that you're here for your appointment."

"Tell them Mrs. Porter is here."

"Thank you, I'll be right back." Grace walked to the PT department where she found Laura on her phone in the supply room.

"Excuse me Laura, Mrs. Porter is here for her appointment."

"Oh, could you do me a favor and let Eric know? Thank you."

Grace found Eric working with another patient. "Excuse me Eric, Mrs. Porter is here for her appointment."

"Thanks Grace, tell Laura to bring her to the second table."

Grace went back to the supply room, but Laura was no longer there. She returned to Mrs. Porter and assisted her to the seating area in the PT dept. Grace didn't know which table was number two, and she didn't want to get Laura in trouble. She turned quickly to check the supply room again and slammed right into Eric. He steadied her with his arms before apologizing.

"Sorry Grace, have you seen Laura?"

"Ahh, she was in the supply room; I'm on my way there now."

"I just came from that area and she's not there."

"Don't worry, I'll take care of Mrs. Porter."

"No, that's okay Grace. You go back to the reception area, it's almost the end of your shift."

Grace could tell that Eric was irritated with Laura's absence. She went back to the reception area while still looking around for her co-worker. Grace left when the next receptionist came for their shift. *Well, I tried to cover for her,* she thought.

The first two weeks at work went by smoothly. Snr. Mr. Reed would open the facility in the morning and stay with Gracie until Eric arrived, then he would leave to manage the boxing gym. The following Monday Gracie received a surprise. Loretta strolled into the gym in full color coordinated athletic gear. "Auntie, you didn't tell me that you were coming this morning," said Grace as she went over to give her a hug.

"Well, I have the day off and thought I should use my gym membership while I still have it. Then we can go to lunch afterwards to celebrate your new job."

"That sounds great to me. Is that the real reason you're here, or are you checking up on me?"

"Hmm, let's just say I wanted to make sure that my niece was being treated well, but don't let me disturb you, I'm here to work out too." Loretta walked over to one of the machines with towel and water bottle in hand.

"Ms. Mitchell? I thought I heard your voice. I haven't seen you in such a long time I almost forgot what it sounded like. It's so nice to see your lovely face again," said Snr. Mr. Reed.

"Now Clayton, you know I come regularly. It's just that I've been busy helping the teachers with the end of semester wrap up. The only time I'm able to get here is 7 p.m. and you're long gone by then." Grace watched the two as they continued to converse. She witnessed her Aunt blush at Snr. Mr. Reed's compliments. She also noticed Mr. Reed's unblinking gaze on her Aunt's smile. Grace smiled to herself as she realized what was going on.

Just then Kenneth stepped in front of her. "Is that smile for me?" he said with a grin. Grace didn't know how to tell him no without sounding rude. Luckily Eric came to her defense.

"Kenneth, stop harassing our staff. Good morning Grace, is that your aunt over there on the elliptical?"

"Good morning Eric, yes, that's my aunt. She's taking me to lunch later."

"That sounds nice; I'll go over and say hello." Kenneth turned around to see whom Eric was talking about.

"Wow, that's your aunt? I see that beauty runs in your family," he said.

"Come on Kenneth, Grace has work to do," Eric shouted at him.

"Alright, alright!" Kenneth shouted back. Before he left Grace, Kenneth turned around and whispered, "One of these days we'll go someplace where we can talk without your boss hovering around."

Grace just smiled while inwardly she hoped he would leave already. *I definitely would not be going out with you or any other man who stares at my chest like you,* she thought. Since she started working behind the counter, she found Kenneth's eyes on her chest more times than she could count. Grace had an excellent view of the gym. She observed Kenneth flirting with all the young women. Seem to her that he was attracted to all females.

At the end of her exercise session, Loretta showered and changed before returning to the reception counter. When Grace's shift ended, the two walked to a nearby restaurant that Mr. Reed recommended.

"What are you ordering, Auntie?"

"Well, Clayton recommended the pulled pork, but that has too many calories for me. I want to lose a few more pounds by the summer. Why don't you try it?"

"Auntie, you are fine just the way you are, you don't need a diet."

"That's exactly what Clayton said."

"Oh, I believe that; it was written all over his face when he saw you," Grace said with a grin.

"Girl, stop looking at me like that. There's nothing going on between me and Clayton, we're just friends."

"You know Auntie, your face really lights up when you say his name."

"Enough about me, who's this Kenneth guy who didn't want to leave you alone?"

"He's just Eric's friend from college. When we first met, I thought he was a nice guy, but he's just trying to get with every woman in the gym."

"Oh, I hate guys like that. They make me think of my past and that's not some place I want to go back to," said Loretta.

"I'm tired of guys like that. At the market store, some of the men would first stare at my chest then ask me for a date. I got rid of them by saying I already had a boyfriend. It usually worked, but some were still unfazed."

"Is that what you're going to say when Kenneth asks you out? You know it's coming."

"Auntie, I'm tired of lying. I'll be as gentle as possible when I let him down. You want to hear something crazy? There is someone who I can't stop thinking of, even though I've tried."

"I can't believe this, Gracie, you've been holding out on me. Tell me who's the mystery man. Is he in one of your classes?"

"No, but I wish he was someone from school."

"Oh, it can't be that bad, tell me already."

"Okay, but you have to keep your voice down and don't laugh; I don't want anyone to overhear this. It's Eric," Grace said dejectedly.

"Gracie, it's wonderful that you like Eric. I think you two would be great together, you're definitely opposites and they say opposites attract," said Loretta excitedly.

"Shhh, Auntie, don't speak so loudly. Someone may hear you; and don't get too excited because I still can't stand him.

He's always watching me as if I'm going to steal something. Anyway, nothing's going to happen because he thinks I'm too young. It's just that ever since I bumped into him and he held me to stop me from falling, he's been on my mind. I keep thinking of his arms around me and how cute his eyes are. Sounds silly doesn't it? Guess I'm falling for the closest man in my environment because I'm pathetic and lonely. There are so many nice guys in the gym, but I have to fall for the guy who never smiles and happens to be my boss."

"Gracie, this sounds like more than loneliness. With all the men who come to that gym, if he's the only man you think of everyday, it's definitely more than loneliness. Has he said anything romantic to you?"

"No, and he never will."

"Gracie, you can't hide behind school and work forever. Don't let the assault you experienced in the past keep you from living your life in the present. You are a beautiful, smart young woman who deserves to be happy. I know fear and I've been there too, but sweetheart, you have to take chances in life. Anything worth having comes with risks. Eric went through a bad time with his previous relationship, so he will be happy to find love again."

"What do you mean by again? Did he have a girlfriend?"

"Clayton told me what he had was a cheating fiancée. Eric dated a young lady he met in his freshman year. They became engaged just before Eric moved to grad school. While they were separated, his fiancée was lonely and hooked up with someone else. That boy was devastated. Many of the ladies in the gym have looked his way, but

Clayton said he hasn't seen him with anyone since. Eric may be just as lonely as you are. Speak to him, Gracie."

"Whoa Auntie, I'm not asking anyone to date me. I don't have enough experience to be that bold anyway. My first and last kiss was at fourteen, and dad made sure nothing happened after that."

"I know your dad went a bit far with overprotecting you, but you have to understand, he was afraid you'd turn out like me. I never told him everything Terrance did, but he found out later what Terrance and I were doing when I was a teenager. He wanted better for you."

"Auntie, Terrance is in the past, you can start fresh with Clayton. I see the way he looks at you, give him a chance. You said yourself that he's a very nice man."

"Gracie, he's famous, he could have any woman. Once he learns about my past his infatuation with me will be over."

"Auntie, you don't know that. You deserve a chance at love again. Besides, I saw you blush when he complimented you. Don't tell me you feel nothing, speak to him."

"Alright, touché. I'll tell you what, if you tell Eric how you feel, I'll ask Mr. Reed out to lunch."

"No, sorry, that's not good enough. You have to tell him that you're attracted to him too."

"Oh no, older men don't like bold women. I can't tell him that."

"Auntie, I've never heard that one before. Are you making this up?"

"No, I just know these things."

CHAPTER SEVENTEEN

"I'm done! That was my last final exam. I can't wait for graduation," said Grace.

"I'm proud of you honey. It wasn't easy, but you did it all on your own. I have an idea. You're not doing anything this summer, why don't we go somewhere together?"

"That sounds wonderful, Auntie, I'll come over after you get home and we can discuss where we should go."

"I'll see you then," said Loretta.

Grace ended her conversation just as Kenneth and Eric walked in. Eric said good morning and kept walking, but Kenneth came over to the counter.

"You seem very happy this morning, who were you talking to, your boyfriend?"

"Ahh no, that was my aunt. I don't have a boyfriend."

"You see, that's something I don't understand. I asked you out but you only want to be friends. Now you say you don't have a boyfriend, so what's the deal?" he said with attitude. Kenneth looked over his shoulder to see if Eric left, but he found Eric watching them intently. "I better go before your uptight boss accuse me of harassing you again."

Grace didn't know what to say, she turned down his date and offered to be friends even though she didn't want any relationship with him. The sarcasm in his voice made her feel uneasy.

Mrs. Porter came in with her grandson. This time he stayed, but he still didn't help his grandmother to sit. Grace came over to assist Mrs. Porter as Laura hadn't arrived yet.

"Oh Grace, I want you to meet my grandson George, he's always around to bring me to my therapy. He's a good man."

Grace was at a loss for words. *I must have a sign on my forehead that says I'm lonely,* she thought. "It's nice to meet you, George," said Grace. Instead of making eye contact with Grace, George licked his lower lip and looked her up and down as he shakes her hand. "Excuse me, I hear my boss calling me," said Grace. Eric wasn't calling her, but it was the only thing she could think of to say before things got awkward.

Eric was busy arranging therapy equipment in his office when Grace walked in. "Excuse me Eric, Mrs. Porter is here."

"Thanks Grace, have you seen Laura?"

"No, sorry I haven't. Why don't I bring Mrs. Porter in, her grandson is with her."

"Oh, that's new, he usually bolts out the door before she sits down," said Eric.

"I think Mrs. Porter has an agenda today. I'll go get them." Grace left before Eric looked up to ask what she meant by agenda.

"Mrs. Porter, you can come in now. George, can you

help your grandmother up? I'll help on this side." When the three walked into the Physical Therapy department, Eric helped Mrs. Porter to the table.

"So, when do you get off work? I was thinking that we could get together sometime," George said to Grace.

"Oh, ahh, sorry, but I'm seeing someone," said Grace.

"It's okay to see other people. I'm sort of seeing someone too, but it's not working out," said George.

"Umm, I also work really, really long hours," Grace said while looking directly at Eric, hoping he would tell George not to harass her. Unfortunately, Eric said nothing. "…and I go to night classes," Grace continued her list of lies.

"I don't mind waiting, maybe I'll meet you after your class," said George.

"Sorry, like I said, I can't go out with you because I'm in a relationship."

"Actually, Grace is seeing me exclusively," said Eric. Grace was shocked and relieved when Eric lied for her, but Mrs. Porter wasn't having it.

"Wait, I never saw the two of you together," she said.

"We try to be as professional as possible," said Grace. Disappointed, George sucked his teeth and left, mumbling to himself. Grace exhaled, not realizing she was holding her breath. She mouthed "thank you," to Eric before leaving him with an upset Mrs. Porter.

After finishing with Mrs. Porter's exercises, Eric came to Grace. "Grace, can I speak with you for a minute?"

"Sure Eric. I'm sorry for putting you on the spot like that with Mrs. Porter's grandson, but he wouldn't leave me alone. I didn't want to be rude when Mrs. Porter was listening to every word. I believe she encouraged him to ask me out."

"Don't worry about that, Grace, I was about to tell him to wait in the reception area. I want to speak with you about something else. You're out of school now, aren't you?"

"Yes, I'll have my graduation at the end of the month. Then I'll continue with my bachelors this fall."

"That sounds great. Would you be interested in working with me until 5 p.m. temporarily? I know it's a lot to ask, but it should only be for a few weeks at the most and you'll receive two salaries. Oh, and I would need you next Saturday too if possible," said Eric.

"Hmm, I'm going somewhere with my aunt Saturday morning, but my afternoon is open. Do you need me to cover the counter until 5 p.m.? Is Matthew out sick?"

"No, you won't have to cover for Matthew, he will be here. You'll cover for Laura. I'll need your help with the patients and you do extremely well with them."

"But Laura's a physical therapy assistant, how can I do her job?"

"Don't worry, I'll show you everything you need to know. I've been watching you. You learn fast and you're great with the patients. They love you by the way. Max was upset when he didn't get a chance to say goodbye to you when he completed his sessions." Looking into Eric's eyes, Grace said yes without thinking.

"That's great," said Eric. He smiled and gave Grace a light hug. A hug too short for her liking. Eric continued to talk, but Grace barely acknowledged what he was saying, her heart continued to pound in response to their touch. They were interrupted by Laura's arrival.

"Excuse me Grace, I have to speak with Laura now." Eric and Laura walked into Eric's office while Grace went back to the counter. A few minutes later, Laura stormed out with her belongings without saying goodbye to anyone. Eric came out later to continue their conversation. "I might as well tell you now that I just fired Laura."

"Oh, I'm sorry to hear that," said Grace.

"I'm sorry too. I tried to work with her, but the constant lateness was affecting the quality of service I provide and that's not something I can tolerate. I'm conducting interviews for a new physical therapy assistant, but I really need your help in the meantime."

"Don't worry Eric, you can count on me."

****

"Hi Auntie, you'll never guess what I did today."

"You don't sound too happy about it, what did you do?"

"I volunteered to work more hours."

"What in the world made you volunteer to do that? You just left a job because you were overworked."

"Well, it's only for a few weeks until he hires new staff."

"Would that 'he' be Eric," said Loretta before she started laughing.

"Why are you laughing, Auntie?"

"Look at yourself, you're not dating the man and yet you can't say no to him. You must really be in love."

Grace couldn't refute what her aunt was saying. She'd

213

never felt this way about anyone before. Just standing next to Eric made her heart dance. Sometimes he'd glance her way when she was behind the counter and for a few seconds, she'd think he knew how she felt about him, but he never approached her. Then again, she thought he's just being a supervisor checking on his employees.

The next morning Grace left her home at the usual time, but halfway to work she realized she didn't bring the lunch she prepared. She greeted Snr Mr. Reed as she came into the facility.

"Hey Grace, congratulations on your new position."

"Thanks, but it's only temporary, Mr. Reed. Eric will find a replacement soon."

"I don't know about soon, he really likes how you are with the patients. Have you ever worked in the medical field before?"

"No, but I did take care of my father when he was sick."

"Oh, I had no idea. Is he okay now?"

"No, he passed away when I was sixteen."

"I'm very sorry to hear that you lost your father at such a young age. Was it just you and your mother then?"

"No, my mother passed when I was three, it was just me and my dad. I sort of had an older brother and cousin."

"Sort of? That sounds complicated. I do know you have a beautiful aunt who loves you. I have two aunts back home in Jamaica. They helped to raise me when my parents moved to New York to give my siblings and me a better life. When they brought us kids here, it was tough. My father worked two jobs and my mother worked too. My brother and sister did well in school, but I struggled. One day, this bully picked on me at school. He didn't know that was his worst day. Man, I had him knocked out cold on the ground in three minutes. What I didn't know was that the assistant principal saw the whole thing. I thought I was going to be suspended, but with my dad's permission, he took me to a boxing gym instead. Turns out I was good at knocking guys out and the rest is history. Did you see these?" Mr. Reed opened the glass case that held his trophies.

"Wow, Mr. Reed, you were really famous! Aren't you afraid someone might steal these?"

"Grace, I'm way ahead of you. These are copies," he whispered. They were laughing when Eric and Kenneth walked in.

"Why're you guys always laughing when we walk in? Isn't anyone working?" said Kenneth.

"Kenneth, you just keep walking with your sourpuss expression. Grace and I have things covered," said Snr. Mr. Reed.

"What's gotten into you Ken, you've been so grouchy lately? I like seeing Grace laugh in the morning, she sets a pleasant tone to the atmosphere," said Eric. Mr. Reed raised his brow at his son's statement.

Some of the work Grace did for Eric was challenging, but she didn't mind because it kept her close to him. He bought her lunch and they ate together while he discussed attributes of the PT equipment. Unbeknownst to him, having lunch with Eric made her day.

The week went by quickly and Grace was tired at the end

of each day. Eric, noticing her fatigue, offered to drive her home each night. Grace happily accepted.

****

Saturday Morning

"I'm here Auntie."

"Gracie, why are you so glum? You don't have to go if you don't want to. Not visiting your father's grave doesn't take away the love you had for him. I think you should visit because you didn't allow yourself to grieve when he passed. Those sleeping pills prevented that."

"Auntie, I feel bad about not going before, but just thinking about dad makes me upset sometimes. I wished he had told me about the surgery before he planned it. I know it sounds silly, but I was angry with him for dying," said Grace.

"That's understandable, it was traumatic for you finding out the way you did. The first time visiting a grave of someone you love is the hardest, but it's something I believe you need to do to help you move on with your life. Why don't you pick out the flowers to put on their graves, it might make you feel better."

They left for the cemetery after 7 a.m. It was a trip Loretta made several times a year. She drove to the florist where Grace picked out two arrangements of violet and white gladiolus before they continued their drive to Evergreens Cemetery. Grace's short boots sunk into the rain-soaked lawn of the cemetery as they walked to the site.

Though she still heard faint sounds of the parkway traffic below, walking up the hills of the expansive cemetery was peaceful. She could hear the birds chirping in the old growth treetops. Loretta bent down to removed dead flowers and water from grave vases. Then she cleaned the gravestones with oil as Grace watched on. Loretta showed Grace where to obtain the water for the flowers. Together, they cut and arranged the bouquets to their satisfaction.

"I'll leave you alone now. You can talk, pray or just be here. It's up to you. I'll be in the car."

"Thanks for bringing me, Auntie. I'll just be a minute." Grace waited until Loretta was out of earshot before speaking.

"Dad, it's me, Grace. I miss you so much, you'll never know. When you died, I felt like a bird abandoned in the nest before learning to fly. I didn't make it at first and some bad things happened to me, but that's in the past. I was angry with you because you left me. You shut me out of what was going on with your health. That made me feel like I wasn't important. Looking back now, I know you did what you thought was best for me. I'm not angry anymore.

"That summer was the worst of my life. I lost three people. You died, JJ stopped speaking to me, and Brandon went to jail. I pushed Aunt Loretta away too, but I'm so glad that she didn't give up on me. Aunt Loretta and Aunt Felicia … they're are all I have right now." The tears she choked on made Grace realize how hard she was crying. She wept for her father more now than she ever had. Grace sat in front of the grave crying profusely until she felt Loretta's hand on her shoulder.

"Gracie, it's time to leave now," said Loretta as she pulled Grace up to stand. She held onto Loretta tightly as they made their way back to the car. "Gracie, it's ten o clock. Let me call Eric to tell him you can't come in today. You don't look well."

"No, I'll be fine, Auntie. I have to do something to take my mind off of dad or else I'll just cry all day."

"Are you sure, you haven't eaten anything this morning. Why don't I make you some breakfast; you really don't need to lose any weight."

"I'm not hungry now, but I'll have a cup of tea when I get to work. I'll be fine."

"Well, okay. I'll give you a lift then." When Grace arrived at work, she quickly changed her clothes before entering Eric's office.

"Good morning Eric, what would you like me to start working on?"

"Hi, Grace. Are you okay?"

"Yes, I'm fine, I just had a really rough morning. Why don't I see who is in the waiting room," she said, wanting to escape the stare Eric was giving her. On her way to the waiting room, Grace peeked at her reflection in the glass wall. She knew her eyes were a little puffy when she looked in the car mirror, but the fluorescent lighting revealed bloodshot eyes staring back at her.

After Eric finished with his first patient, he asked Grace to his office.

"Grace, are you really alright, because you don't look well. You know if you're not well, you can go home. Don't worry about the patients, I'll take care of them."

"No, I'm not sick, but I'll be okay."

"Grace, if something or someone's bothering you, you can talk to me. I can tell that you're upset. Please, let me help you." Gracie had to look away because the tears started again.

"Grace?" Eric walked over and took her in his arms. "Tell me what's wrong, I really want to help." Grace broke down in tears as she held onto him.

"I'm sorry Eric, I'll stop crying."

"It's okay, you go ahead and cry. Please, tell me what's wrong, did someone upset you?"

"No, it's nothing to worry about. I'm ashamed to say why I'm crying. My father died when I was sixteen. I didn't handle it well and I was angry about it for a long time. Today was the first time I visited his grave. It just reopened old wounds I thought were healed. Working usually keeps my mind off thoughts I don't want to dwell on. Just give me a few minutes. I promise I'll get myself together. I don't want to take you away from your work." Grace looked up at Eric, realizing that she was still in his arms. Suddenly, he kissed her gently on the lips, but then he stepped away.

"I'm so sorry, Grace. You're vulnerable right now and I shouldn't have done that..." Before Eric could finish apologizing, Grace placed her hand around the back of his neck and kissed him back. Eric responded with a deeper kiss. Time stood still for Grace as the two held onto each other.

"I've wanted to do that for such a long time, but I wasn't sure that it was what you wanted. I was convinced that you didn't even like me," said Eric.

"This is crazy, I didn't know you felt anything for me. You never said a word," said Grace.

"Grace, you have no idea how hard it was for me to stay away from you. Every time I turned around, Kenneth or some other guy was asking you for a date. I noticed you would step back when someone came onto you, as if you wanted to run away. I didn't know how to approach you and I didn't want you to be afraid of me. You're also my employee. The last thing I needed was a sexual harassment charge. I have to be honest. I wish you were a little older, are you sure that you want a relationship with me?"

"Eric, I haven't been on a date since my freshman year in high school. So, if you're looking for someone with a lot of experience, that's not me, but what I do know is that my heart wants you. Are you okay with that?"

"I'm more than okay with that. It's going to be really tough for me to work with you now but I promise to keep my lips off you outside of this office," said Eric.

"That's fair, you've been distracting me for some time now. We should leave this office before your patients start searching for you."

Eric sighed. "You're right, but we need to talk. Grace, I do think you should go home and rest today."

"Nope, I'm staying. And I promise, no more crying."

The rest of the day went by quickly. Grace popped her head into Eric's office at the end of her shift. "Eric, I'm going home now."

"Please, wait a minute, I'll drop you home."

"Don't you still have a lot paper work to do?"

"Yes, but it can wait. I want to spend some time with you. Please, give me five more minutes."

"Okay, I'll wait in the lunchroom." Grace whipped out her phone on the way to the lunchroom. "Auntie," she whispered when Loretta picked up the phone.

"Gracie? Why are you whispering?"

"I just wanted to tell you that Eric kissed me today."

"Oh Gracie, that's wonderful! Now give me all the details."

"I'll have to do that later, Eric's taking me home now."

"What do you mean he's taking you home? Gracie wait…"

"Auntie, don't worry, he's just dropping me home."

"Oh Gracie, don't scare me like that. Now be careful, Eric's already had a serious relationship, you've never had any."

"Don't worry, Auntie, we're just going to talk. I'll call you tonight."

"You better, I'm not getting any sleep otherwise."

Just then, Eric walked up behind Gracie.

"Okay, I'm ready. Hey, would you like to have dinner before I drive you home?" Eric asked.

"Dinner would be nice as long as I don't get home too late. Cujo would be very upset me."

"Who's Cujo?"

"He's my dog."

"You named your dog Cujo? He must be ferocious."

"He'd like to think of himself that way, but he's really a

sweetheart. The animal shelter staff nicknamed him Cujo. I liked the name so I kept it." They walked to a grill restaurant in the neighborhood. Grace ordered shrimp and spring vegetables while Eric ordered a steak.

"You know, I thought you were a vegetarian. When you eat lunch its usually smoothies or vegetable wraps," said Grace.

"I try to eat light during work so I can keep my energy up for my patients. So, you've been watching me eat, huh? I have to confess that I've been watching you too, though I try to make it look like I'm watching you as my employee."

"Well, you were very convincing to me, I thought you were a micro manager."

"I've had to keep watch over you to protect you from Kenneth. I've seen him wear women down until they give in and say yes to a date. I didn't want that to happen to you."

"You didn't have to worry about Kenneth, he's not my type. You must really like your job. I can tell you put a lot of energy into your work. Sometimes I listen to your conversations with the patients. I think Mrs. Porter looks forward to talking with you. She keeps you talking for a while."

"Yeah I know. Despite having her grandson, she seems lonely. I don't know what the deal is with George, he's not very attentive toward her. It's going to be difficult, but Mrs. Porter's sessions will have to end soon. If she'd follow my exercise instructions, she would have been finished a while ago. But enough about me, tell me about your studies. Dad said you're a music major? What made you choose that field?"

"Well, I've been around music all of my life. My father was a jazz pianist. He taught my brother and me how to play. My brother plays extremely well and has a career in music. My dream is to manage a studio as a music production and sound-engineering specialist. I'm graduating with my two-year degree now and I will continue my studies in the fall. Would you like to come to my graduation? It'd be nice to have you there with Aunt Loretta."

"I would love to come, just say when. It would be nice to meet your brother and the rest of your family, too."

"Well, my brother's been upset with me, so I'm not so sure that meeting will happen. Now I need to learn more about you. What made you want to be a physical therapist?" Grace asked him.

"Well, physical therapy wasn't my first choice. I played basketball in high school; thought I was going all the way to the NBA. Everyone in high school knew who I was. There were a few articles written about how promising my outlook was. Then, during one game I made a sharp turn on the court. I lost my balance and fell awkwardly on my knee. The pain was excruciating. I tore my ACL and had surgery the next day. When I came out, I needed physical therapy and extensive recovery time. After I healed, I just wasn't as quick in the game as I used to be. That killed my basketball dreams because none of the college scouts wanted to touch me after that. Dad was on my back to get what he called a 'real career' anyway. So, I looked into medicine. It interested me. My mother's a nurse. That's how my parents met by the way. When dad had stomach cramps after one of his fights in

Madison Square Garden, my mom was the nurse who took care of him in the hospital. They stayed together long enough to have me, and then they divorced. Anyway, I knew that I didn't want to deal with surgeries because I had no interest in that. I loved to help people and I loved athletics. Receiving therapy for my knee gave me insight into the work. So I chose physical therapy as a career and I'm happy that I did."

"Hmmm, very interesting. My parents divorced right after they had me too. I like your dad. He's told me a lot about his career; he's had a very interesting life. Maybe I'll write a song about him one day."

"You write music as well?"

"Yes, but most has never been heard and I'm going through a dry spell right now."

"You said most, have you written something that's been recorded?"

Hmm, how do I get out of this one? Have to be more careful of what I say. If I tell him about the song, he'll find those terrible articles. "You know, that's another story for another time because I have to get home to feed Cujo."

"Okay, I can't wait to pick up where we left off," said Eric. They arrived at her home shortly after leaving the restaurant. "This is a very nice neighborhood that you live in. Do you live here with your aunt?"

"No, but she's only a ten minute bus ride from here." Eric got out of the car and walked Grace to the door of her basement apartment.

"I know it's short notice, but would you be up to going

on a date tomorrow," said Eric. "Sure, that would be nice. Where are we going?"

"Why don't you tell me what you would like to do."

"Hmm, I'm not sure. Just pick someplace where we can have fun." Eric thought for

a moment before getting an idea.

"Okay, I can do that. Dress casually, we're going to be outside. I'll pick you up at 2 p.m." Cujo was barking up a storm behind the door.

"Wait a minute Eric, someone wants to meet you."

"He's not a biter, is he?"

"No, Cujo's a sweetheart, he just threatens to bite." When Grace opened the door, Cujo jumped out and stood between them, growling at Eric.

"Oh, he's a Chihuahua mix," said Eric as he bent down to rub Cujo's head. After a few sniffs, Cujo warmed up to him and licked his hand.

Grace left them at the door as she hastened inside to fill Cujo's bowl with food. Cujo's ears perked up when he heard the food being poured. He went inside immediately to eat. "Sorry sweetie, I know you were hungry," said Grace as she rubbed his head. She went back to the door to say goodbye to Eric. When she stepped out, Eric pulled her into his arms.

"I like your hair when it's naturally curly like this, do you mind if I touch it?"

"Ahh no, go ahead."

Eric slipped off the band that held her hair in a tight ponytail. Then he cradled the lower back of her head in his hands as he bent down to give her a lingering kiss. When

Grace opened her eyes, she found Eric staring at her.

"Good night, Grace." Eric turned and left before Grace could gather her senses to reply. When she turned around to go inside, she caught site of Mrs. Rivas peeping down at her through the window curtain.

Back inside the studio, Grace sighed with a smile as she leaned against her closed door. It was the end of a long eventful day and she was emotionally exhausted. Noticing her vibrating phone on the table, Grace picked it up. The cellphone screen showed that she missed several calls and texts from Aunt Loretta, so she quickly dialed her back.

"Auntie I'm sorry, I forgot to call you back!"

"Girrrrrl, I was about to go over there to find out what's going on. What took you so long?"

"Eric took me to dinner before he dropped me off."

"And, what else?"

"Oh, and he met Cujo."

"And?"

"And he kissed me and left."

Loretta exhaled. "That sounds nice, Gracie. Now I know that you're an adult and I of all people have no right to tell you what to do, but I hope you don't become intimate. Your father gave you the purity ring you now wear on your necklace instead of your finger. He's no longer here, but you know his wish for you honey."

"Auntie, you have nothing to worry about, Eric is a gentleman and he's so sweet. I can't really explain it, but I feel safe with him. We could have talked for hours and not run out of things to say. He held my hand when he walked me to the door. Oh, and that kiss! When he kissed me, I forgot everything. It was wonderful, Auntie. As far as the ring goes, I have to wear it on a necklace chain. When I worked in the market, it was a magnet for men looking for virgins. You have no idea how many men, including ones with wedding bands, come on to me because of this ring."

"Alright, alright. I just want you to be careful because you're young and inexperienced."

"Auntie, I'll be fine, don't worry. It's been a long day and I'm ready to go to bed, I'll give you a call tomorrow, okay?"

"Okay Gracie. You know I'm just looking out for you and I don't want you to get hurt. I have an idea, why don't you come to church with me in the morning. Maybe we could have lunch afterwards and talk."

"I'm not sure, Auntie. I'm going out with Eric in the afternoon. I'll call you in the morning and let you know if I'm coming."

"Well, okay. You have a good night and I'll speak to you soon."

It was getting late so Grace walked Cujo and prepared for bed, but she was still ecstatic about the kiss. She never longed to be with anyone the way she longed for Eric, yet they shared their first kiss only hours ago. Tomorrow's date couldn't come soon enough, but she had to promise herself to be more careful about what she tells Eric. As far as Grace was concerned, the dark events in her past must stay in her past. She could only imagine what Eric would think of her if he found out about her past addiction and the attempted rape. She wondered if he would look at her the same way those men at church looked her up and down? Would he expect her to be intimate with him? Grace went to bed with these thoughts on her mind.

In the morning, Grace jumped out of bed and quickly prepared to leave. Last night's dream of Eric scared her into making sure she arrived at Aunt Loretta's church on time. She needed divine strengthen to keep the vow she made to her father.

Siting in the pew of Aunt Loretta's church brought back memories of her old church and the people in it. Grace missed seeing Jamal, Brandon and Tasha. Somehow Loretta knew what she was thinking.

"Why don't you call him and apologize? Your father would not want you two to be estranged from each other."

"Auntie, he hasn't called and I still have the same phone number, so, that means he doesn't want to speak to me."

"No Gracie, it means that he's just as stubborn and pigheaded as you are. What about Brandon? Did you try to reach him?"

"I tried to call him but his number was no longer in service. I miss them a lot, but maybe it's good I'm not around to mess up their lives. Besides, JJ has a real sister now."

"Gracie, you need to stop thinking this way. You did not mess up anyone's life. Sometimes bad things just happen. It doesn't mean you separate from your family. Bad events should encourage you to stay closer so you don't feel alone."

Grace sighed. "Okay, Auntie, I'll call JJ, but I'm sure he won't respond."

"Well the Jamal I know was really concerned about you

being safe. Even if he's still mad, I'm sure he'd appreciate hearing from you." After service was over, Loretta dropped Grace home. Grace changed into a fashionable red sundress and wedged heels. This time she left her curly hair unbound after applying a little mousse to tame any frizz. She then applied makeup and topped it off with jewelry. Grace smiled at her reflection in the mirror. She was ready to impress on her first adult date, but Eric wasn't due for another 30 minutes. The smile left her face as Grace sat on her couch with Cujo and picked up her cellphone. The call went to voice mail as she suspected it would, but she left a message anyway.

Hi JJ, it's me Grace. I just called to say I miss you and Brandon. I was hoping to see you guys at some point; guess you're both busy. My graduation is coming up and I thought it'd be nice to have you there, but I know you're really busy. Anyway, send a text when you can. Okay, love you. Bye. Grace was sitting on the couch, mentally critiquing the message she just left, when Eric's knock on her door startled her.

"Hi, Eric," she said as she opened the door.

"Hello. Wow, that's a gorgeous dress. You look like a model, but you should probably wear shorts and sandals for where we're going."

"Um, okay. I'll make a quick change and meet you at the car." Five minutes later Grace entered Eric's Jeep with jean shorts and a tee shirt. "Where are we going?" she asked.

"It's a secret, but you'll be able to guess as we get closer," said Eric.

The sun beaming down on her head in Eric's Jeep took

Grace's mind back to the drive in Jamal's convertible Jaguar. She sighed heavily as she thought of him. Jamal's popularity had soared so much in the past year, she wondered if he even thought of her anymore.

"Hey, why so glum? Are you thinking about your father?" said Eric.

"Ahh, yeah, I was thinking of him, but I'm going to stop doing that and enjoy my present company," Grace said with a smile. She felt bad about lying to Eric, but she convinced herself that it was necessary.

The heavy traffic on the Belt Parkway lengthened their journey. When Eric turned off exit 6S, Grace knew exactly where they were going. "I haven't been to Coney Island in such a long time. Dad used to take me here when I was little."

"My dad used to bring me here, too, I love it. Sometimes I just come to ride my bike on the boardwalk at dawn," said Eric.

After parking the car, they walked hand in hand into Luna Amusement Park. Eric convinced Grace to join him on many rides she'd normally be too frightened to try, but with Eric holding her hand, she had no fear. Afterwards, they ate cotton candy and hot dogs on the boardwalk. It was late in the afternoon when Grace and Eric walked hand in hand on the beach. Eric felt as though he could tell Grace anything. He could not understand why he was so comfortable with her. His reservations about Grace being too young to date were washed away by her smiles. The two sat on a bench by the beach and continued talking until sunset.

Grace's cell phone rang. *"Oh, hi Auntie. Yes, I enjoyed the service at church this morning…. Thanks for the offer but I'm not home now…., No I'm at Coney Island with Eric…… I will Auntie, Love you too, goodbye."*

"Eric, Aunt Loretta said to tell you hello."

"That's nice of her. Please tell her I said hello too. I didn't know you went to church this morning. I hope you didn't have to get up too early. My service starts late, so I was able to get some rest."

"I woke up at eight, but it's okay. I plan to go to bed early tonight because my boss has a lot of work for me tomorrow," said Grace. Eric laughed. "You need to laugh more, you're always so serious at work."

"Yeah, I know, dad tells me that all the time. It's just that I haven't had much to smile about lately, so I just focus on my work."

"I know how you feel, there've been times when it was hard for me to smile too."

"Really? Do you want to talk about it?" asked Eric.

"Ahh, maybe another time. I don't want to chase your elusive smile away."

"Grace, my smiles will never be elusive when you're around." For that compliment Grace rewarded Eric with a kiss.

****

Mrs. Rivas witnessed her tenant coming home hand in hand with the same tall man again. He kissed her at the doorway and left as usual, but the inquisitive landlady wondered if he would soon temp Grace into letting him stay. The elderly lady decided it was time to make a call.

Gracie's extra dose of cheerfulness didn't escape Mr. Reed on Monday morning. "Hmph, I don't have to ask how your weekend went. You're practically glowing," he said. Grace just smiled sanguinely at Mr. Reed while she stocked the refrigerated beverages behind the counter. Eric and Kenneth strolled in at their usual time. Kenneth said hello and kept walking, but Eric came to the counter to greet his father and Grace. The look Eric gave Grace didn't escape Mr. Reed. He wondered what took place on Saturday. After Eric went to the back PT department, Mr. Reed excused himself and joined his son. He had to find out if his suspicion was correct.

"Hey Eric, you know, I've been thinking about adding another employee to work reception in my gym. I think Grace would be perfect for the position. She's young as you said, and she gets along well with kids. She could keep an eye on the kids while they wait for their martial arts class. What do you think of that idea?"

"Um, I don't think that's something Grace is interested in, besides, she's helping me with PT right now."

"Oh, I know she's helping you, but maybe that needs to stop."

"Dad, what do you mean by that?"

"Don't act innocent. I see it all over your face, son. Something happened between you two. Both of your faces were glowing this morning. Do I have to remind you that Grace is your employee? I like Grace. She's a bright and beautiful lady, but it's like you said. She's young and I imagine inexperienced.

Since her father has passed away, I have to ask the question for him. What are your intentions with this girl?"

Eric sighed. "Dad, I have to be honest. I didn't want to have a relationship with Grace. I felt the attraction from the first day she came for the interview, but I closed my heart to it. That's the real reason I tried to dissuade you from hiring her. After she started the job, I tried my best to avoid her, but then I would see other men ask her out. It filled me with fear because I wanted her to be with me. When I decided to fire Laura, I'd already interviewed people for the position and offered the job to the best person. When they accepted, I told them the job starts June because I saw an opportunity to have Grace work closely with me. My hope was for Grace to get to know me better. I didn't know how to divulge my feelings without making us both very uncomfortable.

"When she was upset on Saturday, all I could think of was holding her in my arms. I was willing to do anything to make her pain go away. I have to admit, I kissed her without thinking and I despised myself for losing control. When she kissed me back, I couldn't breathe, I was so happy. It's only been a few days, but dad, she already has my heart. Being with Grace made me realize I never loved Ashley. Yesterday Grace and I talked like we were old friends. There was no tension or pretense."

Mr. Reed sat down and scratched his head. "My goodness, it sounds like you've really fallen for her son. Listen, the two of you see each other every day at work, please be careful and take it slow. I don't want to see either of you get hurt."

****

The week went by quickly for Grace; she believed her life was getting better. She had a new job and a relationship with a wonderful man. Her face lit up in a smile whenever she thought of Eric. As she fondled the purity ring on her necklace, Grace thought about her family. She wanted all of them back in her life and she wanted Jamal to know that she's doing well. *I wonder if JJ and Brandon would approve of Eric as my boyfriend. Is that what he is though? Can I call him that? We talk everyday, but are we boyfriend and girlfriend? I have to find out how to define our relationship before I embarrass myself.*

Workdays flew by too swiftly for Grace and Eric. They ate lunch together every day. The staff noticed the new closeness between their employer and new young co-worker, but Grace didn't care. She wanted all the women to know whom Eric belonged to. Their relationship had been going strong for several weeks. Eric invited Grace to meet his mother at church this Sunday. Grace was happy about meeting Eric's mother, but nervous of the questions she may ask.

CHAPTER EIGHTEEN

"Good morning, Reed Boxing, how can I help you?"

"Good morning to you too, Clayton. You always sound so cheerful on the phone."

"Loretta, is this really you calling me or am I dreaming?"

"You are too funny Clayton. How are you?"

"I'm a thousand times better now that you've called, you have brightened up my day."

"Ha, bet you say that to all the women."

"No, that's where you're wrong because only you can make me feel a thousand times better. Now, what can I do for you?"

"Well, I feel funny asking this, but can I talk to you about Eric and Gracie?"

"Oh, now I'm crestfallen! You don't want me; you want to pump me for information. Well, it's going to cost you. You have to go to dinner with me tonight, then I'll tell you everything I know, and I know a lot."

"Hmm, you drive a hard bargain Mr. Reed. Alright, dinner it is. Where should I meet you?"

Clayton took her number and promised to confirm the location soon. He had hoped Loretta called to take him up on his previous date offer, but he'd take what he could get. *I have to find a way to turn this meeting into a real date*, he thought.

****

Loretta walked into the five-star restaurant foyer feeling uncomfortably underdressed in her plain black linen dress. She drove by this very restaurant many times wondering what it was like inside. The exterior was somewhat plain and the shaded windows gave no opportunity to peek in, but the foyer showed a hint of what was to come. The suited elderly maître d' looked for her name in an old-fashioned ornate reservation book. It was wider than a telephone directory, but the paper stock was of high quality. While being escorted to her table, Loretta looked around in wonder at the intricate Italian renaissance style décor. The drapery reminded her of window coverings she noted in a Vanderbilt mansion tour. The arched ceiling was covered with hand painted tiles and the old-world decorative chandeliers took her to another time and place. The waiter pulled out her chair at the table where Clayton was already seated. Decked out in a single breasted midnight blue suit and open collar cream shirt, the man sitting in front of her no longer looked like the active boxer in sweats. This was a handsome well-built middle-aged man. Clayton rose and kissed Loretta on the hand. Just looking at him made her smile.

"Clayton, what have you done?" Loretta chided. "You invited me to a simple dinner."

"No, I never said the word 'simple.' I just said dinner." Loretta looked around again and wondered if she should rush home to change.

"Clayton, you look so dapper in that suit and I feel so underdressed. This place is wonderful. I never imagined it would look like this inside."

"You look lovely, Loretta. I chose this place because I wanted this dinner to be memorable."

"Thank you for inviting me here," said Loretta.

"I used to come here many times in my boxing days. It's one of the few places that's not really open to the public. You have to be invited by a member. It's perfect for our date."

"Clayton Reed, this isn't a date, we're just friends."

"Loretta, why are you fighting this? You just don't understand how I feel about you," he said while shaking his head. When the waiter came over and took their order, Loretta welcomed the interruption. She loved being in Clayton's company, but she didn't want to spoil their friendship by taking it to the next level. Although, Clayton made it very difficult sometimes.

Clayton started. "Here's what I know about our couple so far. They found out they liked each other the day Grace started working Saturdays. I know my son. I've never seen his face light up the way it did when he looked at Grace that Monday morning. I've also seen the change in Grace. So, I told Eric to take it slow since Grace is much younger. Eric was already thinking the same thing. He didn't tell anyone in the gym they were dating because he thought it might be too much stress for Grace. That said, I have to admit that

Grace is a very mature 19-year-old. She has good common sense and she knows how to greet people professionally and with respect. That's uncommon for her age. That's my scoop, now it's your turn."

"Alright Clayton, I've also advised Gracie to take it slow, but it seems she's completely smitten with Eric. It also seems Eric is very serious about their relationship. Did you know that Eric is bringing her to his church on Sunday to introduce Gracie to his mother?"

"He's doing what?! I had no idea he was at that stage," said Clayton.

"I know Eric had a bad time when he broke up with his fiancée, but Gracie had some bad experiences after the death of her father and I doubt she's recovered fully from them. She's lived on her own since she was sixteen by choice," said Loretta.

"If you don't mind my asking, why didn't she live with you after your brother died?"

Loretta exhaled and broke eye contact with Clayton. "That's a long story. You don't know me Clayton. When I was younger, I did some bad, unforgivable things ... things I regret but can't change. I might as well tell you the reason now. It's also the reason why we should just be friends." Loretta told Clayton her full story. All the sordid details of her actions from when she first met Terrance and what she had to do to keep him from hurting her niece. It was painful for her to relive her past again. Clayton listened quietly and intently while watching the pain etch its way into Loretta's face. After she finished her story, Loretta dried her eyes and waited for Clayton to say something. But he sat, shaking his head with his eyes closed. Loretta took Clayton's silence as confirmation of his disgust with her past. She gathered her handbag and started to rise from the chair, intending to make a quick exit, but Clayton latched his strong hand onto her wrist to prevent her departure. He moved swiftly to her side of the table and took out a handkerchief to wipe her fresh tears.

"Loretta, I'm sorry for what you went through. It should never have happened. You fell in love with a very bad guy and the experience tainted your view of all men, but I'm not like that. Most men are not like that. All I'm asking is for you to give me a chance."

CHAPTER NINETEEN

"Hey Eric, what's going on? Is what I'm hearing true?"

"I don't know Kenneth, what are you hearing?"

"Well, I heard that you and Grace are working long hours together and then you leave together, is that right?"

"Yeah, she's helping me out until the new employee arrives."

"Come on man, I know it's more than that. I saw you two in the restaurant around the corner. No employer holds his employee's hand like that, and everyone notices the way you look at Grace. Why the secrecy? You couldn't tell me you were hitting that?"

"Wait Kenneth, it's not like that. No one is 'hitting' anything. We're just getting to know each other."

"Really? So how much do you know about her? Has she told you about her crazy past? Somehow I doubt it, because if you really 'knew' her, you would be hitting it."

"Kenneth, I told you before, I'm not living my life like I used to. I'm staying celibate for God and what are you talking about anyway? Why are you so concerned about who

I'm dating? Is it because you wanted to add Grace to the long list of women who sleep with you?"

Kenneth laughed, "Man, I'm just looking out for you. You kicked Ashley to the curb for stepping out on you; then you ran back to church, stopped going to the club and stopped dating. Everyday fine women who come here to exercise surround you. Some give you the eye, yet you do nothing. Next thing I know, you pick up someone whose reputation is worse than Ashley's."

"Kenneth, you're not making any sense. Look, I have to prepare for work," said Eric as he walked away. Kenneth was getting on his last nerve. Eric sighed and thought, *Why am I keeping Kenneth as a friend?* He reminisced about those early years in college with Kenneth. Looking back, they shared what he thought were good times. Now he shudders whenever memories of those good times come to mind.

Kenneth was the most popular frat man on campus. All the women wanted him. He was a well-known member that all freshmen aspired to be. It was Kenneth who introduced him to Ashley. She taught him things he never knew. At the time, that seemed like a good thing. Later, he wondered how many men she slept with to learn those talents. Upon obtaining her B.S. degree in Business Management, Ashley continued her studies to obtain her master's degree while Eric was required to change schools to continue his studies.

Kenneth woke up with a different woman in his bed every day, but for Eric, it was only Ashley. The distance between schools meant they couldn't be with each other for weeks on end. Waking up without seeing Ashley's face in the morning was tough. So, Eric called every day, he made it work. When Ashley did visit, they would stay together at Kenneth's place. His mother would never tolerate them sleeping together in her house.

When his dad planned a huge graduation party, Eric seized it as the perfect opportunity for his surprise. After thanking his guests for celebrating his graduation, Eric got down on one knee in front of everyone and asked Ashley for her hand in marriage. There was a slight hesitation before she said yes. Eric believed it was just shock. He wanted to set a date, but Ashley wasn't ready. Later, over the phone, Ashley confessed that she had started seeing someone after Eric left for Grad school. What disgust Eric the most were those times she would come to visit him, she would then go back and have sex with the other guy. To Ashley, their relationship was just physical, she had no interest in being exclusive. Eric was enraged and wished he'd never gave her a ring.

It was his father who made Eric realized he was to blame for what happened. His father told him that he didn't take time to find out who Ashley was. When she offered sex, he accepted, though he knew nothing about her. His father reminded him that he was not raised to have casual sex. Though divorced, his parents raised him with strict Christian values. He threw those values away when easy sex was offered. It was Eric who confused sex with love, not Ashley.

That was a hard pill of truth to swallow, but his dad was right. Eric agreed that his relationship with Ashley shouldn't have happened. Still, it broke his heart. Kenneth's attempts to help Eric out meant going to clubs. Eric followed Kenneth to clubs though his heart wasn't in it. Most of the time he went just to keep Kenneth company. Once Kenneth motioned that he was leaving with a woman, Eric would leave. Many women came on to him, but none were tempting. It took Eric a while to realize that the problem wasn't the women, it was him. He knew he shouldn't be in a club looking for quick sex and he felt convicted. That night, Eric got on his knees and asked the lord to forgive him. He'd strayed far from who he was supposed to be in Christ and he asked for help to remain celibate until God found him the right mate. Since that night, he was determined to keep his mind and body pure. The next day at work, it seemed all the women were coming onto him. Throughout the following weeks, Kenneth tried to con Eric into going back to the club. Eric knew Kenneth thought he was soft when he told him about his commitment. Kenneth didn't understand him anymore and their friendship began to fray. They'd still come into the gym every morning together; Eric to work and Kenneth to take advantage of his free membership, but that was the only thing they did together.

Eric prayed continuously for God to send him a woman who would be true to him, but God had his own timing. To stay on track, Eric poured all his energy into growing his physical therapy practice. It's been open for over a year now and he can see the early fruits of his hard work.

People say be careful what you pray for. Eric initially regretted praying for someone to love when his heart fell for Grace. Before seeing Grace, Eric thought love at first sight was a romantic myth. Then it happened to him. However, this love felt more like a curse. *Why a nineteen-year-old? What could she know about being in a relationship,* he thought. Eric imagined she still kept stuffed animals on her bed. What was worse, he knew she didn't like him. Whenever she said "good morning Eric," it was said between clenched teeth; yet his dad received warm welcomes from Grace. She was cool with Kenneth too in the beginning, but something changed. It seemed she was now avoiding him.

Being in love with a teenager at twenty-seven was torture. His heart was pounding out of his chest during the interview with Grace, yet he suppressed those feelings to stay professional. It wasn't until jealousy entered his heart that he realized he'd risk losing this love if he did nothing. Jealousy and anger rose up in him whenever he saw a man flirting with Grace. Eric kept his eye on Grace every day. It was risky asking her to work more hours, but it was the only chance he saw to keep her closer to him. Eric was caught off guard when he saw how distraught Grace was that Saturday. He felt guilty for making her come in on what should have been her day off. It was obvious to everyone that she had been crying, her eyes were raw. His worst fear was that she had a very bad date. Determined to find out if anyone had hurt her, he brought her into the office. She looked like she needed a shoulder to cry on so he offered a hug. Touching was a mistake. His heart made an unauthorized move that could have gone badly. *The kiss Grace gave me was so sweet. How could I describe such a thing to Kenneth? This is a guy who covered his dorm wall with Playboy centerfolds. No, Kenneth lacked the capacity to comprehend what a sweet moment was with any woman. For him, it's only about physical sex. Now Kenneth is trying to break us up by making up lies about Grace's past. I'd never thought he'd stoop so low. There's Grace now, walking behind the counter. I'd better stop staring and get to work.*

****

Kenneth returned to the gym after Eric completed his session with Mrs. Porter. He walked around to different staff members, showing them something on his tablet. Eric didn't know what Kenneth was up to. Mrs. Porter walked over to Kenneth to see what he was showing everyone. One thing that disturbed Eric was that after viewing the tablet, each person would stare at Grace. Eric walked over to investigate just as Kenneth approached Grace at the counter.

"So, Grace, it seems you've had a lot of fun in your teen years," said Kenneth with a smirk.

Grace looked at him with confusion. "What are you talking about, Kenneth?"

"I'm talking about this, look at it. This article says that you were living with Amal Bliss and another man when you were sixteen." Kenneth pushed the tablet in Grace's face. She immediately lost her composure and stepped back as if he was showing her a snake.

"That story is wrong and it was retracted."

Eric came to the counter and looked at the article in Kenneth's hand.

"Grace, is this you?" Eric asked her.

"It's me, but the article is not true. Amal is my brother."

"Yeah, yeah, yeah, they said that you called him your brother, but he's not your real brother," said Kenneth.

"He's a real brother to me," said Grace as she looked around and saw that everyone, including Eric, was staring at her now. His facial expression disturbed her the most.

"What's going on?" she asked Kenneth.

"Well, I'm trying to find out who you really are since you're dating my buddy now. Okay, let's say that story might not be true, but what about this one? Here's another article where you're pictured with this old rich man. He's hugging you in the picture. The article says this old man was giving you drugs for sex, but then you turned around and accused him of sexual assault. Is this story true?"

Grace's hand started shaking after she viewed her attacker on the tablet. All the suppressed memories of that day came back to her in a flood. Kenneth, the staff, and Mrs. Porter were looking at her waiting for a reply. She looked over to Eric as he continued to read the article. All she could see was the look of repulsion on his face. The overwhelming sense of shame Grace felt brought tears to her eyes, but she held them in. She had to get away now before she broke down. Grace went under the counter to retrieve her handbag. With shaking hands, she removed the keys given to her by Mr. Reed and slammed them down on the counter before bolting for the door.

Eric, startled by the sound, looked up to see Grace quickly exiting from the counter. "Grace, where are you going?" he shouted, but she never looked back. Eric ran to catch up to Grace at the door and held her arm, intending to ask her where she was going, but before he could say a word, she flinched at his touch and turned around.

There were tears in her eyes when she said, "Don't touch me!" That one statement broke his heart and shocked him at the same time. He was confused. Grace was halfway down the block when he called out to her, but she never turned around. Eric immediately took out his phone and called his father to let him know what happened.

"Dad, I have to find her, please come and watch the gym so I could go."

Mr. Reed sighed. "Son, let it go for now. She's upset and rightly so. How in the world did you let Kenneth get into your business?"

"Dad, I had no idea what he was up to. When he shoved the tablet into my hands, I saw pictures of Grace in a completely different life. I was reading the article when I heard her slam the keys on the counter and run for the door. I have to find her dad."

"Listen Eric, she may not go straight home because she's upset. Wait until you finish work and then go to her house. She has to come home at night for her dog and maybe she will be in a better mood by then. I'd better call Loretta to let her know what happened. I'll call you back if she tells me anything."

Eric's mind was racing. He didn't know what to do or think. *Did someone rape Grace? Did she sell her body for drugs? Why did Kenneth do this in front of everyone?*

****

Grace's phone rang again. She made no motion to retrieve the call. Though tears blurred her vision, she continued to walk, though she didn't recognize where she was. Her mind told her to flee, but she had no direction. Shame and self-loathing encapsulated her thoughts. *Why did Kenneth and Eric do this to me,* she thought. Grace remembered Kenneth's smirk and everyone else looking at her, but she couldn't get over the look of on Eric's face. *He believed those things that were written about me,* she thought. Grace continued to ignore every call Eric made to her since she left. Twenty minutes later, she hugged her arms as she sat by her father's grave. Grace cried until she was fatigued. The cell phone ring startled her this time. She was about to silence the ringer before noting that this call wasn't from Eric.

"Aunt Loretta?"

"Gracie honey? Where are you, are you okay?"

"No, I'm not alright. I had a very bad day. I'm at dad's grave."

"Oh honey, that's not a good place to be right now. Listen, you're not far from me. I want you to come here so I can take care of you."

"Auntie, you're working now, I can't talk to you there."

"Don't worry about that. I'll take the rest of the day off as soon as you get here."

"Thanks Auntie, I'm on my way."

Loretta began working with the new assistant principal two months ago. She was a nice amiable young lady who she got along well with.

"Excuse me Miss Morris, I'm sorry to do this, but my

niece is having some problems and she'll be here shortly. Can I leave early today?"

Tasha Morris never saw Ms. Mitchell so distraught. The woman is so caring to the students. Many come in the office at the end of the school day just to tell her goodbye. Tasha would do anything to help Ms. Mitchell. "That's perfectly fine Ms. Mitchell, let me know if there's anything I can do. I'll tell the kids you had to leave early."

"Thank you so much, Ms. Morris, she should be here soon. I'll start putting my files away now."

Grace took out her compact to check her appearance. She patted her hair down and took out a tissue to wiped her tears away before walking up the steps of the middle school. She didn't want to look the way she felt. After showing her ID to the security officer, Grace was allowed inside the building. Thankfully, all the students were in the classrooms so the hallways were clear. She could hear the teachers speaking behind the classroom doors as she walked toward the main office.

A woman in a fitted teal skirt suit hurriedly stepped out of the office and walked in her direction. When she saw Grace, she stopped and stared for a few seconds before saying, "Gracie, is it really you?"

"Tasha?" said Grace, as she recognized the woman as her old friend. The two hugged tightly.

"Girl, I missed you so much. Where have you been? No one has seen you at church or in the neighborhood. Even Brandon asked me if I knew where you were."

"Brandon? Brandon's back in Brooklyn? I thought he was still in California."

"No, he's been back over a year now."

"Where is he? I really need to see him."

"I'll be happy to take you to him myself. I'm going to see him this Sunday, we can go together. Wait! You're Ms. Mitchell's niece? You even resemble each other. I don't know why I never made the connection before," Tasha said while smacking herself in the forehead. "I have to go to a meeting now but I don't want us to lose contact. Give me your phone. I'll put my number in your phone and yours in mine. Text me your address and I'll pick you up on Sunday. We have a lot of catching up to do and I want to hear about everything you've been up to." They hugged again before Tasha ran to her meeting.

Loretta was turning off her desktop as Grace entered the office. She gave Grace a huge hug. "Let's go home to talk so we could have privacy," said Loretta.

During the drive, Loretta took quick glimpses of Grace's sullen face. Her heart went out to her niece who sat in the passenger seat, withdrawn into her thoughts. When they entered Loretta's home, Grace told Loretta all of what happened.

"Gracie, Clayton called me after he received a frantic call from Eric. He said that Eric didn't realize what Kenneth was doing until it was too late. He regrets that he didn't say anything and he's sorry about that. Have you told him how he made you feel?"

"Well, the last and final thing I told him was 'don't touch me.' He's been calling and texting me to say he's sorry, but it's over."

"What do you mean, Gracie?"

"I mean our relationship is over and I don't want to see him again."

"Gracie, you're saying this now because you're hurt, you may feel differently later."

"Auntie, you weren't there. Kenneth was showing everyone those terrible articles about me. Instead of coming to my defense, Eric stood by his friend and read the articles on the tablet. I could never look him in the eye again. They made me feel like that 16-year-old screw up who almost killed herself, all over again. Because of my stupidity I was almost raped, Brandon went to jail and I messed up JJ's career. It took me a long time to bury those memories, but when Kenneth showed me that picture of Ronnie, I relived that day all over again. Am I going to go through this for the rest of my life?"

"No Gracie, you don't need to feel this way again. Sweetheart, you need counseling so you can move beyond your past. I sought counseling after my ordeal. It really helped me to manage my feelings. Gracie, you were never a screw up. You made some bad decisions when you were grieving the death of your father. You're human and you are not responsible for your assault. The sleeping pills you took did not make that skank give Jamal's keys to that old man so he could rape you. Brandon and Jamal love you. Brandon went to jail because he was protecting someone he loved and Jamal never said the publicity messed up his career. Gracie, don't let what Kenneth did steal your peace and destroy your relationship."

"It's too late Auntie, he's already accomplished that. I

can't go back to my job with everyone wondering if I was sleeping with that old man."

"What about Eric? I know he has strong feelings for you. You can't just leave him like this."

"It's over Auntie." Grace picked up her vibrating phone and shut it off while Loretta was speaking. The screen showed Eric's number again. Loretta later tried in vain to get Grace to eat dinner, but she was too distraught to eat.

"Auntie, I have to get home to take care of Cujo."

"Gracie, why don't you spend the night here, I can pick up Cujo and bring him here."

"Thanks for the offer, but I just want to go home now."

"I understand. Give me a few minutes and I'll drop you off."

Grace was exhausted when she arrived at her studio. She picked up Cujo and hugged him when he greeted her at the door. Grace filled his bowl and prepared to lay down until he was ready for his walk. The doorbell rang just before she sat down. "Auntie, did you forget something?" Grace called out. There was no reply.

Eric was standing in the doorway when Grace opened the door. He had a pained expression on his face. "Grace, please talk to me. I didn't know that Kenneth was going to do what he did. I would never try to hurt you." Cujo left his food and ran to Eric who bent down to rub Cujo's head. Grace sighed and kept her eyes down before replying. "I'm sorry Eric, I should have called you back, but I wasn't ready to speak. I can't see you anymore. I shouldn't be in a relationship because I haven't dealt with what happened to me in the past."

"Grace, I'm sorry for what you went through in the past, but please don't give up on us now," he pleaded.

"Eric, this won't work."

"Grace, don't do this. I love you, we can work this out."

"I'm sorry, but I can't deal with a relationship now. You have to leave." Grace scooped Cujo from the doorway and closed the door without looking at Eric.

Sunday came quickly. Grace stared at the new dress she purchased to wear to Eric's and his mother's church. She sighed before shoving it out of sight to the rear of her closet. There were no new texts from Eric. Grace had already deleted all the old ones; all except for one where he said he loved her.

It proved impossible to forget him. Eric dominated her every thought. She missed the

scent of his aftershave, the way his brown eyes lit up when he smiled and the way she felt when he kissed her. Grace forced herself to get dressed so she would be ready when Tasha picked her up. She hadn't seen Brandon in such a long time, but she prayed he received help for his drinking.

Tasha picked her up on time and they were on their way. Grace was anxious about seeing Brandon. *What if he hates me because I'm the reason he went to prison,* she thought.

"Tasha, does Brandon know I'm coming?"

"Nope, it'll be a surprise for both of you."

"Why are you being so secretive, is he alright?"

"Brandon is fine, he's at work now so we'll have to wait a while to see him."

Grace was perplexed. *What kind of work is he doing 9:00 on Sunday morning?*

Tasha drove down Herkimer Street as quickly as the Sunday morning traffic would allow. After securing a tight parking spot on a side street, she took Grace by the arm and hurriedly walked down the street to the front of an old dilapidated church. There was scaffolding attached to the upper facade of the church. Cracked stucco and peeling paint spoke of neglect the building suffered for some time. The stucco on the lower portion of the building's exterior, however, had been beautifully restored.

"Tasha, are we really going in here? Is this building safe to enter? Is Brandon doing construction work?" Suddenly Grace stopped abruptly.

"What?" said Tasha as she turned to see why Grace stood still.

"This isn't a homeless shelter, is it?"

"Oh my goodness, Gracie, just trust me and come inside."

Grace entered the building hesitantly. The inside foyer was surprisingly clean and freshly painted. As they walked to the doors of the sanctuary, Grace heard many voices coming from inside. The voices came from a packed church, which was more spacious than she initially anticipated. A lady usher gave the two a warm greeting and handed them church programs. Tasha quickly snatched the program from Grace's hand as they walked toward an usher.

"Tasha, what's wrong with you?"

"Gracie, I promise to explain everything after the service starts. Please, be patient with me."

After being seated, Grace's thoughts immediately went to Eric. She imagined him at his mother's church this very moment explaining why she wasn't the woman he thought she was. Tasha, noting her sadness, touched her arm.

"Gracie, what's wrong?"

"I'm still thinking about the day you saw me. I was a mess. Someone at my job found out about my past. They showed everyone those tabloid articles about me. My boyfriend read them too. Things didn't go well and our relationship came to an end."

"Oh Gracie, I'm so sorry to hear that, but if he left you because of the lies written in those trash articles, he doesn't deserve you."

"Actually, I left because of it. I watched him while he read the articles, the disgusted expression on his face made me feel like damaged goods. Ending the relationship makes it better for both of us. He can move on without feeling guilty." Tasha put her arm around her old friend as Grace placed her head on Tasha's shoulder.

The choir began singing softly as the musicians chimed in with their instruments. Grace could discern their talent by the way they played. The soloist sung a familiar song. Both she and Tasha sang along to VaShawn Mitchell's song, "Joy." The church was busting at the seams as more congregants made their way to the last available pews in the back. Grace looked around at the people. The congregants were an odd eclectic crowd of young adults and teens, whereas her old church was filled with seniors. Some congregants wore suits and others wore jeans and casual clothes. As the choir finished singing, a casually dressed man sitting to the side stood up and walked to the altar. There was something familiar about his stride. He wore jeans and a white button-down shirt with rolled up cuffs. The man was tall and broad with a thick beard. Grace sat up in her seat and squinted at the stage.

She whispered, "Hey Tasha, he looks just like…." As Grace turned to look at Tasha, she saw her mischievous smile. It was then that she realized Brandon was the pastor.

"Gracie, close your mouth and stop gaping at him, people will stare," Tasha whispered.

Grace could not believe what she was seeing. *Brandon a pastor? The man who got drunk every night, slept with one-night stands and refused to take her to church. How could this be,* she thought.

"Brandon?" Grace blurted out.

"Shhh, it's Pastor Brandon now, and keep your voice down," Tasha whispered. Grace covered her mouth with her hands and stared at the man who adjusted the microphone.

"Good Morning Church," said Brandon. The church responded with good mornings and hooting's. After they quieted, Brandon began to speak. "I'm going to pick up from where I left off last week. Turn in your bibles to Isaiah 61:7. 'For your shame, you have a double portion; therefore, in their land, they shall possess double; they shall have everlasting joy.' Now I want to expound on the meaning of this verse…." Brandon stopped speaking and closed his eyes. "Hmmm, I want to continue, but for some reason the Holy Spirit is prompting me to give my testimony again. Maybe someone out there needs to hear it. I know many of you have already heard this and some of you have your own stories, so please bear with me.

"For those of you who don't know, I was raised in a Baptist church pastored by my father. So, that makes me a preacher kid. My older brother and I lived by strict rules. We were also taught to respect our elders. We couldn't go to parties in non-Christian households. Every Sunday was devoted to the church. Every Wednesday night was bible study. Dad said we represented him so we had to be respectable. I had no problem with it; it was the life I knew and I loved to please my father.

"When I was seven, my father was visited by Bishop Rodney Evers. The Bishop's Maryland church was very well known and respected. Dad was overjoyed that the Bishop came all the way from Maryland to visit his church. There was some special event going on at our church, but I don't remember what it was. I remember dad making many preparations for the Bishop's arrival. He beamed with joy when Bishop Evers preached at our church. The Bishop stayed at our house, ate meals with the family and even played basketball with my brother and me. Anyway, two weeks after the Bishop left, he called my father. It seems the Bishop had an annual camping trip he takes some of the boys from his congregation on. He had a last-minute cancellation and thought it would be a good opportunity for me to come. He said that our family had been so gracious to him that he wanted to do something for us. My dad was more excited about the trip than I was. Camping in the woods did not appeal to me at all. Dad thought it was great that the busy Bishop thought of me for his trip. My mother didn't want me to be so far away, but dad convinced her that this would be a good experience for me. So, against the advice of my mother, he packed me up and drove me to Maryland for my trip.

"When I got there, I saw other boys who looked like they were my age so I thought maybe this trip would be fun. The Bishop took us hiking through the woods. He took us fishing, showed us how to identify poisonous plants and some other things. Before night came, he helped us to set up our tents. At the time I thought the tents were set far apart from each other, but no one else seemed to be bothered. I didn't think any more of it until that night.

"He made dinner and told us to eat all our food so the wild animals wouldn't smell it and come after us. After eating we each went to our tent. I remember being drowsy, which was weird because I wanted to stay awake in case the wild animals came.

"Later that night I heard my sleeping bag being unzipped. I was still drowsy, but I knew it was the Bishop. He took my clothes off and raped me. When I screamed in pain, he put his hand over my mouth. I couldn't fight him off. I didn't understand why he did this to me, but I knew it was wrong. I stood up to him the next morning and told him what he did. He got angry and told me to shut up. The Bishop told me no one, not even my father, would believe such a thing. I cried angry tears. I couldn't wait to tell my dad because I knew my dad would help me.

"On pick-up day, the Bishop first talked to all the parents while he made us pack up our things. My dad was strangely silent when we started the drive back. When I started telling dad what the Bishop did to me, he became angry with me. He said the Bishop told him that he chased another boy out of my tent after he heard us fooling around. My own father called me stupid for letting another boy mess with me. Then he told me not to bring it up with my mother because it would just upset her.

"I was lost emotionally. My own father didn't believe me. He never took me to a doctor or anything. I was in misery for a long time and there was no one to talk to about what happened to me. Sometimes thoughts of killing myself entered my head. Later, my heart was filled with hatred toward my father and our relationship soured. Though I still had to do whatever he told me to, I no longer trusted or respected him. When I entered my teens, things got worst. I started drinking alcohol in secret. My family and friends had no idea of what I was doing. My drinking followed me into college. The space under my dorm bed was kept littered with empty liquor bottles.

"Just before I graduated with my bachelors in social work, the media ran a story about the great Bishop Evers. He was accused of molesting several boys throughout the years at his camp. He lost his church and was ousted from the Baptist Church organization. My father called me that same day. He was weeping and apologizing for not believing me. I've never heard my father cry before, but it didn't matter to me, I let him have it. All the mean things I thought about him came out. I cursed him and called him a useless sorry excuse for a father. His apology was fifteen years too late for me. When my mother found out why I was disrespecting my father, she argued with him too. When my brother found out that I was the reason my parents' marriage was in turmoil, and he stopped talking to me. I thought fine, I don't need any of you anyway.

"My best friend lived in L.A. He asked me to come out, so I moved to California for my graduate degree, but my drinking intensified and my grades plummeted. Instead of studying, my free time was spent picking up women for sex and drinking until I passed out. My parents were paying for my tuition and apartment, yet they had no idea I was failing my classes. At this stage, I couldn't sleep without drinking. It got so bad that my friend, who hated clubs, went to them with me just to make sure I didn't drive drunk.

"What's funny is that in the midst of this, I felt God calling me to preach the gospel. Can you believe that? I wasn't trying to hear from God. I'd shut him and my father out of my life a long time ago. My mind wondered how could a man of God like a bishop rape me? What I didn't understand was that Jesus warned us about people like that; I'll expound on that later. In my mind, life was good. The sad truth was that my life was on a destructive path. Bad grades forced me to drop out of school. Sleep never came without drinking because the withdrawal symptoms drove sleep away. I didn't care.

"All that changed one day. My friend's teen sister, someone I watched grow up from a baby, snuck one of my vodka bottles to get drunk. That convicted my heart because I knew she got the idea from watching me. It tore me up inside because I didn't want her to end up like me. On this night my friend was having a huge party. I didn't want to mess up his party by confronting her at that time. Instead, I decided to keep checking on her. That turned out to be the best thing I could do for her. During one of my checks, another powerful old man was attacking her. My mind snapped because the next thing I remember was the police telling me I almost killed the guy. My blood covered swollen knuckles were the only evidence to me that I did what they said. The attacker was messed up pretty bad, so they sent me to jail for three months. I didn't care. I was happy to stop someone from going through what I went through, but then the police were sending me to a notorious prison. Now I'm a big guy, but to be honest, I was scared of the prisoners. The night before my transfer, I was on my knees asking God to help me get through this. That was my first prayer in years.

"There were some really bad guys in prison, but to my surprise, the inmates treated me with respect. So there I was, in the midst of hardened criminals. They were offering me cigarettes and other things. I didn't understand why until one of them told me that inmates don't like pedophiles and they heard what I did to one. The prison offered regular church services. I still had my issues with God, but I attended the service anyway just to pass the time. I was shocked to hear many testimonies of rape, molestation and other forms of abuse the inmates suffered in the past. That's when I realized prison was full of men suffering from abuse and trauma; and most like me, gave up on God.

"One night I was restless and couldn't sleep. Then I felt

it again, God nudging me to preach. I thought, he had nerve. After all, what did God ever do for me? What's scary was his answer. Immediately, I knew I wasn't an alcoholic anymore. I'd spent twenty days in prison and every night I slept like a baby with no craving for alcohol and no withdrawal.

"The next morning, I took a bible from the prison library and just started reading. Being a PK, I already knew the scriptures and could quote verses with my eyes closed, but on that day, the words came alive for me! I understood the meanings and interpretations. During the next service, I stood to testify. The faces before me were nodding in acknowledgement because they suffered the same experiences. God nudge me again and this time I was in agreement with him. From that day, I began preaching the word. I told them God is not the author of sexual abuse, he is against it. I quoted Deuteronomy 22:25-27. It says the man who raped the virgin shall die. I read Genesis 19, where the men of Sodom were breaking down Lot's door because they wanted to rape the male angels who entered his home. Those wicked men were blinded by God so they could not find Lot's door. Then, after Lot escaped, God destroyed that city of Sodom because he couldn't find ten righteous men in the whole city.

"I began praising God continuously. Then the Holy Spirit came upon me and I started speaking in tongues. Others in the congregation experienced the Holy Spirit too. Many gave their life to Christ that day, including yours truly. That was a powerful service. Since that day, we held our heads up instead of living life behind our shameful secrets. Those secrets had eaten away at our self-esteem and purpose.

Jesus took off our yokes of shame and replaced them with garments of praise.

"Most people regret their time in prison; I believe that my time saved my life. Don't get me wrong, I'm not telling anyone to go to prison to find Jesus; Jesus will meet you wherever you're at. God used prison to save my life and he gave me an incredibly strong desire to preach to those who've been hurt by sexual abuse. Millions of people in the world are looking for relief from the mental anguish caused by sexual abuse.

"With the help of my best friend and my father, I opened this church last year. Yes, I said my father. I forgave him because there's no way I can remain in God's peace and hold anger toward someone at the same time. This building was a wreck. My dad and I have worked on it for some time and we still have much more to do. Someone asked why open the church before renovations were complete? My reason? The people who come for help need it now. How can I turn someone away who needs help because the building wasn't pretty?

"There are too many victims struggling with life because of their assault. I believe the church must to do their part to save and heal all victims. We've partnered with other churches, including my father's church, to educate our congregants on sexual assault so they can help themselves and their children. We have kids' programs where they learn about inappropriate touching. Some say we shouldn't teach kids things like that. I say, if we love our children, how can we not teach them about such things? We can't just tell them to not accept candy from strangers. We have to tell them why that stranger wants to entice them to come closer. Now, we are going to have an alter call for those who want to give their life to Christ and invite him in to help with your pain. We're here if you need to rededicate your life to Christ, too. Whoever you are, if you want Jesus to remove your yoke, come to the alter now and accept him into your life. Jesus said whatever you ask in his name, God will grant. Our prayer team members are here to help you receive Christ and receive his healing."

Hordes of people flocked to the alter. The isles were filled with crying congregants lining up for prayer. Grace didn't realize she was crying until she felt Tasha rubbing her back. She stood up and made her way through the crowd of people. When she reached the alter, one of the prayer team members laid a hand on her shoulder and began praying for her. She answered yes when he asked if she wanted Christ as her lord and savior. Grace closed her eyes as the man prayed. She felt another hand grasp her other shoulder. When the second person started praying over her, she knew it was Brandon. Grace tried to turn to see him, but the hand held firm.

"Please stay still, I'm not finished praying," said Brandon. She kept still as the two continued. Then Brandon began praying in tongues. In the midst of her thoughts, she marveled at Brandon. Any doubt she had of him being a real pastor ceased in that moment.

Slowly, she felt a warm sensation on her head. It continued down her body, infusing her with a happy, peaceful sensation. Her tears were now tears of joy. Brandon stood looking at her with his own tears of joy. He gave her a great big bear hug.

"I knew you were coming, I just didn't know when," he said with a smile. "Welcome to the body of Christ!" Grace was ecstatic, all she could do was hug Brandon and smile. The joy she felt from receiving Christ and finding Brandon took her words away. Brandon told her to wait in his office while he prayed for others. Remembering Tasha, Grace went back through the crowd and found her at their pew.

"Gracie, it was so amazing to see you two praying together," said Tasha as they hugged. The two made their way to Brandon's office.

When Brandon arrived, both Tasha and Gracie stood up to hug him. "You have no idea how much I've missed you and JJ," said Grace. Brandon pulled back and looked at Grace. "Just a minute, you moved away from us," said Brandon.

"At the time, I thought it was the best thing for all of us. I was miserable and I was destroying your lives. You went to prison because of me and JJ's public image was tarnished by me."

"Is that how you really saw things? Gracie, you couldn't have been more wrong. First of all, didn't you hear my testimony? Prison helped me. I went to jail for my actions and I wasn't just beating Ronnie for you. I beat him like I did because of what happened to both of us. As far as Jamal goes, all the publicity and media attention heighten his career. He received more interview requests than ever. No, you didn't hurt his career, but you hurt his feelings when you left. He believes you left because you blame him for everything that happened."

"Why does he think that? None of it is his fault."

Brandon sighed. "The two of you need to start talking again."

"It's too late for that. JJ doesn't want to hear from me and he doesn't return my calls. I've invited him to my graduation, but he never called back."

"Gracie, don't worry. I know Jamal; your graduation is something he'd want to attend. You have no idea how much he worries about you. And, he does check on you." Grace and Tasha looked at Brandon with a confused expression.

Brandon laughed. "I think it's time for you to know something. Jamal knows where you live, where you work; he even called to tell me you started dating someone." Grace's mouth gaped open. "He didn't want me to reveal anything to you. That's why he wouldn't tell me where you lived."

"He knows where I live? How?"

"Think about it, Gracie. You live in a very expensive part of Brooklyn. How do you think you could afford your studio?"

"Wait a minute, I pay the rent."

Brandon laughed again. "You think you pay the rent. Jamal hired the real estate agent to find a landlord who was willing to keep an eye on you. He pays the full rent for your studio. The money you give the landlady is the extra she receives to look out for you. Who did you think added the clause to your lease about no sleep overs?"

Grace sat down because she was shocked. "All this time, I thought Mrs. Rivas was just a nice nosey old lady. But why hasn't JJ contacted me?"

"He's afraid you'd move if you found out he knew where you lived. The argument you guys had was really bad. Sounded like both of you said things you didn't really mean," said Brandon.

Grace exhaled, "I did say some mean things."

"Jamal was really angry with you at first, but when you left, he worried about what would happen to you. That's why he tricked you into renting the studio. How do you feel about all of this? Don't be mad at Jamal, he did what he thought was right. He just wanted you to be safe," said Brandon.

Grace sighed, "Well, it's a blow to my ego. I've had a lot of those lately. I'm not mad at JJ, I just feel pathetic. I thought I was a strong independent woman, but I've been fooling myself with this and my relationship with Eric."

"I take it Eric is the guy you're dating? What happened? Did he try something? Do you need me to talk to him?" said Brandon.

"No, it's nothing like that. Everyone in the gym, including Eric, saw what the media said about me, even that lie about me being Ronnie's girlfriend. Eric was disgusted and shocked. When I saw that picture of me with Ronnie's arm around my waist, I had the worst panic attack of my life. I was angry with Eric at first; I thought he asked his friend to look up my background. I found out later that his friend did it on his own. Still, I had to end our relationship. Eric's normal, he doesn't need someone with issues."

"Don't you miss him," asked Tasha.

Grace shook her head yes. "Every day. I don't think I can forget Eric."

"How did Eric respond when you ended your relationship?" asked Brandon.

"He didn't want to end it."

Brandon sighed, "Gracie, I want you to start our counseling program as soon as possible. Sometimes sexual assault victims suffer from PTSD and certain events can trigger flashbacks to the time when the assault occurred."

"That sounds like what happened to me, but I wasn't raped. Why am I having flashbacks?"

"Sexual assault is still a traumatic experience, especially for minors. Penetration doesn't have to occur for a victim to be traumatized. I want you to promise me to make an appointment with us for counseling."

"I promise Brandon, I'll do whatever it takes to not experience another flashback. You mind if I ask you and Tasha to come to my graduation this Friday afternoon? I know it's short notice, but I didn't know where you guys were. Aunt Loretta will be there sitting by herself. I'd love to have as much family as possible, and you guys are family to me. Please say yes."

"I'd love to come, as long as I don't have to sit next to Jamal, just send me the details," said Tasha.

"Thanks Tasha, I'm grateful you can come; and don't worry about JJ. He won't be there," said Grace.

"Count me in too, pest, I'd love to be there. Don't count Jamal out though, hold a seat for him," said Brandon.

"I can't hold a seat for JJ if he doesn't contact me, the graduation is ticketed. If he doesn't get a ticket from me, he can't get in."

CHAPTER TWENTY

The outdoor ceremony was held on the University football field. Faculty and honored guests sat in their robes along one side of the temporary stage. Over 200 graduates sat in perfectly aligned rows of seats in front of the stage. The mid-afternoon sun made the event extremely hot and sticky. Some students fanned themselves as they sweated under long black graduation robes. All friends and family members of the graduates sat under shaded bleachers that surrounded the field. Occasionally someone called out to their graduate after spotting them on the field. This time, it was Loretta who called out to Grace. Grace spotted Loretta's loud yellow dress in the crowd and waved to her. Loretta stood and waved furiously back. Brandon and Tasha waved back as well.

Grace was extremely happy that they came, but Jamal not being there stole some of her joy. His lack of response to her call was Grace's confirmation that he no longer wanted to be a part of her life. It made no sense to her that he would pay her rent yet stay out of her life. Determined not dwell on what she didn't have, Grace made a small prayer of thanks to God for bringing her aunt, Brandon and Tasha to her graduation. From her recent counseling sessions, Grace learned to live in the moment and in this moment, she was grateful for who she had in her life. Grace turned around again and waved at Loretta and her two old friends

The college president started the ceremony with welcomes and introductions. Other staff followed with boring speeches and well wishes. The guest speaker was introduced and everyone applauded respectfully. As the speaker continued talking, Grace's mind drifted to other things. This was the first leg of education she'd planned for herself. Already signed up for the fall semester at New York University, this summer Grace was set to work for a four-week piano lesson job at a youth summer enrichment program. She wished her dad was here to see her. Grace knew he would be proud of her accomplishments. She opened the program to see how many more had to speak before the ceremony would be over. The guest speaker had just completed his oration and exited the stage.

According to the program, the honor professor was next to give his speech, but there seemed to be some confusion at the podium. Grace and other graduates continued to fan themselves with their programs as the cloudless sky allowed the sun to beam mercilessly on their heads. Finally, the college president came to the podium microphone to speak.

"Ladies and gentlemen, please bear with us. We have a second guest speaker ..." The audible groans from the graduates drowned out the president's last words. They were ready to get out of the heat and leave with their families, but the president continued. "We are very pleased to introduce to you a man who needs no introduction …" The president was interrupted again, but this time there were cheers and clapping instead of groans. Grace and the other graduates sitting in the back stood up to see who was on stage. Cellphones throughout the crowd were flashing photos of the new speaker. Grace craned her neck to get a glimpse of the guest speaker, but she found it impossible to view the stage over the graduates who stood in front of her.

"Good afternoon graduates!" Shouted the speaker. Grace knew that voice, but she had to be sure. While the graduates were standing and cheering, Grace climbed on top of her chair and stood in her four-inch stiletto heels to view the stage. Nearby graduates were staring at her as if she was crazy, but she didn't care. Standing on the chair allowed her to see Jamal at the podium. Grace got down quickly and sat in her chair. Her shaking hands struggled to retrieve tissue from her purse so that she could wipe the tears from her eyes. Grace was so excited Jamal came to her graduation that she wanted to rush the stage and hug him. She couldn't focus on a word he was saying until she heard....

"… my sister's graduation. Gracie, if you're out there, raise your hand!" Grace instantly stood on her chair, stuck her hand up and waved vigorously. The other graduates gave her a different look this time. Jamal ended his speech by welcoming all graduates to the music industry. The applause he received was deafening. Jamal quickly exited the stage with security close behind him.

Grace's previous small circle of student friends grew into

throngs of students who wanted to connect with her. The college president came back to the podium and ordered everyone to go back to their seats. He then instructed them to move their tassels to the left of their hats in unison before proclaiming them official graduates. There were cheers and shouts as hats flew in the air. All the graduates exited quickly, each looking to meet their family. Grace and Loretta previously arranged to meet at Loretta's parked car on the next block. Still in cap and gown, Grace exited the university grounds with the other students. All were walking in different directions, although many looked her way to see who she would meet up with. Grace set out for her meeting location with inextinguishable happiness. She wondered where Jamal had exited to because she wanted to see her brother ASAP. Grace walked around the corner toward Loretta's black Accord, but the car was empty. She leaned against the vehicle and she whipped out her phone to call Loretta, but she had to text Jamal first.

"JJ, I'm so happy you came to my graduation!" She received a reply as she was texting Loretta.

"I'm happy that you wanted me there," was his reply. *"Where are you?"* she texted back.

"Gracie!" She heard her aunt call her name and spun around to see her sitting in the back of a white stretch limo. It pulled up next to the black Accord. The back windows were rolled down. Both Felicia and Loretta stuck their heads out.

"Aunt Felicia? You came to my graduation!" Grace ran to the car door and kissed Felicia on the cheek.

"Of course I came. I wished you'd invited me, though."

"I didn't know you'd want to come all the way from Maine to see me," said Grace.

"Girl please, I'm your auntie too, remember?"

"Come in so we can go," said Loretta. Grace kissed Loretta on the cheek as she settled in next to her.

"Thanks Auntie." Brandon and Tasha were also seated in the limo. She leaned over to give them hugs while she thanked them for coming.

Grace knew the limo was compliments of Jamal, but he wasn't inside. She didn't mind because his coming to her graduation was the best present she could ever receive. Now she knew that she was forgiven.

"I can't stop smiling, I'm so happy you guys came to my graduation. I know it's only a two-year degree, but it means a lot to me to have everyone here." She hugged Loretta again and reached out and held Felicia's hand.

"Gracie, it's not just a two-year degree. You went through a lot to get here. Your father would be very proud of you," said Felicia.

The limo wasn't going in the direction of the restaurant Aunt Loretta told her about.

"Auntie, are we going to a different restaurant?"

"Yes, it was a last-minute change, but I'm certain you'll like it," she said while giving Felicia a knowing wink. The limo drove on as they all conversed. It stopped outside of what looked like an upscale restaurant by the bay. As they walked toward the entrance, Grace turned around to Loretta.

"Auntie, we're having dinner here, are you sure?"

"Gracie, stop worrying and go inside, everything is fine," said Loretta. Upon entering, they were welcomed in like royalty. Their group was escorted to a private room where Jamal was already present.

"JJ, you're here!" Gracie yelled as she rushed to hug him.

Upon seeing Jamal, Tasha halted and looked back at the door to make a quick exit. "Oh no you don't," said Brandon as he took her arm. "It's time for you two to face each other as adults and leave the past behind."

"Where else would I be when my sister is graduating?" Jamal said as Grace teared up. "Okay, okay stop, no crying," said Jamal as he patted her hair.

"I can't, it's been too long since I've seen you and I know it's all my fault," said Grace.

"No Gracie, that's not true," said Jamal.

Tasha came over and rubbed Grace's back. "Don't cry Gracie, none of the past was your fault. You were just exposed to too much," she said as she gave Jamal a wayward look.

Jamal whispered to Tasha, "What do you mean by that?"

Tasha whispered back, "Jamal, you know exactly what I mean, but let it go, this is Gracie's day." Unfortunately for Tasha, Jamal wasn't about to let her dig at him go unconfronted.

"Hold up a minute, everyone, there's a buffet and tables set up in the next room for us. Please go in and help yourself, I'll be there in a minute. Gracie, you go in and hold a seat for me, we have a lot of catching up to do." Tasha was about to follow Gracie, but Jamal touched her on the arm. "We need to talk," he said.

Grace sat closest to the entrance of the room and attempted to listen to the conversation between Jamal and Tasha. She was ready to intervene if necessary. Jamal looked like he was ready for a fight, but she didn't want him to argue with Tasha. She loved them both and wanted everyone to have a peaceful dinner. Grace remembered the last time Tasha, JJ and Brandon were together with her. They were all kids having fun at church; she wanted this event to be a joyful reunion.

A few minutes passed. Grace could hear Tasha and Jamal raise their voices as they argued. *Should I go in there and make them stop?* she wondered. The others were enjoying the buffet. It contained an extensive mixture of Italian and traditional American dishes. Grace smiled to herself because Jamal remembered how much she loved Italian food. Her stomach rumbled in anticipation of the meal, but she didn't want to start eating without Tasha and Jamal. So, she got up to peek in the other room. What she witnessed made her smile. Unable to keep what she saw to herself, Grace went back to the buffet and pulled Felicia's arm to make her stand up. Felicia gave her a questioning look, but when Grace whispered in her ear, she hastened to follow. When Felicia peered in the next room, Jamal and Tasha were still locked in a kiss. Felicia looked to the ceiling and mouthed *"thank you God."* Wondering where everyone went, Brandon and Loretta got up to investigate. They also stood silently watching the long kiss. When Tasha and Jamal's lips parted, they turned and saw everyone watching. Tasha wore a sheepish expression while Jamal smiled like a kid who just received the best birthday gift ever.

Everyone walked back to the buffet room. Grace insisted Tasha sit in her chair so that she and Jamal would be together while Grace sat between Brandon and Felisha. The servers catered to all the guests, so no one had to get up from the table.

Watching Jamal and Tasha rekindle their relationship made Grace's heart ache for the relationship she gave up. One look at her face told Loretta instinctively who was on Grace's mind.

"You know, Eric misses you too; the two of you really should talk."

"Have you seen him recently?" asked Grace.

"No, but Clayton said Eric is distraught. He's really worried about him."

"Gracie, remember it's best to reveal you're in therapy before you enter a serious relationship," said Brandon.

"I know Brandon. I didn't realize it at the time, but I was in a serious relationship, I really do love Eric." All conversations stopped around the table when they heard Grace's declaration.

"Gracie, are you certain about that? You haven't dated anyone else so you have no experience to compare your feelings to," said Jamal.

Tasha turned to Jamal and asked, "You didn't have any comparison's when you said you were in love with me. Were those other women you went out with comparisons?"

"Tasha, no. It wasn't like that. Back then, when I told you I loved you, I knew it was real, but I was young and stupid. Those other relationships weren't comparisons, they were really bad decisions."

Tasha turned to Grace. "When Jamal was sixteen, he told me that he was in love with me. At that time, he'd never dated any other girl to compare his feelings to. Today, Jamal told me that he's still in love with me, so don't doubt your love because you're young or haven't dated others."

"Gracie, you know I'm just looking out for you. I don't want you to get hurt," said Jamal.

"I know JJ, and I appreciate you looking out for me, but it doesn't matter. I can't be in Eric's life again. He's a really great guy. He deserves someone better, someone without an embarrassing past."

"That's one of the reasons you shouldn't date until you finish therapy. That statement should never come out of your mouth. There are many men out there who would want a relationship with you, but if you feel like you're unworthy, they will take advantage of your low self-esteem," said Brandon.

"It's my fault, I should have gotten therapy for Gracie after she left the hospital. Since you weren't raped, I thought you would be okay, but now I know that I was wrong. I'm sorry about that and for not changing the locks after Serena left," said Jamal.

"Serena's actions are not your fault JJ, you can't control what people do," said Grace.

"I know, but it happened in my house, the one place you should have been safe. It took me a while to figure out that you left because you didn't feel safe."

"That's not entirely true, though I didn't want to sleep in that bedroom anymore. I left because of all the damage I did to you guys. In less than six weeks I ruined your relationship and your career. I sent Brandon to prison and I overdosed at your birthday."

"Gracie, you didn't ruin anything for me. You rescued me from Serena's trap," said Jamal.

"Amen to that, you spared me from having gold-digger grandbabies!" interjected Felicia.

"And Gracie, all the bad publicity boosted my career, and prison saved Brandon's life," said Jamal.

"Yeah, it forced me to reconcile with God and become a pastor."

"The thing that scared me the most was when you lost consciousness in the ambulance. I didn't know if you were going to make it. I'd just lost your dad and I was praying that I didn't lose you too. That would have been too much," said Jamal.

"I'm sorry, JJ. I was too stupid to realize mixing pills and vodka could kill me."

"Gracie, you weren't stupid; you were grieving and I had no idea how much."

"Gracie, you should call Eric. Let him know how you feel. Tell him about the counseling you're receiving. He doesn't understand why the two of you broke up," said Loretta.

"You're right, Auntie. I have to talk to him and explain everything."

"Gracie, if this Eric is the man for you, he will wait until you're ready to date again," said Brandon.

"Thanks guys, I'm so happy that you're all back in my life. Promise you won't let me cut myself off again, no matter what."

"Pest, that day will never come," said Brandon. Both Jamal and Brandon got up and hugged Grace.

"Stay right there, I've got to take a picture of this," said Felicia.

"Me too," said Loretta as she got up.

****

It was dark when everyone piled into the limo to go home. Gracie was the first to be dropped off since she had to feed Cujo. Jamal and Brandon promised to come by in the morning so the three of them could have breakfast together. Brandon wanted to discuss Grace joining his church music ministry and Jamal wanted to discuss her career.

Grace gave everyone hugs and kisses before she stepped out of the limo. As she approached the steps that led to her doorway, a figure stepped out of the shadows. Startled, Grace screamed before she noticed that it was Eric. At the sound of her scream, Cujo started barking on the other side of her door. Grace heard quick footsteps from behind and turned around to see Jamal and Brandon directly behind her.

"It's okay guys, this is Eric," she said quickly. Eric stepped forward and apologized for scaring everyone. Jamal and Brandon didn't step back until Grace told them that she'll see them in the morning. They climbed back into the limo, but the vehicle remained parked with the windows wound down.

"I'm so sorry, Eric, I should have called you."

"It's alright, I just wanted to see you and apologize again. Grace, I'd never do anything to hurt you. Looking back, I know I should have stopped Kenneth, but I was caught off guard."

"I know Eric. I realize that now, but at the time I wasn't just upset with you. I was having flashbacks of my assault and I couldn't handle it. I convinced myself that I shouldn't be in any relationship after that, but I started therapy now and it's helping me a lot. Eric, I love you."

Elated, Eric grabbed Grace's hands and responded, "That's wonderful news because I'm in love with you too."

"Eric, I need to fix my problem now so it won't be a problem between us in the future. My therapy's not done. We won't be able to date for a while, will you be patient and wait until I'm done?"

"Grace, I'd do anything for you as long as you're giving me another chance." Eric pulled her close into a kiss. The sound of Brandon loudly clearing his throat in the limo brought them back to the realization that they had an audience. Grace turned around and saw five pair of eyes watching her every move.

"I didn't know you guys were still here." Grace yelled, "Good night everyone!" She waved goodbye but the limo still did not budge.

"I guess they're waiting for me to leave. I'm going to call you every day. Is that okay?" Eric asked her.

"Yes, I'd love that." Eric gave Grace a chaste kiss on the forehead before leaving. She turned and waved goodbye again to her family as she opened her door. This time the limo pulled off.

CHAPTER TWENTY-ONE

TWO YEARS LATER - GRACE

It was another sizzling hot day for graduation, but I'm not complaining. This time JJ told me his plans. JJ and Mrs. Tasha Bliss rented a rooftop restaurant with a beautifully shaded outdoor garden for my graduation party. We have the whole place to ourselves. Best of all, we're enjoying breezes on the rooftop that none of the pedestrians walking the pavement below could experience.

There's a large crowd here. My circle of friends and family have grown since my last graduation. I've invited new friends from church, Eric's gym and a few new friends I made at my university. Eric's mother, dad's friend Eddie, Aunt Felicia, Jonathan, Tasha's parents and Brandon's whole family are also here.

"Sweetie, is that smile for me?" I'm holding this beautiful baby girl in my arms. She just finished her bottle and rewarded me with a huge smile, or maybe it was gas. Little Gabrielle Reed has the cutest dimples and bright brown eyes, just like Eric's. Here he comes now, bringing me a slice of cake. He sits down next to me and whisperers in my ear, *"I can't wait until we have one of these."* I sucked my teeth and turned to him. "You know what Eric, please take your sister so I can eat my cake." Eric laughed heartily while he gathers little Gabby in his strong arms. He loves to tease me, but I have a way to fix his baby craze. I turned around to my Aunt Loretta, aka Mrs. Clayton Reed. "Auntie, the next time Gabby puts out a big one, please let her brother handle it. He wants the baby experience."

Everyone laughed. They know Eric loves teasing me despite the fact that we've already settled this subject during pre-marital counseling. That's when he informed me of his desire to have five kids. At first, I thought he was joking. This is where the age thing becomes an issue. He's ready to populate the world whereas I'm focused on my career, but even if I were 29, there's no way I'm going through five pregnancies! During counseling we agreed to wait three years before starting a family.

Eric and I have come a long way. After completing my personal therapy, Eric and I slowly resumed dating. At the same time, Aunt Loretta caved into Clayton Reed's charms and started a romance with him. Six months later, they were walking down the aisle. I'd never seen Aunt Loretta so happy and Mr. Reed was so overwhelmed with joy, he cried during their vows. Everyone could tell that Clayton Reed really loved my Auntie. At their wedding, Aunt Felicia was the matron of honor and I was the maid of honor. Eric was the best man.

Mr. Reed was 53 years old while Aunt Loretta was 40

when Gabrielle was born, nine months after their wedding. Like I said, Mr. Reed really loves my auntie. No one was expecting to see little Gabby, but now that she's here, we can't imagine life without her. I'm secretly hoping Aunt Loretta gives me another cousin soon. Turns out, I like babies more than I thought I would, but I dare not mention that to Eric.

JJ didn't waste any time with Tasha either. He stayed in Brooklyn until their rekindled relationship was solid. They married eight months after my first graduation and I was the maid of honor for the second time.

Just before his sister was born, Eric confessed that dating was no longer enough for him. He proposed during my midterms. I was ecstatic, but then he said we should marry during spring break. He had it all planned out, talk about stress! I wasn't stressed about getting married. I always knew we would marry one day, but I didn't think he wanted to do it so soon. I convinced him that marrying after my graduation would be so much better. Between exams and internship, my final semester was hectic. I wanted to give Eric my full attention when we marry. I also did not want a rushed wedding since for me, this is a once in a lifetime event! He understood in the end.

Eric's mother and Tasha helped me plan our wedding. The planning was a bit difficult for me. I've always expected my dad to escort me down the aisle, but JJ said that was his job now. Of course Brandon, as my pastor, will perform our wedding ceremony. JJ and Brandon are always there for me. I don't know what I did to deserve such a wonderful brother and cousin.

Today I obtained my bachelors in Music Business from New York University. The work I've done with JJ was invaluable. JJ's also helping me with plans to build my studio when Eric and I find a home. The money dad left me and my royalties will cover the studio cost and much, much more. My career is ready to take flight! Eddie said he's expecting big things from me as the daughter of Gregory Mitchell. I told him that he won't be disappointed because I expect to do great things. And, with JJ as my mentor, I know he will keep me from falling off my path to success.

I can't help but think about the time when I felt so alone and unloved after my father's death. Now, the very same people I pushed away, surrounds me. Aunt Loretta, JJ and Brandon. They've all shown me so much love. I don't understand how I didn't feel it when I was sixteen. I'd never thought that I would have so many people who care about me and I for them. And now, the love has multiplied. I love my little cousin/future sister in law. And I can't wait to be an auntie to JJ and Tasha's baby when he or she arrives. Brandon had convinced me to work with the music ministry team at his thriving church. Through my work, I've gained many new friends and relationships. There's never been a time in my life when I felt this fulfilled.

But there are days when I realize what I don't have. I look at JJ, who invited both of his parents and his half-sister to his wedding. They took a family picture together after taking one with Brandon and me separately. It made me think about never having a family photo with my parents. There's also the time when Brandon had a church revival event after completing the renovations on his church building. His parents and brother were there, along with members of his father's church. Brandon's father put his arms around him and hugged him. His father had tears in his eyes because he was so happy that Brandon forgave him and accomplished so much with his ministry in such a short time. I thought to myself that no matter what I accomplish in my life, I will never receive a hug like that because my parents are dead.

Sometimes I dwell on these thoughts, my mind grows dark and my heart heavy with longing. I long for the love of my parents and I question God's decision to allow them to die early. There are those thoughts and thoughts of anger. Anger toward my deceased parents because they chose their addictions over me.

Pastor Brandon taught me that these are dangerous places for my thoughts to dwell. He said on those days when you're feeling like you were short changed on your blessings, open your mouth and praise God for what you do have. Sing songs to him, count your blessings and thank him for each one. So, when I pray, I thank God for placing Aunt Loretta, JJ and Brandon in my life. Where would I be without their love and guidance? Aunt Loretta's unconditional love saved me from the lonely life I inflicted on myself. JJ has looked out for me even after I kicked him out of my life. In both I see a part of my dad and the love he had for me. And what can I say about Brandon? He's my cousin, guardian angel, pastor, counselor, life coach, and the list goes on. I don't know where I'd be in life today if Brandon wasn't in it. It was Brandon who, through counseling, made me aware of the anger and shame I had toward my mother. You see, dad purchased matching burial plots when my parents married. Whenever I visited my father's grave, I'd never acknowledged my mother's grave, which was right next to his. It was Aunt Loretta who always looked after both gravesites. Now it's my job and I'm happy to do it. When I visit the cemetery, I talk to both of my parents, and whenever someone asks how my mother died, I tell them the truth. She overdosed on heroine, but she loved me.

That first night after visiting my mother's grave, I dreamed of my father. In the dream he said he was happy now. It was a strange dream, and I awoke feeling happy. Did my father's spirit visit me? Who knows? What I do know is, my life is so much better since I stopped hanging onto anger and hurts from the past.

Now, what can I say about Eric? My Eric, the love of my life who's been a major blessing. He's been so patient with me and my therapy. I'm amazed at how much he cares for me. Like the time when JJ let me drive his old Jag after I completed driver's education. I was driving down a local road when I swerved to avoid hitting a cat that ran in front of me. The Jag slid into a ditch and I gave myself a mild concussion. When Aunt Loretta told Eric about my little fender bender, he canceled all of his appointments for the next three days and flew out to me ASAP; just to make sure I was well. I didn't think my concussion was a big deal, but Eric was so worried about me. He tested my reflexes and encouraged me to sleep as much as possible.

JJ was his usual mean self. He didn't want Eric to stay in

his house because he didn't think it was proper. Can you believe that? The hot R&B artist, Amal Bliss, was acting like somebody's daddy. Luckily, Mrs. Tasha Bliss had the last word and Eric stayed. Eric took great care of me. He would carry me into the great room after my naps because he didn't want me to walk too much. JJ would give Eric the evil eye and mumble, *"Y'all not married yet."* Eric also made sure I knew how to take care of myself before he flew back to New York.

After our engagement, whenever he called me at school he would say, "May I speak to the future Mrs. Eric Reed please?" It gave me goosebumps whenever he said that in his deepest voice. I do love that man.

So, here I am. In the midst of people who love and care about me. Today's one of those events you cherish forever because it's like a little slice of heaven on earth; having all of your friends and family gathered around to celebrate with you. Just think, some people only get this at their funeral!

Now, I know every day isn't filled with rainbows and sunshine, but with the love of Jesus and the love of my friends and family, I will overcome whatever life throws at me.

-END.

ABOUT THE AUTHOR

Irene Williams received her Bachelor's in Marketing from Baruch College and she has worked in Marketing for over twenty years. Originally born in Brooklyn, Irene currently resides in the borough of Queens with her husband and daughter.